VIRGIN PRINCESS,
TYCOON'S
TEMPTATION
BY
MICHELLE CELMER

AND

THE SECRET CHILD
& THE COWBOY CEO
BY
JANICE MAYNARD

MILLS
& BOON

"It would be okay if you kissed me now."

Louisa gazed up at him, a dreamy look on her face.

Oh, Garrett wanted to. So much that it surprised him a little. "Are you sure that's what you want?" he asked.

"Just because my family treats me like a child doesn't mean I am one."

There was nothing childish about her, which she proved by not even waiting for him to make the first move. Instead, she reached up, slid her hands behind his neck, pulled him down to her level and kissed him. Her lips were soft but insistent and she smelled fantastic—delicate and feminine.

Louisa expelled a shudder of breath and rested her head against his chest. "Now, that was a kiss."

He couldn't exactly argue.

"It probably isn't proper to say this," Louisa said. "But I can't wait to see you naked."

VIRGIN PRINCESS, TYCOON'S TEMPTATION

BY
MICHELLE CELMER

All the characters in this book have no existence outside the imagination of
the author, and have no relation whatsoever to anyone bearing the same name
or names. They are not even distantly inspired by any individual known or
unknown to the author, and all the incidents are pure invention.

Published in Great Britain 2011
by Mills & Boon, an imprint of Harlequin (UK) Limited,
Eton House, 18-24 Paradise Road, Richmond, Surrey TW9 1SR

© Michelle Celmer 2010

ISBN: 978 0 263 88310 7

51-0711

Harlequin (UK) policy is to use papers that are natural, renewable and
recyclable products and made from wood grown in sustainable forests. The
logging and manufacturing processes conform to the legal environmental
regulations of the country of origin.

Printed and bound in Spain
by Blackprint CPI, Barcelona

To my grandson, Cameron James Ronald

Bestselling author **Michelle Celmer** lives in southeastern Michigan with her husband, their three children, two dogs and two cats. When she's not writing or busy being a mom, you can find her in the garden or curled up with a romance novel. And if you twist her arm really hard you can usually persuade her into a day of power shopping.

Michelle loves to hear from readers. Visit her website, www.michellecelmer.com, or write to her at PO Box 300, Clawson, MI 48017, USA.

Dear Reader,

Welcome to my ROYAL SEDUCTIONS series, the story of Princess Louisa Josephine Elisabeth Alexander and real-estate king Garrett Sutherland.

As an author, I love all the books I write and the characters I create, but every so often one comes along that I hold a special fondness for. This is one of those books, and Princess Louisa is definitely one of those characters. It is her innocence, and her unshakable faith in the people around her, that makes her so likable. And frankly so much fun to mess with. It was quite a challenge for me, tearing her down and stripping away her illusions. But, hey, it had to be done. And I'll tell you, she was a tough nut to crack.

The same could be said for Garrett, whose single-minded determination made him as appealing as he was obtuse. What can you do to a guy who thinks he has all the answers? (Insert evil laughter here.) That's right— tear him down, too.

Are you getting the feeling I really enjoy this?

Usually I have a pretty good idea going into a story how it will end, but I have to say, these two kept me guessing right up until the very last page. They genuinely surprised me, and I think they'll surprise you, too.

Enjoy!

Michelle

One

A genuine believer in fate and fairy tale romances, Princess Louisa Josephine Elisabeth Alexander knew that if she was patient, the man of her dreams would eventually come along. And as their eyes met across the crowded ballroom, beneath a canopy of red and white twinkling lights, shimmering silver tulle and pink, white and red heart-shaped balloons, she could swear she felt the earth move.

She just knew he was the one.

Her family would probably remind her that she'd felt that way about men before. Aaron would tease her and call her a hopeless romantic. Chris, the oldest, would just sigh and shake his head, as if to say, "Here we go again." Her twin sister Anne would probably sneer and call her naive. But this time it was different. Louisa was sure of it. She could *feel* it, like a cosmic tug at her soul.

He was the most intriguing, handsome and *tallest*

man—by several inches—at the charity event, which was what drew her attention to him in the first place. With raven hair, a warm olive complexion and striking features, he was impossible to miss.

Was he an Italian businessman, or a Mediterranean prince? Whoever he was, he was rich and powerful. She could tell by the quality of his clothing and the way he carried himself. Most people knew better than to openly stare at a member of the royal family, but this man gazed intently at her with dark, deep-set eyes, as though they already knew one another. Which she was sure they didn't. She definitely would have remembered him. Maybe he didn't realize she was royalty, although she would imagine the diamond encrusted tiara tucked within her upswept hair would be a dead giveaway.

Another woman might have waited for him to make the first move, or manufactured a scenario in which their paths accidentally crossed, but Louisa didn't believe in playing games. Much to the chagrin of her overly protective siblings. The youngest member of the royal family by a mere five minutes, and labeled as too trusting, Louisa was treated like a child. But contrary to what her family believed, not everyone was interested in her money and title, and those who were, were fairly easy to recognize.

She set her empty champagne glass on a passing server's tray and headed in his direction, the full skirt of her gown—in her customary shade of pink—swishing soundlessly as she crossed the floor. Never once did his eyes leave hers. As she approached, he finally lowered his gaze and bowed his head, saying in a voice as deep as it was smooth, "Her Highness is enchanting tonight."

Not a half-bad opening line, and he spoke with a

dialect not unlike her own. Almost definitely from Thomas Isle, so why didn't she recognize him? "You seem to have me at a disadvantage," she said. "You obviously know me, but I don't recall ever meeting you."

Most people, especially a stranger, would have at least offered an apology for staring, but this man didn't look like the type who apologized for *anything*. "That's because we've never met," he answered.

"I suppose that would explain it," she said with a smile.

Face-to-face, he was a little older than she'd guessed. Mid-thirties maybe—ten years or so her senior—but she preferred men who were older and more experienced. He was also much larger than she thought. The top of her head barely reached his chin. It wasn't just his height that was so imposing, either. He was big all over, and she would bet that not an ounce of it was fat. Even through his attire, he seemed to have the chiseled physique of a gladiator. She couldn't help noticing that he wasn't wearing a wedding ring.

This was, without a doubt, *fate*.

She offered a hand to shake. "Princess Louisa Josephine Elisabeth Alexander."

"That's quite a mouthful," he said, but she could see by the playful grin that he was teasing her.

He took her hand, cradled it within his ridiculously large palm, lifted it to his mouth and brushed a very gentle kiss across her skin. Did the ground beneath her feet just give a vigorous jolt, or was that her heart?

"And you are...?" she asked.

"Honored to meet you, Your Highness."

Either he had no grasp of etiquette, or he was being deliberately obtuse. "You have a name?"

His wry smile said he was teasing her again and she felt her heart flutter. "Garrett Sutherland," he said.

Sutherland? Why did that sound so familiar? Then it hit her. She had heard her brother speak of him from time to time, a landowner with holdings so vast they nearly matched those of the royal family. Mr. Sutherland was not only one of the richest men in the country, but also the most mysterious and elusive. He never attended social gatherings, and other than an occasional business meeting, kept largely to himself.

Definitely not the kind of man who would need her money.

"Mr. Sutherland," she said. "Your reputation precedes you. It's a pleasure to finally make your acquaintance."

"The pleasure is all mine, Your Highness. As you probably know, I don't normally attend events such as these, but when I heard the proceeds would benefit cardiac research, for your father's sake at the very least, I knew I had to make an appearance."

A testament to what a kind and caring man he must be, she thought. Someone she would very much like to get to know better.

His gaze left hers briefly to search the room. "I haven't seen the King tonight. Is he well?"

"Very well, under the circumstances. He wanted to make an appearance but he has strict orders from his doctor not to appear in public."

Louisa's father, the King of Thomas Isle, suffered from heart disease and had spent the past nine months on a portable bypass machine designed to give his heart an opportunity to heal and eventually work on its own again. Louisa took pride in the fact that it had been her idea to hold a charity ball in his honor. Usually her family wrote off her ideas as silly and idealistic, but for the first time in her life, they seemed to take her seriously. Although, when she had asked to be given the responsibility of planning the affair, they had hired a team of professionals instead. Baby steps, she figured. One of these days they would see that she wasn't the frail flower they made her out to be.

Across the ballroom the orchestra began playing her favorite waltz. "Would you care to dance, Mr. Sutherland?"

He arched one dark brow curiously. Most women would wait for the man to make the first move, but she wasn't most women. Besides, this was destiny. What could be the harm in moving things along a bit?

"I would be honored, Your Highness."

He held out his arm, and she slipped hers through it. As he led her through clusters of guests toward the dance floor, she half expected one of her overprotective siblings to cut them off at the pass, but Chris and his wife Melissa, enormously pregnant with triplets, were acting as host and hostess in their parents' absence. Aaron was glued to the side of his new wife, Olivia, a scientist who, when she wasn't in her lab buried in research, felt like a fish out of water.

Louisa searched out her sister Anne, surprised to find her talking to the Prime Minister's son, Samuel Baldwin, who Louisa knew for a fact was not on Anne's list of favorite people.

Not a single member of her family was paying attention to her. Louisa could hardly fathom that she was about to dance with a man without *someone* grilling him beforehand. He took her in his arms and twirled her across the floor, and they were blissfully alone—save for the hundred or so other couples dancing. But as he drew her close and gazed into her eyes, there was no one but them.

He held her scandalously close for a first dance—by royal standards anyhow—but it was like magic, the way their bodies fit and how they moved in perfect sync. The way he never stopped gazing into her eyes, as though they were a window into her soul. His were black and bottomless and as mysterious as the man. He smelled delicious, too. Spicy and clean. His hair looked so soft she wanted to run her fingers through it and she was dying to know how his lips would taste, even though she felt instinctively they would be as delicious as the rest of him.

When the song ended and a slower number began, he pulled her closer, until she was tucked firmly against the warmth of his body. Two songs turned to three, then four.

Neither spoke. Words seemed unnecessary. His eyes and the curve of his smile told her exactly what he was thinking and feeling. Only when the orchestra stopped to take a break did he reluctantly let go. He led her from the dance floor, and she was only vaguely aware that people were staring at her. At them. They probably wondered who this dark mysterious man was dancing with the Princess. Were they an item? She would bet that people could tell just by looking at them that they were destined to be together.

"Would you care to take a stroll on the patio?" she asked.

He gestured to the French doors leading out into the garden. "After you, Your Highness."

The air had chilled with the setting sun and a cool, salty ocean breeze blew in from the bluff. With the exception of the guards positioned at either side of the garden entrance, they were alone.

"Beautiful night," Garrett said, gazing up at the star-filled sky.

"It is," she agreed. June had always been her favorite month, when the world was alive with color and new life. What better time to meet the man of her dreams? Her soul mate.

"Tell me about yourself, Mr. Sutherland."

He turned to her and smiled. "What would you like to know?"

Anything. *Everything.* "You live on Thomas Isle?"

"Since the day I was born. I was raised just outside the village of Varie on the other side of the island."

The village to which he referred could only be described as quaint. Definitely not where you would expect to find a family of excessive means. Not that it mattered to her where he came from. Only that he was here now, with her. "What do your parents do?"

"My father was a farmer, my mother a seamstress. They're both retired now and living in England with my brother and his family."

It was difficult to fathom that such a wealthy and shrewd businessman was raised with such modest means. He had obviously done quite well for himself.

"How many siblings do you have?" she asked.

"Three brothers."

"Younger? Older?"

"I'm the eldest."

She wished, if only for a day or two, she could know what that felt like. To not be coddled and treated like a child. To be the person everyone turned to for guidance and advice.

A chilly breeze blew in from the bluff and Louisa shivered, rubbing warmth into her bare arms. They should go back inside before she caught a cold—with her father's condition it was important that everyone in the family stay healthy—but she relished this time alone with him.

"You're cold," he said.

"A little," she admitted, sure that he would suggest they head back in, but instead he removed his tux jacket and draped it over her shoulders, surrounding her in the toasty warmth of his body and the spicy sent of his cologne. What she really wanted, what she *longed* for, was for him to pull her into his arms and kiss her. She already knew that his lips would be firm but gentle, his mouth delicious. Heaven knows she had played the scene over in her mind a million times since adolescence, what the perfect kiss would be like, yet no man had ever measured up to the fantasy. Garrett would, she was sure of it. Even if she had to make the first move.

She was contemplating doing just that when a figure appeared in the open doorway. She turned to find that, watching them, with a stern look on his face, was her oldest brother, Chris.

"Mr. Sutherland," he said. "I'm so pleased to see that you've finally accepted an invitation to celebrate with us."

Garrett bowed his head and said, "Your Highness."

Chris stepped forward and shook his hand, but there was an undertone of tension in his voice, in his stance.

Did he dislike Garrett? Mistrust him? Or maybe he was just being his usual protective self.

"I see you've met the Princess," he said.

"She's a lovely woman," Garrett replied. "Although I fear I may have monopolized her time."

Chris shot her a sharp look. "She does have duties."

As princess it was her responsibility to socialize with *all* the guests, especially in her parents' absence, and duty was duty.

Another time and place. Definitely.

"Give me a minute, please," she asked her brother.

He grudgingly nodded and told Mr. Sutherland, "Enjoy your evening." Then he walked away.

Louisa smiled apologetically. "I'm sorry if he seemed rude. He's a little protective of me. My entire family is."

His smile was understanding. "If I had a sister so lovely, I would be, too."

"I suppose I should go back inside and mingle with the other guests."

His look said he shared her disappointment. "I understand, Your Highness."

She took off his jacket and handed it back to him. "I was wondering if you might like to be my guest for dinner at the castle."

A smile spread across his beautiful mouth. "I would like that very much."

"Are you free this coming Friday?"

"If not, I'll clear my schedule."

"We dine at seven sharp, but you can come a little early. Say, six-thirty?"

"I'll be there." He reached for her hand, brushing

another gentle kiss across her bare skin. "Good night, Your Highness."

He flashed her one last sizzling grin, then turned and walked back inside. She watched him go until he was swallowed up by the crowd, knowing that the next six days, until she saw him again, when she could gaze into the dark and hypnotizing depths of his eyes, would be the longest in her life.

Two

Garrett sipped champagne and strolled the perimeter of the ballroom, eyes on the object of his latest fascination. Everything was going exactly as planned.

"That was quite a performance," someone said from behind him, and he turned to see Weston Banes, his best friend and business manager, smiling wryly.

He pasted on an innocent look. "Who said it was a performance?"

Wes shot him a knowing look. He had worked with Garrett since he bought his first parcel of land ten years ago. He knew better than anyone that Garrett would have never attended the ball without some ulterior motive.

"I've hit a brick wall," Garrett told him.

Wes frowned. "I don't follow you."

"I now own every available parcel of commercial land that doesn't belong to the royal family, so there's only one thing left for me to do."

"What's that?"

"Take control of the royal family's land, as well."

A slow smile spread across Wes's face. "And the only way to do that is to marry into the family."

"Exactly." He had two choices, Princess Anne, who he'd commonly heard referred to as *The Shrew,* or Princess Louisa, the sweet, innocent and gullible twin. It was pretty much a no-brainer. Although, considering the way she'd looked at him, as responsive as she was to his touch, he wondered if she wasn't as sweet and innocent as her reputation claimed.

Wes shook his head. "This is ruthless, even for you. Anything to pad the portfolio, I guess."

This wasn't about money. He already had more than he could ever spend. This was about power and control. To marry the Princess, the monarchy would first have to assign him a title—most likely Duke—then he would be considered royalty. The son of a farmer and a seamstress becoming one of the most powerful men in the country. Who would have imagined? If he played his cards right, which he always did, someday he would control the entire island.

"We can discuss the details later," Garrett told him. "I wouldn't mind your input, seeing how this involves you, as well."

"This is really something coming from the man who swore he would never get married or have children," Wes said.

Garrett shrugged. "Sometimes a man has to make sacrifices."

"So, how did it go?"

"Quite well."

"If that's true, then why are you here, and she's way over there?"

His smile was a smug one. "Because I already got what I came for."

"I'm afraid to ask what that was."

Garrett chuckled. "Get your mind out of the gutter. I'm talking about an invitation to dinner at the castle."

His brows rose. "Seriously?"

"This Friday at six-thirty."

"Damn." He shook his head in disbelief. "You're good."

He shrugged. "It's a gift. Women can't resist my charm. Just ask your wife."

Wes turned to see Tia, his wife of five years, standing with a throng of society women near the bar. "I should probably intervene before she drinks her weight in champagne and I have to carry her out of here."

"You need to let her out more," Garrett joked.

"I wish," Wes said. Despite considerable means, Tia was the kind of nervous new mother who believed no one could care for their child as well as she and Wes, but he worked ridiculous hours and because of that she didn't get out very often. In fact, this was the first public function they had attended since Will's birth three months ago.

"Join us?" Wes asked, gesturing in his spouse's direction.

Garrett gave one last glance to the Princess, who was deep in conversation with a group of heads of state, then nodded and followed Wes to the bar. He already had a game plan in place. What he would say to her and what he wouldn't, when they would share their first kiss. The trick with a woman like her was to take it very slow.

He had little doubt that in no time, probably next Friday, he would have her eating out of the palm of his hand.

Louisa had been right.

It had been a murderously *long* week waiting for Friday to arrive, and when it finally did, the day seemed to stretch on for weeks. Finally, when she thought she couldn't stand another second of waiting, at six-thirty on the dot, a shiny black convertible sports car pulled up in front of the castle and Garrett unfolded himself from inside.

She watched from the library, surprised that someone of his means didn't have a driver, and wondering how such a big man fit into such a tiny vehicle. Maybe someday he would take her for a drive in it. With her bodyguards following close behind of course, because no member of the royal family was allowed to leave the castle unescorted. Especially not since the threats began late last summer.

Louisa peeked out from behind the curtain, watching as Garrett walked to the door. He looked so handsome and distinguished in a dark gray, pinstripe suit. And *tall*. She'd almost forgotten just how big he was.

Her brother Chris hadn't been happy about the short notice when she'd informed him this morning that she had invited Garrett for dinner. She knew though that if she'd told him sooner, the family would have teased and harassed her mercilessly all week.

As it was, everyone had managed to get their digs in this afternoon. Chris of course questioned Garrett's motives, as though no man would appreciate her for anything but her money and connections. Aaron voiced concern about the age difference—which, as Louisa had guessed, was just over ten years. Anne, who had been particularly cranky since the ball, warned her that a man like Garrett Sutherland was way out of her league and only interested in one thing. Louisa would love to know how Anne knew that when she didn't even know Garrett. Even her parents, who had been relying on Chris's judgment lately, were reserving their opinion. She wished, just this once, that everyone would mind their own business.

When Chris married an illegitimate princess, everyone just had to smile and go along with it for the good of the country, and when Aaron announced that he was going to marry an American scientist, an orphan who had not even a trace of royal blood, barely anyone voiced an objection. So what was the big deal about Louisa dating a rich and successful businessman?

She had checked up on him this week, purely out of curiosity of course, and though she hadn't been able to find too much information, none of it had been negative.

She was sure, though, that since her announcement this morning, Chris had ordered Randall Jenkins, their head of security, to dig up all the information he could find on Garrett. Louisa wasn't worried. She knew instinctively that he was a good person because she was an excellent judge of character.

The bell rang and she scurried over to the sofa to wait while Geoffrey, their butler, let Garrett in. She sat on the edge of the cushion and smoothed the wrinkles from the skirt of her pale pink sleeveless sundress, her heart pounding so hard it felt as though it might beat right through her chest.

Under normal circumstances she would have worn something a bit more conservative, like a business suit, for a dinner guest, but this was a first date and she wanted to look her best. Make a good first impression.

It seemed to take a millennium before the library door opened and Garrett strolled into the room. She rose to her feet to greet him.

Garrett wore his confidence like a badge of honor. So different from the cocky young royals she'd been introduced to in the past, who reeked of wealth and entitlement, as though their name alone afforded them everything their greedy and spoiled hearts desired.

Louisa and her siblings had been raised with wealth and privilege, but taught not to take anything for granted. Life, they had learned, especially since their father's illness, was fragile, and family was what mattered above all else.

Maybe it was wishful thinking, but she had the distinct feeling Garrett shared those values.

When he saw her standing there, a gorgeous smile curled his lips. He bowed his head and said, "Your Highness, a pleasure to see you again."

"I'm so glad you could make it," she replied, even though she'd never had a single doubt that he would show. What had happened between them on the dance floor had been magical and she was certain that they were destined to be together. Besides, his assistant had phoned hers this morning to confirm.

"Would you care for a drink, sir?" Geoffrey offered.

"Scotch, please," Garrett said, and his manners made Louisa smile. There was nothing she despised more than a man who treated the hired help with disrespect.

Especially Geoffrey, who had been with them since before Louisa was born and almost single-handedly kept the household running like clockwork.

"White wine, Your Highness?" Geoffrey asked her.

She nodded. "That would be lovely, thank you."

She gestured to the sofa and told Garrett, "Please, make yourself comfortable."

He settled onto the cushion, looking remarkably relaxed, as though he dined with royalty on a daily basis, when she knew for a fact that the charity ball had been the first time he had visited the castle under social circumstances. She sat at the opposite end, all but crawling out of her skin with excitement. When their drinks were poured, Geoffrey excused himself and they were *finally* alone. No family breathing down her neck, no bodyguards watching their every move.

"I was looking forward to my parents meeting you, but unfortunately they won't be joining us this evening."

"Your father isn't well?" he asked, looking concerned.

"He's going in for a procedure soon and has to stay in tip-top shape. The fewer people he's exposed to, the less likely he is to contract illnesses. His immune system is already compromised by the heart pump."

"Another time," he said. Was that his way of suggesting that he wanted to see her again? Not that she ever doubted he would. This was destiny.

It was still nice to hear the words out loud, to know what he was thinking.

"I'll warn you that tonight might feel more like the Spanish Inquisition than a dinner," she told him.

Garrett smiled. "I expected as much. I have nothing to hide."

"I Googled you," she admitted.

Her honesty seemed to surprise him. "Did you?"

"Earlier this week, although I didn't find much."

"There isn't much to find. I am a simple man, Your Highness. What some may even consider...boring."

She seriously doubted that. Everything about him intrigued her. He was so dark and serious, yet his smile was warm and inviting. She liked the way his eyes crinkled slightly in the corners when he smiled, and the hint of a dimple that dented his left cheek.

She opened her mouth to tell him that she would never consider a man like him boring, but before she could get the words out, her family appeared in the doorway. The entire lot of them.

Fantastic bloody timing. God forbid they let her have a little time alone with the man she planned to marry.

As everyone piled into the room, Garrett rose and Louisa stood to make the introductions.

"Garrett, I believe you already know my brothers, Prince Christian and Prince Aaron."

"A pleasure to see you again." Garrett bowed his head, then accepted a firm and brusque shake from each of them. Very businesslike, but with an undertone of possessiveness, a silent notification that he was being carefully assessed.

"This is my sister-in-law, Princess Melissa," Louisa said.

"Just Melissa," she added in the southern drawl she had adopted while living in the States. She shook his hand firmly and with purpose. For a southern belle, she didn't have a delicate or demure bone in her body. "It's a pleasure to finally meet you, Mr. Sutherland. I've heard so much about you."

"Please call me Garrett," he said. "I understand you're expecting. Congratulations."

"Kind of tough to miss at this point," she joked, laying a hand on her very swollen middle.

"I understand it will be soon."

"They prefer I make it to thirty-six weeks, so the babies' lungs have enough time to mature. Preterm labor is a possibility with multiples, but I can hardly imagine another month of this. I feel like an elephant."

"I've always believed there's nothing more beautiful than an expectant mother," Garrett said with genuine sincerity.

Melissa grinned widely and Louisa knew that he'd instantly won her over.

Aaron stepped forward and said, "This is my wife, Princess Olivia."

Liv smiled shyly, still unaccustomed to her role as a royal. A botanical geneticist, she was reserved and studious and would much rather be in her basement lab studying plant DNA than interacting with people. But she shook Garrett's hand and said, "Nice to meet you."

Anne, not waiting to be introduced, stepped forward and announced, "I'm Anne." She stuck out her hand, shaking Garrett's so firmly that Louisa worried she might challenge him to an arm wrestle.

What was her problem?

If Anne had been expecting a negative reaction from her confrontational introduction, she got the opposite.

"A pleasure to meet you, Your Highness," Garrett said with a smile, the picture of grace and etiquette, and Louisa all but beamed with pride. The situation couldn't be more tense or uncomfortable, yet he'd handled it with ease.

"I'll admit I was surprised when Louisa informed us this morning that you were joining us for dinner," Chris said, and Louisa wanted to punch him. Garrett had to be wondering why she would wait until this morning to tell them. She didn't want him to get the wrong idea, to think that she was ashamed of him or uncertain of her invitation.

Instead of appearing insulted, Garrett looked her way and flashed her that adorable, dimpled smile. "And I was a bit surprised when she asked." His eyes locked on hers with a look so warm and delicious she almost melted. "I could hardly believe I was lucky enough to draw the attention of the most beautiful woman in the room."

The honesty of his words and the admiration in his eyes warmed her from the inside out. The fact that he would speak so openly of his feelings for her, especially in front of her family, made her want to throw her arms around his neck and kiss him. But who wanted an audience for their first kiss?

Geoffrey appeared in the study door and announced, "Dinner is ready."

Melissa held out her arm for Chris to take. "Shall we?"

"Go ahead without me. I'd like to have a private word with our guest."

Louisa's heart nearly stopped. Why did Chris need to see him alone? She prayed he wouldn't say something embarrassing, or try to scare Garrett off. But if she made a fuss, it might only make things worse.

At Melissa's look of hesitation he added, "We'll only be a minute."

Louisa flashed Garrett an apologetic look, but he

just smiled, looking totally at ease as Melissa ushered everyone from the room.

With any luck, Garrett wouldn't decide that pursuing a princess was just too much hassle and bring an end to their first date before it even began.

Three

And so it begins, Garrett thought as the rest of the family walked, or in Melissa's case, waddled, from the room, leaving only himself and Prince Christian. He wondered if, had he been a royal, the Prince would feel this chat was necessary.

Well, it wouldn't be long before Garrett had a royal title, garnering him all of the respect he had earned. Though time wasn't an issue, he would still push for a quick engagement. The sooner they were married and settled, the sooner he could relax and begin enjoying all the fruits of his labor.

"Under normal circumstances it would be the King having this conversation with you," Chris said.

But the King wasn't well enough, so Garrett was stuck with the Crown Prince instead. He hadn't yet decided if that was a good or a bad thing. "I understand."

The Prince gestured to the sofa, and after Garrett

sat, Chris took a seat in the armchair across from him. "As a precaution, I had a thorough background check performed on you."

He had anticipated that, and as he had told Princess Louisa, he had nothing to hide. "Did they find anything interesting?"

"Actually, they didn't find much of anything at all. Though ruthless in your business practices, as far as I can tell you've always kept it legal and ethical, and you seem to be a fair employer. You donate a percentage of your income to worthwhile charities—most having to do with education for the underprivileged—and as far as any brushes with the law, you've never had so much as a parking ticket."

"You sound surprised."

"I would expect that a man so elusive might have something to hide."

"I certainly don't mean to be elusive," he said. "I simply lead an uncomplicated life. My work is my passion."

"It shows. Your accomplishments are quite impressive."

"Thank you."

The Prince paused for a second, as though he was uncomfortable with what he planned to say next. "While I see no clear reason to be concerned, I'm obligated to ask, on the King's behalf, what your intentions are regarding Princess Louisa."

It seemed ridiculous to Garrett that, at twenty-seven years old, Louisa wasn't allowed to make her own decisions regarding who she wanted to see socially. "Her Highness invited me to dinner and I accepted," he said.

The simplicity of his answer seemed to surprise the Prince. "That's it?"

"I admit I find your sister quite fascinating."

"Louisa is...special."

He said that as though that was an impediment, and Garrett felt an odd dash of defensiveness in her honor. Which was a little ridiculous considering he barely knew her.

"I've never met anyone quite like her," he told the Prince.

"She tends to be a bit naive when it comes to the opposite sex. Men have taken advantage of that."

Maybe if her family stopped sheltering her, she would learn not to be so gullible. However, that particular trait was working in his favor, so he could hardly complain. "Rest assured, I have nothing but the utmost respect for the Princess. I pride myself on being a very honorable man. I would never do anything to compromise her principles."

"I'm glad to hear it," Chris said. "But of course I will have to discuss the matter with the King."

"Of course, Your Highness."

The shadow of a smile cracked the serious expression. "We've known each other a long time, Garrett. Call me Chris."

With that request Garrett knew he was as good as in. Chris needing to speak with his father was merely a formality at this point. "I'm very much looking forward to getting to know you better," Garrett told him.

"As am I." Chris paused, his expression darkening, and said, "However, if you did take advantage of my sister, the consequences would be...unfortunate."

The fact that Garrett didn't even flinch seemed to

impress Chris. Still, Garrett was going to have to be very cautious while he courted Louisa.

Chris rose from his chair and said, "Shall we join the others?"

Garrett stood and followed him to the dining room. The first course was just being served, and as soon as they entered the room, Louisa shot from her seat and gestured him to the empty chair beside her.

When they were seated again, she leaned close to him and whispered, "I'm so sorry he did that. I hope he wasn't too hard on you."

He gave her a reassuring smile. "Not at all."

If he thought the worst was over, he realized quickly that it had only begun. He barely had a chance to taste his soup before Anne launched into the inquisition portion of the meal.

"I understand your father was a farmer," she said, her tone suggesting that made him inferior somehow.

It had only been a matter of time before someone broached the subject of his humble beginnings, but he wasn't ashamed of his past. He was instead very proud of his accomplishments. Although for the life of him he never understood why his parents hadn't strived to better themselves. Why they settled for a life barely a step above poverty when they could have done so much more for themselves and their sons.

"All of his life," Garrett told her. "My earliest memories are of working beside him in the fields."

"Yet you didn't follow in his footsteps," Anne noted, her words sounding an awful lot like an accusation. Much the way his father had sounded when Garrett had informed him that he planned to leave the island to attend college.

"No, I didn't. I wanted an education."

"How did your father feel about that?"

"Anne," Louisa said, plainly embarrassed by her sister's behavior.

"What?" Anne asked, her innocent look too manufactured to be genuine. He wasn't sure if she was jealous of Louisa, or simply being difficult because she could. If there was one thing Garrett knew for sure, he'd definitely chosen the right sister. Had he picked Anne, he would be asking for a life of misery.

"Stop being so nosy," Louisa said.

Anne shrugged. "How else can we get to know Mr. Sutherland?"

"Please call me Garrett," he told Anne. "And in answer to your question, my father wasn't at all happy with me. He expected me to take over the farm when he retired. I wanted to do something more with my life."

"Which you certainly have," Chris said, and maybe Garrett was imagining things, but he almost sounded impressed.

"If there's one thing I've learned," Garrett said, "it's that you can't live your life to please other people." He glanced over at Louisa, catching her eye for emphasis. "You have to follow your heart."

"I believe that, too," Olivia said. She reached over and placed a hand on her husband's arm. "Aaron is starting back to school in the fall. Premed."

"I'd heard that," Garrett said. He made it his business to know everything about his stiffest competition. Aaron's leaving the family business would create the convenient opening he required to insinuate himself inside.

"He's going to be a brilliant doctor," Olivia said,

beaming with pride. She was a plain woman, very young and unassuming, but pretty when she smiled… and quite the brilliant scientist from what he understood. The previous autumn, an unidentifiable blight potentially threatened all the crops on the island. The effects would have been devastating on the export trade, the main source of income for the country, and Olivia had been hired by the royal family to find an eco-friendly cure.

"I've heard that your own brilliance saved the livelihood of every landowner in the country," Garrett told her. "Myself included."

Olivia grinned shyly and blushed. It would seem that he had won over at least three-quarters of the females at the table. Anne seemed a lost cause at this point. Chris and Aaron, he wasn't sure about, but it looked promising. Now it was time for a change of subject, and he'd done his research.

"I understand you spent quite a lot of time in the States," Garrett said to Melissa.

"I was born on Morgan Isle but raised in New Orleans," she told him.

"A lovely city," he commented.

"You've been there?"

He nodded. "Several times in fact. For business. Terrible what happened during Katrina."

"It was. I started a foundation to fund the rehabilitation of the city."

"I had no idea. I'd love to make a donation."

Melissa smiled. "That would be lovely, thank you."

"I'll have a check sent round next week."

"What other places have you visited?" Louisa asked him, and they launched into a conversation about traveling abroad, and everyone's favorite vacation spot.

Garrett was pleasantly surprised to find that, with the exception of Anne, they were a friendly bunch, and not nearly as uptight as he'd expected. The tone of the conversation was not unlike those of his youth, when his family gathered for supper. In fact, by the time dessert was served, Garrett realized that he was actually enjoying himself.

Louisa didn't say much, but instead spent most of her time gazing up at him, seemingly mesmerized by every word that passed his lips.

After dinner, Chris pushed back from the table and asked Garrett, "Up for a friendly game of poker? We play every Friday evening."

Before he could answer, Louisa said, "Garrett and I are taking a walk in the garden." Which he took as his clue to decline their offer, when the truth was he would much rather play cards than take a leisurely stroll, but securing his position with Louisa took precedence for now.

"Maybe some other time," he told Chris.

"Of course." Chris turned to Louisa, his expression serious, and said, "Not too far, and I want you inside before sundown."

"I know," Louisa replied, sounding exasperated, and Garrett didn't blame her. He knew her family kept a tight grip on the reins, but telling a woman of twenty-seven that she couldn't stay out past dark bordered on the absurd.

Louisa slipped her arm through his and smiled up at him. "Ready?"

He thanked her family for dinner, then let Louisa lead him through the castle and out onto a patio that opened up into acres of lush flower gardens. The evening was a warm one, but a cool breeze blew in from the bluff.

She kept a firm grip on his arm as they started down the path, as though she feared the instant they were in the clear he might run for his life.

"I'm really sorry about my family," she said, looking apologetic. "As you probably noticed, they treat me like a child."

"They are quite...*protective*."

"It's humiliating. They think I'm naive."

Maybe they weren't so far off the mark, he thought wryly. She was unsophisticated enough to fall for his charms without question or doubt. Not that he would ever mistreat her, or compromise her honor. She would never suffer as his wife.

"I'm sure they mean well," he told her. "I imagine it would be much worse if they didn't care at all."

"I guess you're right," she conceded. "But since the threats started they've been a lot worse than usual. They think everyone I meet is a spy or something."

"I had seen something on the news about the security being breached in your father's hospital suite in London. I understand no one was able to identify the suspect from the surveillance footage."

"He calls himself the Gingerbread Man."

"Seriously?"

"Strange, I know. It started last summer with e-mail. He hacked into our computer system and sent threatening messages to us from our own accounts. They were all twisted versions of nursery rhymes."

"Nursery rhymes?" That didn't sound very threatening to him.

"Mine said, 'I love you, a bushel and a peck. A bushel

and a peck, and a noose around your neck. With a noose around your neck, you will drop into a heap. You'll drop into a heap and forever you will sleep.'" She looked up at him with a wry smile and said, "I memorized it."

On second thought, that was rather ominous. "What were the others?"

"I don't remember them word for word, but the common theme was burning alive."

Ouch. No wonder the family was being so cautious.

"At first we thought it was just an elaborate prank, until he managed to slip through castle security and get on the grounds. They think he scaled the bluff."

That explained the seemingly excessive security the night of the ball. "Was anyone harmed?"

"No, but he left a note. It said, 'Run, run, as fast as you can. You can't catch me. I'm the Gingerbread Man.' That's how we learned his name. We haven't heard anything from him lately, but that doesn't mean he's stopped. Things will be quiet for a while, then just when we think that he's given up, he'll leave another note somewhere or send an untraceable e-mail. He sent a gift basket full of rotten fruit for New Year's, then he sent flowers for Melissa and Chris congratulating them on the pregnancy. *Weeks* before the official announcement was made. He even knew that they were having triplets."

"Sounds like someone on the inside."

"We thought so, too, but everyone checked out."

At least her family's protectiveness made a bit more sense now. He just hoped it didn't interfere with his plans. It could be difficult courting a woman who wasn't allowed to leave her home.

"Enough about my family drama," she said, waving

the subject away like a pesky insect. "What is your family like?"

"Simple," he said, then quickly added, "Not intellectually. But they prefer to live a...*humble* lifestyle." One that didn't include him.

"What do your brothers do?"

"Two own a business together in England. They sell farming equipment. My youngest brother is something of a...wanderer. Last I heard he was working a cattle ranch in Scotland."

"I'd like to meet them," she said, with an eagerness that surprised him. "Maybe they could all come to the castle for a visit."

Considering he was trying to impress the royal family, that probably wouldn't be wise. "I'm not so sure that would be a good idea."

She frowned. "You're not ashamed of them?"

Once again, her directness surprised him. "I'm afraid it's quite the opposite."

Her eyes widened. "They're ashamed of *you?*"

"Maybe not ashamed, but they're not very pleased with the path I chose."

"How is that possible? Look how well you've done. All that you've accomplished. How can they not be proud?"

He'd asked himself that same question a million times, but had long ago given up trying to understand their reasoning. He no longer cared what they thought of him. "It's...complicated."

She patted his arm. "Well, I think you're amazing. The instant I saw you I knew you were special."

He could see that she truly meant it, and in an odd way he wished he could say the same of her. He was sure that Louisa was very special in her own right, and maybe someday he would learn to appreciate that.

"Tell me the truth," she said. "Did my family scare you off?"

He could see by her expression that she was genuinely concerned, but he was a man on a mission. It would take a lot more than a grilling by her siblings to get in his way.

He gave her arm a squeeze. "Absolutely not."

Her smile was one of relief. "Good. Because I really like you, Garrett."

Never had he met a woman so forward with her feelings, so willing to put herself out on a limb. He liked that about her, and at the same time it made him uncomfortable. He was taught by his father that showing affection made a man weak. If he loved his sons, his father never once said so.

But Garrett had the feeling that if he was going to make this relationship work, he was going to have to learn to be more open with his feelings. At least until he had a royal title and Louisa had a ring on her finger.

He smiled and said, "The feeling is mutual, Your Highness."

Four

Louisa gazed up at Garrett, looking so sweet and innocent. So...*pure*. He felt almost guilty for deceiving her.

"I think at this point it would be all right for you to call me Louisa," she said.

"All right, Louisa."

"Can we speak frankly?"

"Is there ever a time when you don't?"

Her cheeks blushed a charming shade of pink and she bit her lip. "Sorry. I have this terrible habit of saying everything that's on my mind. It drives everyone crazy."

"Don't apologize. It's a welcome change. Most women play games." Unless this was some sort of game she was playing. But his instincts told him that she didn't have a manipulative bone in her body.

"You should know that I'm not looking for a temporary

relationship. I want to settle down and have a family."
She stopped walking and looked up at him. "I need to
know that you feel the same. That you're not just playing
the field."

"I'm thirty-seven years old, Louisa. I think I've played
the field long enough."

"In that case, there's something else I should probably
mention."

Why did he sense that he wasn't going to like this?

"We should talk about children."

She certainly didn't pull any punches, although oddly,
he was finding that he liked that about her. "What about
them?"

"I want a big family."

He narrowed his eyes at her. "How big?"

The grip on his arm tightened, as though she was
worried he might try to make a run for it. "At least six
kids. Maybe more."

For a second he thought she might be joking, or testing
him, then he realized that she was dead serious.

Six kids? Bloody hell, no wonder she was still single.
Who in this day and age wanted that many children?
He'd never felt the desire or need to have one child, much
less half a dozen of them! Marrying a royal, he knew at
least one heir would be expected. Maybe two. But *six?*

Despite his strong feelings on the matter, he could
see by her expression that this was not a negotiable point
for Louisa and he chose his next words very carefully.
"I'll admit that I've never given any thought to having a
family that large, but anything is possible."

A bright and relieved smile lit her entire face and he
felt an undeniable flicker of guilt, which he promptly
shook off. This was business. Once they were married,

he would lay down the law and insist that two children at most would be plenty and she would eventually learn to live with that. Or maybe, after the first child or two, she would change her mind anyway. He'd seen the way his parents struggled with a large family, the emotional roller coaster rides. Who would want to subject themselves to that?

Louisa gazed up at him, a dreamy look on her face. "It would be okay if you kissed me now," she said, then added, "If you want to."

Oh, he wanted to. So much that it surprised him a little. The idea had been to wait until their second date before he kissed her, to draw out the anticipation. Did she intend to derail each one of his carefully laid plans? "Are you sure that's what you want?" he asked.

"Just because my family treats me like a child, that doesn't mean I am one."

There was nothing childish about her, which she proved by not even waiting for him to make the first move. Instead, she reached up, slid her hands behind his neck, pulled him down to her level and kissed him. Her lips were soft but insistent, and she smelled fantastic. Delicate and feminine.

Though he had intended to keep it brief, to take things slowly, he felt himself being drawn closer, as though pulled by an invisible rope anchored somewhere deep inside his chest. His arms went around her and when his fingers brushed her bare back, what felt like an electric shock arced through his fingers. Louisa must have felt it, too, because she whimpered and curled her fingers into the hair at his nape. He felt her tongue, slick and warm against the seam of his lips and he knew he had to taste her, and when he did, she was as sweet as candy.

He was aware that this was moving too far, too fast, but as she leaned in closer, pressing her body against his, he felt helpless to stop her. Never had the simple act of kissing a woman aroused him so thoroughly, but Louisa seemed to put her heart and soul, her entire being, into it.

To him, self-control was a virtue, but Louisa seemed to know exactly which buttons to push. Not at all what he would have expected from a woman rumored to be so sweet and innocent. Which had him believing that she really wasn't so sweet and innocent after all.

Her hands slipped down his shoulders and inside his jacket. She stroked his chest through his shirt and that was all he could take. He broke the kiss, breathless and bewildered, his heart hammering like mad.

Louisa expelled a soft shudder of breath and rested her head against his chest. "Now *that* was a kiss."

He couldn't exactly argue. Although the whole point of this visit had been to prove to her family that his intentions were pure, yet here he was, practically mauling her out in the open, where anyone could see. If someone *was* watching, he hoped they hadn't failed to notice that she'd made the first move and he'd been the one to put on the brakes.

She nuzzled her face to his chest, her breath warm through his shirt. He curled his hands into fists, to keep from tangling them through her hair, from drawing her head back and kissing her again. He wanted to taste her lips and her throat, nibble at her ears. He wanted to put his hands all over her.

"It probably isn't proper to say this," Louisa said, "but I can't wait to see you naked."

Bloody hell. He backed away and held her at arm's

length, before he did something really stupid like drag her into the bushes and have his way with her. "Do you ever *not* say what's on your mind?"

"I just gave you the censored version," she answered with an impish grin. "Would you like to know what I'm really thinking?"

Of course he would, but this was not the time or place. "I'll use my imagination." He glanced up at the darkening sky and said, "It's getting late. I should get you back inside."

"Lest I turn into a pumpkin," she said with a sigh and took his hand, as naturally as if they had known each other for years, and they walked down the path toward the castle.

"I had a good time tonight," he said.

"Me, too. Although I get the feeling that I'm not quite what you expected."

"No, you're not. You're more intriguing and compelling than I could have imagined."

As she smiled up at him, he realized that was probably the most honest thing he'd said all night.

Louisa stood in the study, watching as Garrett's car zipped down the drive, until the glow of his taillights disappeared past the front gate.

She sighed and rested her forehead against the cool glass. This had been, by far, one of the best nights of her life. Kissing Garrett had been…magical. Even if she had been the one to make the first move. Later, when he had kissed her goodbye, it was so sweet and tender she nearly melted into a puddle on the oriental rug.

He was definitely the one.

"He's using you."

Louisa whipped around to find Anne leaning in the study doorway, arms folded across her chest, her typical grumpy self. Typical for the last week or so, anyway.

"Why would you think that?" she asked.

"Because that's what men like him do. They use women like us. They feed us lies, then toss us aside like trash."

Louisa knew that, like herself, Anne hadn't had the best luck with men, but that reasoning was harsh, even for her. "Are you okay, Anne?"

"He's going to hurt you."

Louisa shook her head. "Garrett is different."

"How do you know that?"

"How do *you* know that he isn't?"

Anne sighed and shook her head, as though she pitied her poor, naive sister. Louisa would have been upset, but she knew that attacking her was Anne's way of working through her own anger. Not that she didn't get a little tired of being her sister's punching bag.

"I can take care of myself," Louisa told her.

Anne shrugged, as though she didn't care one way or another. Which she must, or she wouldn't have said anything in the first place. "Don't say I didn't warn you."

"Did something happen to you?" Louisa asked, and she could swear she saw a flicker of pain before Anne carefully smothered it with a look of annoyance.

"You think that just because I don't like Garrett, something is wrong with *me?*"

"You can talk to me, Anne. I want to help."

"You're the one who needs help if you think that man really has feelings for you." With one last pathetic shake of her head, Anne turned and left. Her sister was obviously hurting, and Louisa felt bad about it, but she wished Anne would stop trying to drag Louisa down with her. Why couldn't Anne just be happy for her for once?

Maybe she was jealous. Maybe Anne wanted Garrett for herself. Or maybe, like Louisa, she wanted someone to love her, to see her for who she really was. Even though Anne could be a real pain in the neck sometimes, deep down there was a sweetness about her, a tender side, and she was loyal to the death to the ones that she loved.

"You'll meet someone, too," Louisa whispered to the empty doorway, knowing with all her heart that it was true. Even though Anne was a little pessimistic and occasionally cranky, there was a man out there who would appreciate all her gifts and overlook her faults. He would love her for who she was, just the way Garrett would love Louisa.

Worried for her sister, she started out the door, intending to collect her Shih Tzu, Muffin—who had spent the afternoon with his groomer and behaviorist—and tell him all about her day, but she ran into Chris in the foyer.

"Poker game over already?" she asked. Typically they played well past eleven. Louisa didn't play cards, unless you counted War and Solitaire, but occasionally she liked to sit and watch them.

"Melissa was tired and Liv wanted to get back to the lab. Some new research project she's working on. I assume your evening was a success."

She smiled and nodded.

"Have you got a minute?"

"Actually, I was just on my way to get Muffin."

His expression darkened. "I suppose you heard what

your little mutt did to the pillows on the library sofa. There was stuffing everywhere."

She cringed. "Yes. Sorry."

"The day before that it was Aaron's shoes."

"I know. I offered to replace them."

"He's a menace."

"He just wants attention."

"What he's going to get is a nice doghouse in the gardens."

Even if she thought Chris was serious, that wouldn't work either because every time Muffin was let outside unsupervised he made a run for it.

"I'll keep a closer eye on him," she promised. "What did you want to talk about?"

"Let's go in the study."

She couldn't tell if this would be a good talk, or a bad talk. But she had the sneaking suspicion that it had something to do with Garrett.

Louisa sat on the sofa while Chris fixed himself a drink. In preparation for his role as future King, Chris had always been the most responsible and aggressive sibling. He honored the responsibility, oftentimes to his own personal detriment. Still it surprised and impressed Louisa, since having to take their father's place while he was ill, how effortlessly Chris had slipped into his place and taken over his responsibilities. She had no doubt that if, God forbid, their father didn't recover, Chris would make a fine king.

But she had every confidence that their father would make a full recovery. He simply *had* to.

"I want you to know," Chris said, his back to her, "I didn't appreciate you waiting until this morning to announce that you had invited Garrett to dinner."

So he'd asked her here to scold her. Wonderful. "Can you really blame me? Had I said anything earlier I never would have heard the end of it."

He turned to her, took a swallow of his drink, then said, "You could have been putting the family in danger."

She rolled her eyes. "You say that like you haven't known Garrett for years. If he was dangerous, I'm sure we'd have heard about it a long time ago."

"You still have to follow the rules. We've all had to make sacrifices, Louisa."

As if she didn't know that. If they didn't treat her like a child, she would have been more forthcoming. This was more her siblings' fault than hers. They drove her to it. Sometimes she just got tired of being the obedient princess.

"I'm assuming that he must have checked out," she guessed, "or he never would have made it through the front gate."

"Yes, he did."

"I knew he would, and I didn't need a team of security operatives to tell me."

He shook his head, as though she was a hopeless cause. He crossed the room and sat on the sofa beside her. "I had a talk with Father about this earlier today, regarding his wishes concerning the matter."

Louisa held her breath. If the King disapproved of a man she wanted to date, she would be forbidden. Those were the rules. "And?"

"He told me to use my discretion."

Louisa wasn't sure if that was a good or a bad thing. At least she knew their father would be fair. Would Chris forbid her to see Garrett to teach her a lesson?

This was probably something she should have considered when she waited until the last second before telling Chris about Garrett's visit.

"And what did you decide?" she asked, flashing him the most wide-eyed and hopeful look she could manage.

He regarded her sternly for a moment, then a grin tipped up the corner of his mouth. "It's clear that you have feelings for the man. Of course you can see him."

She let out an excited squeal and threw her arms around Chris, hugging him so hard that his drink nearly sloshed onto the sofa. "Thank you! Thank you!"

"You're welcome," he said with a chuckle. *"However…"*

Oh boy, here came the conditions. She sat back and braced herself.

"No more stunts like you pulled this morning."

She shook her head. "Never. I promise. I swear, it won't happen again."

"In addition, you will not leave the premises without a minimum of two bodyguards, and I need at least two days' advance notice before you visit any sort of public place or attend a function. No exceptions, or I will not hesitate to place you on indefinite house arrest."

Inconvenient, but definitely doable. "No problem."

"And please, let's try not to give the press anything to salivate over. With Father's health, the last thing the family needs is more gossip and rumors."

She refrained from rolling her eyes. Now he was being silly. "Honestly, Chris, have I *ever* been one to create a scandal?"

"It's not necessarily you I'm concerned about."

"You don't have to worry about Garrett, either. He's

a complete gentleman. So much so that when it came to kissing, I had to make the first move."

Chris cringed. "I really didn't need to know that. I'm counting on you to be...diplomatic."

Diplomatic? He made it sound as though she and Garrett were forming a business partnership. Besides, she knew for a fact that Chris hadn't been very "diplomatic" when he was first seeing Melissa. They couldn't seem to keep their hands off each other.

What he was really saying was that he expected her to live up to her reputation as the innocent and pure princess. Eventually her family was going to have to accept that she was a woman, not a child.

If only he knew what went on in her head, how curious she was about sex and eager to experiment. Most modern women didn't make it to twenty-seven with their virginity intact. He would probably drop in a dead faint if he knew about all of the reading she had done online about sex. When it came to intimacy, boy, was she ready. It was all she'd been able to think about since she had danced with Garrett on Saturday night.

"You don't have to worry about me or Garrett," she assured him and left it at that, and Chris looked relieved to have the subject closed.

"I want you to know that I like Garrett," he added.

"But...?"

"No buts. I think you and he would be a good match."

She eyed him skeptically. "Even though he isn't royal?"

"Liv isn't a royal," he reminded her.

True. Liv was an orphan from the States who didn't even know who her parents were, but there was always that double standard. A prince could get away with marrying a commoner. A princess on the other hand was held to a higher standard. She imagined that Garrett's money was probably his only saving grace. She would never be allowed to date a man of modest means.

"Given his background," Chris continued, "Garrett would be the perfect choice to take over Aaron's position now that he's going back to school. If you marry him, that is."

Oh, she would. The fact that he was already making plans to include Garrett in the family business was more than she could have hoped for. "I think that's a wonderful idea!"

"However," he added sternly, "I don't want you to think this means you should rush into anything."

How could she rush fate? Either it was or it wasn't meant to be. Time was irrelevant. Besides, Chris was one to talk. He'd asked Melissa to marry him after only two weeks. Of course, at the time, he'd expected nothing more than an arranged, loveless marriage. Boy, did he get more than he'd bargained for. But destiny was like that. And there was no doubt that he and Melissa were meant for one another.

Just like Louisa and Garrett.

She pictured them a year from now, married and blissfully happy, hopefully with their first baby on the way. Or maybe even born already. She would very much like to conceive on her honeymoon. What could be a more special way to celebrate the union of their souls than to create a new life? Some women dreamed of a career, and others liked to travel. Some spent their lives donating their time to charitable causes. All Louisa had ever wanted was to be a wife and mother. Archaic as some believed it to be, it was her ultimate dream. A man to cherish her, children to depend on her. Who could ask for more?

"By the way," Chris said. "Melissa and I are planning to go sailing Sunday."

"Is she allowed to do that so close to her due date?"

"As long as she takes it easy and stays off her feet. We figure we should get in as much time on the water before the babies come. You're welcome to join us. Garrett, too, if you'd like to invite him."

Her parents were leaving for England on Sunday morning for testing on her father's heart pump, and Anne was going with them. If Chris and Melissa were going to be gone, too, that would mean that she and Garrett could have some time alone, without her entire family watching over their shoulders. She wondered if there was any way she could get rid of Aaron and Liv, as well.

"Maybe next time," she told Chris. "I already have plans."

At least, she would have plans, just as soon as she called Garrett and invited him over.

Five

Garrett had just walked in the door of his town house when his cell phone rang. He looked at the display and saw that it was Louisa's personal line. When they had exchanged numbers earlier, he hadn't expected a call quite this soon. In fact, he'd just assumed he would be the one calling her.

It shouldn't have surprised him that she wouldn't let him make the next move. This so-called shy and innocent Princess seemed to have everyone snowed, because as far as he could tell, she didn't have a shy bone in her body. As for innocence, she certainly didn't act like an inexperienced virgin.

When he answered, she asked, "I'm not bothering you, am I?"

"Of course not." He dropped his keys and wallet on the kitchen counter then shrugged out of his jacket and draped it over the back of a chair. "I just walked in the door."

"I wanted to tell you again what a wonderful time I had this evening."

"I did, too." Things were progressing even more quickly than he'd hoped.

"I was wondering what you're doing Sunday afternoon. I thought you might like to come over."

He chuckled. "I suppose it's too much to expect that I might get to ask *you* on a date."

"Am I being too forward?" she asked, sounding worried.

"No, not at all. I like a woman who knows what she wants."

"I just wanted to catch you before you made other plans."

"If I'd made other plans, I would cancel them. And in answer to your question, I would very much like to come over. If it's all right with your family, that is."

"Of course it is. They love you."

That must have meant he'd passed the initiation. Not that he ever doubted he would. It was just nice to know that he'd scaled the first major obstacle.

"I thought maybe we could have a picnic," Louisa suggested. "Out on the bluff, overlooking the ocean."

"Just the two of us?"

"My parents and Anne will be leaving for England, and Chris and Melissa are going sailing. Liv will probably be tied up in the lab and lately Aaron has been down there assisting her. And as long as I stay on the grounds I don't need security at my heels, so we'll be alone."

He didn't miss the suggestive lilt in her tone, and

wondered what she expected they might be doing, other than picnicking that is.

"Muffin will be there, too, of course," she added.

"Muffin?"

"My dog. You would have met him today, but he was with the groomer and then his behaviorist. He's a Shih Tzu."

So, Muffin was one of those small yappy dogs that Garrett found overwhelmingly annoying. He preferred real dogs, like the shepherds and border collies they kept on the farm. Intelligent dogs with a brain larger than a walnut.

"He can be a bit belligerent at times," Louisa said, "but he's very sweet. I know you'll love him."

"I'm sure I will," he lied, and reminded himself again that this relationship would require making adjustments. It was just one more issue he could address after they were married.

The front bell rang and Garrett frowned. He wasn't expecting anyone. Who would make a social call this late?

"Was that your door?" Louisa asked.

"Yes, but I'm not expecting anyone."

"Could it be a lady friend perhaps?" Her tone was light, but he could hear an undercurrent of concern.

"The only woman in my life is you, Your Highness," he assured her, and could feel her smile into the phone.

The bell rang again. Whoever it was, they were bloody well impatient.

"I won't keep you," she said.

"What time would you like me there Sunday?"

"Let's say 11:00 a.m. We can make a day of it."

"Sounds perfect," he said, even though he'd never really been the picnicking type. He would much rather take her out to eat—preferably at the finest restaurant in town—but the heightened security was going to make dating a challenge.

They said their goodbyes and by the time Garrett made it to the door, the bell rang a third time. "I'm coming," he grumbled under his breath. He pulled the door open, repressing a groan when he saw who was standing there.

"What, you're not happy to see your baby brother?"

Not at all, in fact, but he did his best not to look too exasperated. "Last I heard you were working a cattle ranch in Scotland."

Ian shrugged and said, "Got bored. Besides, I have something big in the works. A brilliant plan."

In other words, he was let go and had formulated some new get-rich-quick scheme. One that, like all his other brilliant plans, would undoubtedly crash and burn.

"Aren't you going to invite me in?" Ian asked with forced cheer, but the rumpled clothes, long hair and the week's worth of beard stubble said this was anything but a friendly social call.

Letting Ian in was tantamount to inviting a vampire into the house. He had a gift for bleeding dry his host both emotionally and financially and an annoying habit of staying far past his welcome.

It was hard to believe that he was once the sweet little boy Garrett used to sit on his knee and read to, then tuck into bed at night. For the first eight years of Ian's life, he was Garrett's shadow.

"Mum and Dad turn you away?" Garrett asked, and

he could see by Ian's expression that they had. Not that Garrett blamed them.

The cheery facade fell and Ian faced him with pleading eyes, looking tired and defeated. "Please, Garrett. I spent my last dime on a boat to the island and I haven't had a proper meal in days."

Or a shower, guessing by the stench, and it was more likely that he'd conned his way to the island than paid a penny for passage. But he looked so damned pathetic standing there. Despite everything, Ian was still his brother. His family. The only family who would bother to give him the time of day.

Knowing he would probably regret it later, Garrett moved aside so his brother could step into the foyer. The cool evening air that followed him inside sent a chill down Garrett's back and when Ian dropped his duffel on the floor, a plume of dust left a dirty ring on the Italian ceramic tile. He would consider it a bad omen if he believed in that sort of thing.

"Spacious," Ian said, gazing around the foyer and up the wide staircase to the second floor. "You've done well for yourself."

"Don't touch anything." Things had a mysterious habit of finding their way into Ian's pockets and disappearing forever. "And take off your boots. I don't want you trailing mud on my floors."

"Could I trouble you for a shower?" Ian asked as he kicked off his boots, revealing socks so filthy and full of holes they barely covered his feet.

"You can use the one in the spare bedroom." It was the room that possessed the least valuable items. "Up the stairs, first door on the right. I'll fix something to eat."

Ian nodded, grabbed his duffel and headed up the

stairs. Garrett considered wiping up the dust on the floor, but there would probably be more where that came from, so he decided to take care of it in the morning after Ian was gone. He walked to the kitchen instead and put a kettle on for tea, then rummaged through the icebox to see what leftovers his housekeeper had stashed there. He found a glass dish with a generous portion of pot roast, baked red skin potatoes and buttered baby carrots from last night's dinner.

He reached for a plate then figured, why dirty another dish, and set the whole thing in the microwave.

While he waited for it to heat, he noticed his wallet lying on the counter and out of habit slipped it into his pants pocket. He wasn't worried about the cash so much as his credit and ATM cards. The last time Ian had stayed with their brother Victor, he'd run off with his Mastercard and charged several thousand pounds' worth of purchases before Vic even realized the card was missing. Electronic equipment mostly, which Garrett figured Ian had probably sold for cash.

Garrett wasn't taking any chances. After a shower and a meal and a good night's sleep, he would loan Ian a few hundred pounds—that he knew would never be repaid—and send him on his merry way. With any luck, he wouldn't darken Garrett's doorway again for a very long time.

Ian emerged a few minutes later, freshly shaven, his hair still damp, wearing rumpled but clean clothes. "Best shower I ever had," he told Garrett.

"I made you tea."

He saw the cup and scowled. "I don't suppose you have anything stronger."

Garrett shrugged and said, "Sorry." Unless he wanted

his liquor cabinet cleaned out, Garrett was keeping it securely locked for the duration of his brother's visit. Besides, Ian probably had a bottle or two stashed in his duffel. Given the choice between a meal and a bottle of cheap whiskey, the alcohol always won.

"Well, then, tea it is," Ian conceded, as though he had a choice. "You just get in from work?"

"Why do you ask?"

"Came by earlier, but you weren't here. I waited for you in the park across the road."

It was a wonder he wasn't arrested for loitering. The authorities in this neighborhood had no tolerance for riffraff. "I wasn't working."

"Got a lady friend then, do you? Anyone I know?"

Garrett nearly chuckled at the thought of Ian socializing with the royal family. "No one you know."

The microwave beeped and Garrett pulled out the dish.

Knowing Garrett couldn't cook worth a damn, Ian eyed the food suspiciously. "You made that?"

"Don't worry, my housekeeper prepared it."

"In that case, slide it this way," Ian said, rubbing his work-roughened hands together in anticipation. Garrett watched as he shoveled a forkful into his mouth, eating right there at the kitchen counter, standing up.

"Delicious," he mumbled through a mouthful of beef and potatoes. He followed it with a swallow of tea. He wolfed down the food with an embarrassing lack of regard for the most basic table manners. Their mum would have been horrified. They may have lived like paupers but his mum had always insisted they carry themselves with dignity.

"So," Garrett asked, "why did you get fired this time?"

"Who says I was fired?" Ian asked indignantly.

"Please don't insult my intelligence."

He relented and answered, "The owner of the ranch caught me in the hay barn with his youngest daughter."

"How young?"

"Seventeen."

Garrett was about to say that a twenty-eight-year-old man had no business chasing a girl more than ten years his junior, but that was almost exactly the age difference between himself and Louisa. But that was different. Louisa was an adult—even if her family didn't treat her like one. Not to mention that Garrett intended to marry her, while he was quite sure his brother was only using the young girl in question.

"Don't give me that look of disapproval," Ian countered. "It wasn't my fault. She seduced me."

Of course. Nothing was ever his fault. Someone else was always to blame for his irresponsibility. "Did you ever consider telling her no?"

"If you'd seen her, you wouldn't have told her no, either."

Unlike his brother, Garrett wasn't a slave to his hormones. He had principles. He didn't take advantage of women. Not sexually, anyway. Besides, he wasn't taking advantage of Louisa. If she married him, she would never be denied a thing she desired. With the exception of a few children, that is.

"What are you going to do now?" he asked Ian.

"Like I said, I have something fantastic in the works.

A sure thing. I just need a bit of capital to get it off the ground."

He didn't say it, but Garrett knew exactly what he was thinking and saved him the trouble of having to ask. "Don't look at me. I've thrown away enough money on your so-called sure things."

Ian shrugged. "Your loss."

Garrett doubted that.

Ian finished his dinner, stopping just shy of licking the dish clean. "Delicious. Best meal I've had in weeks."

"I assume you need a place to stay."

He leaned back against the countertop and folded his arms over his chest. "There's a very comfortable bench in the park I could sleep on."

"You're welcome to use the spare bedroom. For *one* night," he stressed. "And I expect everything to be as you found it when you go."

"I'll even make the bed."

"Well then, I'm off to bed," Garrett said.

"Already? I thought we might catch up for a while."

"I have an early breakfast meeting."

Ian looked appalled. "You're working on a Saturday?"

"Sometimes I work Sundays, as well." A concept Ian, who worked as little as possible, would never grasp. "Help yourself to whatever you find in the icebox, and I have satellite television if you want to watch it. I'll see you in the morning."

"See you in the morning," Ian parroted as Garrett walked from the room. He felt uncomfortable leaving his brother to his own devices, but short of staying awake all night, he didn't have much choice.

Consequently, Garrett didn't see Ian in the morning.

When he rolled out of bed at 6:00 a.m., Ian had already left. With half the contents of the liquor cabinet and Garrett's car.

The e-mail showed up in Louisa's personal in-box late Saturday afternoon. At first when she saw the blank subject line she assumed it was junk mail, then she noticed the return address—G.B. Man—and her heart nearly stopped.

That couldn't be a coincidence. It had to be him.

Not now, she thought to herself. Not when things were going so well. She took a deep breath, preparing herself for the worst, and reluctantly double clicked to open it. The body of the e-mail read simply, Did you miss me, Princess?

No gruesome nursery rhymes or threats of violence this time, still a cold chill slithered up her spine. This was going to put everyone into a panic and security back on high alert. Which meant her chances of leaving the castle and going on a normal date with Garrett were slim to none. Why did the Gingerbread Man have to choose now to start harassing them again?

She leaned over for the phone to ring security, when she noticed the time stamp on the e-mail and realized it had actually been sent yesterday morning. Louisa didn't check her in-box daily, but her brothers did. If they had gotten one, too, wouldn't she have heard about it by now?

Was it possible that the Gingerbread Man had sent a message to her alone? And if so, was it a coincidence that it started at the same time she began seeing Garrett? Was he trying to complicate things?

She sat back in her chair, wondering what she should

do. The e-mail hadn't been threatening at all. Just a reminder that he was still there, which they all had assumed anyway. If he had planned to actually harm a member of the family, wouldn't he have done it by now?

If she accidentally forgot to mention this to security, what difference would it really make?

She sat there with her finger hovering over the delete button, weighing her options. If it turned out her brothers and sister had gotten an e-mail, too, she could just tell them that she must have erased hers accidentally, assuming it was junk mail. She hated to lie, but this was her future on the line. Her relationship with Garrett might be destiny, but even destiny had its limits. Would Garrett want to court a woman who wasn't even allowed to leave the house, and by dating her very possibly make *himself* a target?

It would be best, for now, if no one else knew about this.

Before she could change her mind, she stabbed the delete key, promising herself that if he contacted her again, threatening or not, she would let the family know. Until then, it would be her secret.

Six

It was after noon when Garrett's meeting finally ended. He was in the company limo on his way to the club to play squash with Wes, when he received a call from the police informing him that his car had been in an accident. Apparently, in his haste to flee Garrett's town house, Ian had run off the road and into a tree.

"He was pretty banged up," the officer told him. "But he was conscious and alert when they put him in the ambulance."

Despite everything, Garrett was relieved Ian wasn't hurt too badly. If he'd died, Garrett would have been the one to break the news to his family. Since it was Garrett's car Ian had been driving, they would likely pin the blame on him. Not that he cared what they thought of him any longer. It was just a hassle he didn't need.

"Did he say how it happened?" Garrett asked.

"He claims he swerved to avoid hitting an animal in the road, a dog, and lost control."

Ian had always had a soft spot for animals. Dogs especially, so it was a plausible excuse.

Garrett dreaded the next question he had to ask. "Was alcohol involved?"

"We assumed so at first. There were a dozen or so broken bottles of liquor in the car. Expensive stuff, too."

Tell me about it, Garrett wanted to say.

"He denied being intoxicated, but we won't know for certain until we get the results of the blood test. He must have been going quite fast though. I'm sorry to say that the car is totaled."

It wouldn't be the first car Ian had demolished with his careless driving. Or the last. Besides, Garrett had never expected to get it back. He didn't have the heart to report it as stolen and Ian would have eventually sold it. At least now Garrett would get the insurance money, and Ian would have to face what he'd done while the wounds were still fresh.

He thanked the officer for the information and instructed his driver to take him to the hospital instead, then rang Wes to cancel. With any luck, this fiasco wouldn't find its way into the papers, or, if it did, he hoped no names were released. With the royal family keeping a close eye on him, the last thing he needed was a scandal. Not that he should be held accountable for his brother's actions, but in his experience royals had a… *unique* way of looking at things.

Garrett should have listened to his instincts and never let Ian in the house. Or maybe this time Ian would finally learn his lesson.

The limo dropped him at the front entrance of the hospital and Garrett stopped at the information desk to get his brother's room number. Ian's was on the third floor just past the nursing station, but when Garrett walked through the door, he was totally unprepared for what he saw. He'd expected Ian to have suffered a few bumps and bruises, maybe a laceration or two, but his baby brother looked as though he'd gone a dozen rounds with a prize fighter.

His face was swollen and bruised, his nose broken and both eyes blackened. His right wrist and hand were wrapped in gauze, and he'd suffered small nicks and cuts on both arms. From the broken bottles, Garrett figured. His left leg was in a cast from foot to midthigh and suspended in a sling.

Garrett shook his head and thought, *Ian, what have you done to yourself?*

Instead of seeing Ian the troublemaker lying there, under the bandages and bruises Garrett could only picture the little boy who used to come to him with skinned knees and splinters, and his anger swiftly fizzled away.

"Garrett Sutherland?" someone asked from behind him.

He turned to find a doctor standing just outside the room. "Yes."

"Dr. Sacsner," he said, shaking Garrett's hand. "I'm your brother's surgeon."

"Surgeon?"

"Orthopedics." He gestured out of the room. "Could we have a word?"

Garrett nodded and followed him into the hallway.

"Your brother is a lucky man," the doctor began to say.

"He doesn't look so lucky to me."

"I know it looks bad, but it could have been much worse. The fact that he suffered no internal injuries is nothing short of a miracle."

"What about his leg?"

The doctor frowned. "There he wasn't so lucky. His lower leg was crushed under the dash. The impact shattered the fibula and snapped his tibia in three places. The only thing holding it together are rods and pins."

"But he'll recover?"

"With time and physical therapy he should make a full recovery. The first six weeks will be the most difficult. It's imperative he stay off the leg as much as possible and keep it elevated."

"So he'll stay here?"

"For another day or two, then he'll be released."

Released? Where was he going to go?

He realized, by the doctor's expression, that Garrett was expected to take Ian home.

Bloody hell. He didn't have time for this now. Nor did he feel he owed his brother a thing after all the grief he'd caused. But who else did Ian have? Where else could he stay?

"I know it sounds like a daunting task," the doctor said. "But if money is no object, you can hire twenty-four-hour care if necessary." His pager beeped and he checked the display. "I'll be back to check on him later."

"Before you go, was it determined if alcohol was involved?"

"That was a concern at first, since he came in smelling

like a distillery. We were hesitant to give him anything for the pain, but he swore he wasn't drinking, and the tox screen came back clean. No drugs or alcohol in his system."

So he had just been driving too fast and lost control. If that wasn't Ian's life story. As a kid he was always pushing the limits and hurting himself. If there was a tree too high or dangerous to climb, Ian wasn't happy until he reached the highest branch. By the time he was eight, he'd suffered more broken bones and received more stitches than most people did in a lifetime.

Maybe this time he would learn his lesson.

"You didn't have to come here," he heard his brother say, his voice rusty from the anesthesia.

Garrett turned and walked to his bed. "Someone has to pay the bill."

Ian gazed up at him, bleary-eyed and fuzzy. "I guess 'I'm sorry' isn't going to cut it this time."

"It might if I thought you meant it." But Ian wasn't sorry for all the trouble he'd caused. Only that he'd been caught.

His eyes drifted shut, and Garrett thought that maybe he'd fallen asleep, then he opened them again and said, "I was going to bring it back."

"The car or the liquor?"

"Both."

Garrett wished he could believe that.

"I got a few miles from your house and I started to feel guilty."

That was even more unbelievable. "You don't do guilt."

"Apparently I do now. I thought if I got back fast

enough you would never know I'd left. Then that damned dog darted out in front of me." Ian studied him for several seconds. "You don't believe me."

"Is there a reason I should?"

He sighed. "Well, whether you believe me or not, I'm tired of living this way. I'm going to change this time. I swear I am."

Garrett might have believed his brother if he hadn't heard the same thing so many times before. "Let's just concentrate on getting you healthy. The doctor says you have to keep off the leg for six weeks. With my hectic schedule, I'll have to hire a nurse to stay with you."

"You don't have to do that."

And he didn't expect a penny of it back. "Where else would you go? You think Mum and Dad would let you stay with them?"

His expression said he knew the answer to that question was no. Even if their mother still had a soft spot for Ian, their father would put his foot down.

"I'll figure something out," Ian declared.

"You have a friend who will take you in?"

Ian was silent. They both knew that Ian had never made a friend he didn't eventually betray. Unfortunately, Garrett was all he had. "You're staying with me."

"I owe you too much already," Ian said, and Garrett wished the regret he heard in his brother's voice was genuine. He wasn't counting on it though.

"Face it, Ian, we're stuck with each other. If you really mean what you say about turning over a new leaf—"

"I do. I swear it."

"Then you can spend the next six weeks proving it to me."

* * *

Louisa woke early Sunday morning, planning her picnic with Garrett before she even got out of bed, until she heard the low rumble of thunder and the thrum of rain against her bedroom window.

Oh, damn!

Rubbing the sleep from her eyes, she climbed out of bed, rousing Muffin, who gave a grumble of irritation before settling back to sleep. She walked to the window and shoved the curtains aside. Dense gray clouds rolled in from the northwest, and a fierce wind pummeled the trees and whipped rain against the windows.

She sighed. It looked as though the weather front that was supposed to miss the island had changed course sometime during the night. It was only 7:00 a.m., but even if the rain stopped it would still be too wet for a picnic. She'd been so sure it would be a sunny day, she hadn't bothered with a plan B. Her options were limited considering she couldn't leave the castle with Garrett without giving Chris a two-day warning. And with the weather so dreary, she doubted that he and Melissa would be doing any sailing today.

So much for her and Garrett having some time to themselves. If they had to stay inside the castle, someone would be constantly looking over their shoulders, watching their every move.

She frowned. Being royalty, especially royalty under house arrest, could be terribly inconvenient.

But she refused to let this small setback dampen her spirits. She was sure if she put her mind to it, she could come up with something for them to do, some indoor activity they would both enjoy. Maybe a tour of the castle or a game of billiards. Or maybe they could just sit and talk.

On her way to the shower, Louisa passed her computer and was half tempted to log on, just to see if she had gotten another e-mail from their stalker. No one had said anything about getting the e-mail yesterday, so she could only assume his latest communication had been sent exclusively to her. She couldn't help wondering if her relationship with Garrett was the catalyst or if it was just a coincidence that he chose now to pick on her individually.

Maybe she should check, just in case. She took a step toward her computer, then stopped. What would be the point of checking? If he e-mailed her, he e-mailed her and nothing would change that, and the way she looked at it, what she didn't know wouldn't hurt her.

She gave her computer one last furtive glance and headed to the bathroom instead.

She showered using her favorite rose-scented body wash and took extra care fixing her hair. Instead of the conservative bun she typically wore, she used hot rollers then brushed her hair smooth, until it lay loose and silky down her back. She dressed in pale pink capris and a crème-colored cashmere sweater set, then slipped her feet into a pair of pink leather flats. She rounded out the look with mascara and pink, cherry-flavored lip gloss with a touch of glitter.

She stood back to examine her reflection, happy with what she saw, sure that Garrett would be pleased, too.

Anticipation adding an extra lift to her step, she headed downstairs to the dining room for a spot of tea, Muffin trailing behind her, but Geoffrey intercepted her at the foot of the stairs.

"Prince Christian asked that you call him as soon as possible."

She frowned. "Call him? Did they go sailing? The weather is horrible."

"No, Your Highness. He took Princess Melissa to the hospital early this morning."

Her heart skipped a beat. "What for?"

"He didn't say. He just asked that you call him as soon as you're up."

"Are Aaron and Liv up yet?"

"Not yet."

She was going to ask him to wake them, but there was no sense in starting a panic before she even knew what was wrong. It might be nothing.

"Could you see that Muffin is fed and let out?" she asked Geoffrey.

"Of course. Come along, Muffin."

Muffin just stood there looking back and forth between them.

"Breakfast," Geoffrey added, and Muffin scurried excitedly after him.

Forgetting about her tea, Louisa hurried back to her room and dialed her brother's cell phone. As soon as he answered she asked, "What's wrong? Is Melissa okay? Are the babies all right?"

Chris chuckled and said, "Relax, everyone is fine. Melissa started having contractions last night."

"Why didn't you wake me?"

"There was nothing you could have done and Melissa didn't want you to worry."

"Is she in labor? I thought it was too early."

"She was, but they gave her a drug to stop it. Unfortunately she's already dilated two centimeters, so she's on complete bed rest. They're keeping her in the hospital until she delivers."

"Oh, Chris, I'm so sorry. Is there anything I can do?"

"Actually, yes. Melissa made a list of things she needs. Makeup and toiletries and things like that. Could you gather everything and bring it to the hospital?"

"Of course." She grabbed a pad of paper and a pen and jotted down the list. "I'll be there as soon as I can."

"I want to stay here as often as possible, so I'd like you to meet with my assistant about taking my place at a few speeches and charity events."

For a second she was struck dumb. He never would have trusted her to a task like that before. She almost asked, what about Aaron or Anne, but caught herself at the last minute. She didn't want him to think she didn't want to do it.

"Of course I will," she told him instead. "Anything."

"Thanks, Louisa. I'll see you soon."

She hung up and was turning to leave her room when she remembered her date with Garrett and stopped dead in her tracks.

Bloody hell.

Well, as much as she wanted to see Garrett, family always came first. Especially now, when Chris seemed to be seeing her as a capable adult. She would just have to call him and reschedule. Maybe they could see each other later in the week.

She picked up the phone, mumbling to herself about bad timing, but as she put it to her ear there was no dial tone. She nearly jumped out of her skin when a deep male voice said, "Hello?"

"Garrett?"

"Well, that was strange," he said.

"What just happened?"

"I called your number, but before it could even ring, I heard your voice."

"Seriously? Because I just picked up the phone so I could call you!"

Garrett chuckled. "We must be on the same brain wave or something."

"I guess. Why were you calling?"

"Regrettably, something came up and I have to break our date for this afternoon."

Louisa laughed and said, "Seriously?"

Garrett paused for several seconds, then said, "Well, that wasn't exactly the reaction I'd been expecting."

"I'm laughing because I was calling you to say that *I* have to cancel our date."

"Hmm, that is pretty weird, isn't it?"

"I thought maybe we could get together later this week."

"We could do that. The first half of the week will be a little hectic for me, but maybe Thursday evening?"

That seemed so far off, but at least it would give her time to visit with Melissa while she adjusted to being confined to a hospital bed. "Just to warn you, if you want to take me off the palace grounds, Chris will need two days' warning to arrange for security."

"Well, then, I guess I'll call you Tuesday." There was a commotion in the background, and what sounded like a voice over a PA system, but she couldn't make out what they were saying. "I'm sorry, Louisa, but I have to go. I'll talk to you Tuesday."

Before she could say goodbye, he disconnected, and

she realized she hadn't even asked why he had to cancel today. Oh well, she was sure that it must have been very important. They could talk about it Tuesday.

She hated the thought of having to wait until Thursday to see Garrett again, but the anticipation would make their next date that much more special.

Seven

Sunday morning became a blur of doctors and nurses and representatives from the private home care facility that Garrett was hiring to look after his brother while his leg healed. And since Ian was being released tomorrow morning, there wasn't much time to get everything squared away.

Though Garrett wasn't too keen on the idea of his brother staying in his house for another six weeks or so, at least this time Ian would be physically incapable of running off with his belongings. The only time he was allowed out of bed was to bathe and use the loo, or he risked the bones shifting and healing incorrectly, leaving him with the threat of more surgeries and possible permanent disabilities. And while Ian could be irresponsible and self-absorbed, he wasn't stupid.

It was going on three when all the arrangements were completed and the appropriate paperwork signed. Garrett was walking down the hall to the elevator when someone called his name. He turned to see Louisa standing behind him, flanked by two very large and ominous looking bodyguards.

Oddly enough, his first instinct was to pull her close and kiss her, and he might have were it not for the risk of being tackled by her security detail.

"I thought that was you," she said, breaking into a wide smile. "What are you doing here? Did you come to see Melissa?"

"Melissa?" he asked.

She walked toward him, and with a subtle wave of her hand the guards fell back several steps. "Princess Melissa, my sister-in-law."

"No. Is she here?"

"In the family's private wing," she said, gesturing behind her. "She was brought in last night for early labor. That's why I had to postpone our date."

"I had no idea. I'm here visiting…an associate. He was in an accident yesterday."

"Oh, I'm so sorry. Is he okay?"

"He's banged up, but he'll recover."

"Is that why you had to break our date? To come here?"

He nodded. "Weird, huh?"

"Very weird. If we knew we were both coming here we could have carpooled," she joked.

He grinned. "Except I was already here when I called you."

"He must be a special friend for you to stay here all day with him."

"We've known each other most of our lives." He knew he should probably tell her the truth, but he just didn't feel like explaining. With any luck Ian would heal, then be out of Garrett's life forever, and the royal family would never be the wiser. "Is Melissa all right?"

"They managed to stop her labor, but she's on strict bed rest for at least four weeks, and they're keeping her in the hospital just to be safe."

"Please send her and Chris my best."

"She's having some tests right now, but I'm sure she would love a visit from you later. She's only been here a few hours and already she's crawling out of her skin."

Normally he wouldn't visit a stranger, but under the circumstances, it couldn't hurt. Besides, he'd liked Melissa from the moment he met her. She wasn't a typical royal. Of course neither was Liv, or Louisa for that matter. Maybe there was nothing unusual about any of them. Maybe it was his preconceived notion that was way off.

"I'd like that," he said. "As long as it's not an imposition."

"Of course not. Chris and Melissa really like you. In fact, Chris told me..." She paused and pressed her fingers to her lips.

"Chris told you what?"

Her cheeks flushed to match the pink of her pants. "Forget it."

He smiled. "You're blushing, Your Highness."

"I'm not sure if I should have said anything."

He folded his arms over his chest. She was usually so poised and self-confident. He liked that she had a vulnerable side. "Maybe you shouldn't have, but now you've piqued my curiosity. It wouldn't be fair to leave me hanging with no explanation, would it?"

"I suppose not." She glanced over at the busy nurses' station, then whispered, "Not here."

Whatever she had to say, it was apparently private in nature. All the more reason for him to know what was said. "Where?"

"I was on my way back to our private waiting room," she told him. "You could join me."

"I'd like that," he told her, realizing it was true, and not just for the information. Meeting like this in the hospital hallway could have been awkward, but instead he felt totally at ease with her. In fact, the moment he saw her standing there, some of the stress from the last few days seemed to melt away.

He held out his arm and she slipped hers through it. Thankfully the guards didn't knock him to the ground and cuff him. "Lead the way, Your Highness."

Louisa led Garrett into the royal family's private waiting room. She was relieved to find it empty. If this was the only time they could be alone, she could think of worse places.

"This is nice," Garrett said, gazing around. "More like a hotel suite than a hospital."

"It didn't used to be so modern, but the last few years, with my father's condition, we've spent a lot of time here so it was renovated."

"I expected Chris to be here."

"He's with Melissa. She's having a test to determine the development of the babies' lungs." She turned to set down her purse and felt Garrett's hands settle on her shoulders. A warm and delicious feeling poured through her like honey and the purse dropped with a clunk on the table.

"Does that mean we're alone?" he asked, and something in his tone made her heart skip a beat. Until now, she was the one to instigate the physical contact. It was exciting, and yes, maybe a little scary, that he had taken the upper hand.

"I guess we are."

His hands slipped off her shoulders and down her arms. His palms were smooth and felt hot to the touch. "Security won't barge in at any second?"

"Only if I call them."

"Are you going to call them?"

Now that they *finally* had some time alone? *Not bloody likely.* "I wasn't planning on it."

"Even if I do this?" He pulled her hair over one shoulder and brushed a kiss on the back of her neck. Goose bumps broke out across her skin, and her legs suddenly felt limp. Men had kissed her before, but it had been a long time since one made her tingle all over or feel the warm tug of arousal between her thighs and in her breasts.

He kissed her shoulder and she willed him to touch her, to cup her breasts in his palms, to slide his hand down, inside her panties. She almost moaned out loud imagining it, but she knew this wasn't the time or the place.

"I like your hair this way," he said, running his fingers through it. "You should wear it down all the time."

"Maybe I will."

"You were going to tell me what Chris said," he reminded her, his breath warm on her nape where he dropped soft kisses.

"I'd hoped you'd forgotten about that." She let her head fall to the side, giving him more area to explore, and he didn't disappoint. "Chris might be upset that I told you."

"We'll keep it between you and me."

"You promise?"

He turned her to face him and brushed his lips across hers. "Cross my heart and hope to die."

Even if she'd wanted to tell him no, there was no way she could. He could ask her the royal family's most intimate secrets right now and they would spill willingly from the lips he so skillfully nibbled. "I was talking to Chris the other day and he mentioned that if…well, if you and I were to get married, you would be a good choice to replace Aaron when he goes back to school."

He stopped kissing her. "He said that?"

"Just the other day."

"Well, I'm…I'm a bit speechless, actually. I'm flattered that he would even consider me."

"Nothing is set in stone, of course, which is why I never should have said anything in the first place. Me and my big mouth."

He smiled and made a growling sound deep in his throat. He cradled her face in his hand and brushed the pad of his thumb across her lower lip. "Hmm, I love your mouth."

She loved the way it felt when he touched it. Especially when he used his lips.

"Chris also insinuated that we shouldn't 'rush' things," she said.

"Are we rushing?"

She grinned up at him. "As far as I'm concerned, we're not moving fast enough. In fact, would you find it totally inappropriate to make out on the sofa in a hospital waiting room?"

"If it were only kissing, maybe not, but I'm having a tough time keeping my hands off of you."

She sighed and laid her head against his chest, heard the steady thump of his heart. "There has to be someplace we can go to be completely alone."

"I have a place in Cabo," he offered. "Maybe with enough advance warning, your family would let you go."

"I would *love* that! I'll talk to Chris about it."

"Unless security issues aren't his only concern."

She didn't have to ask what he meant. "I'm twenty-seven. My sex life is none of my family's business. And believe me when I say that they're in no position whatsoever to pass judgment. I hate that we have to even talk about this, that we can't just be a normal couple, let things happen naturally."

He led her to the sofa, pulling her close beside him as they sat. "All couples have issues, Louisa."

She drew her legs up over his thighs and curled against his chest. "Sometimes I wish I could lead a normal life. I'd like to shop in a store without a team of security parked outside, or eat dinner in a restaurant without a thorough background check of every employee." She looked up at him. "Have you ever considered what it would be like to be in a relationship with someone like me? The freedoms you would have to sacrifice? You'd be a fool not to run screaming in the opposite direction."

"Those things don't matter to me, Louisa." He cradled her chin in his hand and gazed into her eyes. They were so dark and compassionate and earnest it made her want to cry. "The way I feel about you, I'd be a fool not to stay."

He brushed his lips against hers, so tenderly. So sweet. But she didn't want tender and sweet. She was tired of that. She wanted fire and passion. She wanted to feel sexy and desired.

She slid her hands around Garrett's neck, pulled him down and kissed him. A kiss that was anything but tender. At first he resisted a little, until she drew herself up on her knees and straddled his lap.

"I can't seem to control myself when I'm with you," he mumbled against her lips.

"Good, because neither can I." She rocked her hips and rubbed against him. Garrett growled deep in his throat and tunneled his fingers through her hair, feeding off her mouth. She could feel his erection growing between them and she wanted so badly to touch him. She was so far gone, she didn't care that Chris could walk through the door at any second.

Which incidentally, he did.

Somewhere in the back of her hormone-drenched brain she heard the door open, then the exaggerated rumble of a throat clearing. She peeled herself away from Garrett and looked over to find Chris in the waiting room doorway, one brow lifted. She knew exactly what he was thinking. This was her idea of discretion?

She heard Garrett mumble a particularly colorful curse under his breath—one most men wouldn't dare speak in front of a princess—as he lifted her from his lap and dropped her onto the sofa beside him.

"Sorry to interrupt," Chris said, "but Melissa is back in her room and eager for visitors."

Louisa should have asked how Melissa was doing, or if the babies were okay, but to her surprise, and apparently her brother's surprise as well, the first thing out of her mouth was, "I'm going to Cabo with Garrett and you can't stop me."

Demanding she be allowed to leave the country with Garrett probably hadn't been the wisest course of action for Louisa to win a little freedom. Especially when Chris had just walked in on them making out like two lust-driven youths. Garrett was quite sure, considering her brother's look of exasperation, she wouldn't be leaving the country anytime soon. With Garrett or anyone else.

So much for convincing her family that he wasn't compromising her honor.

Garrett assumed Chris would be furious with him, but when he pulled the Prince aside later to apologize for his inappropriate behavior, Chris only laughed.

"I know you're smarter than that, Garrett. I don't believe for a second that my sister wasn't the aggressor. Just, if you could, try to keep her in check, at least when you're in public. I would appreciate it."

Garrett had been so stunned, he couldn't form a coherent reply, which seemed to amuse Chris even more.

"You think I don't know what my sister is like?"

"She can be...tenacious," Garrett said.

Chris chuckled. "That's putting it mildly. I've spent the better part of my life keeping her out of trouble. She whines incessantly that we shelter her, yet she refuses to exercise any common sense. If she wants something she goes after it, all pistons firing. Usually with no regard to the rules, or oftentimes her own safety. And if what she gets isn't what she wanted, watch out.

"Don't get me wrong, I love my sister to death. She has a heart of gold and you'll never meet a woman more loyal to her family and friends. I would lay down my life for her. I also believe that she'll make a fantastic wife and mother. But she is a handful. Let your guard down and she'll walk all over you."

In other words, her so-called reputation of being sweet and naive was *bollocks*. He'd basically figured that out already. He just hadn't realized the extent of her defiance. Some men might have considered that a negative quality, and maybe he should have, too, but the idea that she wasn't at all what he expected only intrigued him more.

The question was: what did Chris have to gain by his honesty? Was he trying to scare Garrett away? And why would he after he'd told Louisa that he was considering offering Aaron's position to Garrett?

"Why are you telling me this?" he asked Chris.

"I think you should know what you're getting yourself into. Louisa needs a man who's just as headstrong and determined as she is, and I see those qualities in you. She needs someone who can…rein her in."

He made it sound as though Louisa needed a babysitter more than a husband. Did the royal family cling to the archaic values that deemed women should be seen but not heard?

He wasn't sure if he should feel grateful for Chris's candid advice, or offended on Louisa's behalf. And since when did Garrett feel the need to defend her? When did he start caring about her feelings?

Probably right around the same time she smiled up at him and said she couldn't wait to see him naked.

"By the way," Chris said. "Send me a copy of your itinerary and I'll see what I can do. It will take at least two weeks to arrange."

It took a second for Garett to realize he was talking about the trip to Cabo. "I assumed that wasn't going to happen."

"If I tell her no, there's a good chance she'll go without permission. Besides, maybe some time away would do her good. With our father in fairly stable condition, I think we could all use a vacation."

Garrett, too, was looking forward to some time away. With his brother around, the less time he spent at home, the better as far as he was concerned. He and Ian had nothing left to say to one another, and all that talk about Ian changing his ways was rubbish. Ian would never change.

After a short visit with Melissa, who was indeed climbing the walls, Garrett said goodbye to Louisa, sealing their departure with another enthusiastic kiss. He made a short trip to the office to get a few documents that needed his attention. Then, because the cook had Sundays off, he picked up dinner on his way home.

Later, as he lounged in front of the television, mindlessly surfing the channels, he thought about calling Louisa to see if Melissa's tests came back favorable. Only, as usual, she called him first.

He picked up the phone after the first ring and said, "You probably won't believe this, but I was just about to call you."

"Were you really?" a sultry voice purred in his ear. "And here I thought you'd forgotten all about me."

The unfamiliar voice threw him for a moment, then he looked at the caller ID and realized it wasn't Louisa after all. It was Pamela, a woman he dated on occasion. Although to call what they did "dating" was a gross overstatement. They had sex. Unemotional, uncomplicated, no-strings-attached sex. Just the way he liked it.

"Pamela, sorry, I thought you were someone else," he said. "How have you been?"

Her voice dripped with the promise of something naughty. "Missing you terribly, love."

He used to find her sultry drawl warm and sexy. Now he recognized it for what it was: as insincere as her affection for him. She was using him, just as he had used her. Up until today that hadn't bothered him in the least, in fact he'd preferred it that way, but now it just seemed…sleazy.

"I've been busy," he said, but she totally missed what he'd hoped was a direct brush-off.

"Well, if you're not busy tonight, why don't I stop by for a while? We could get…reacquainted."

It wasn't the only time she'd offered herself up freely to him, but for the first time, he wasn't the least bit interested. Not that he had no appetite for female companionship, but the female he was interested in right now was Louisa.

"I'm afraid this isn't a good time," he told Pamela.

"How about tomorrow night instead?"

"That won't be a good time, either."

The sexy tone wavered, as though she was finally starting to catch on that something was up. "When *would* it be a good time?"

How about never? "The thing is, Pamela, I'm seeing someone."

"So?"

Admittedly, in the past, that wouldn't have stopped him. "What I mean is, I'm seeing someone...*special*."

There was a pause, then a short burst of laughter. "Are you saying that you're in a serious relationship?"

"I am," he said, relieved that he didn't have to spell it out. Sometimes he could hardly believe it himself.

"Is she pregnant?"

"No, she's not pregnant."

"Blackmailing you?"

He laughed. "Is it so hard to believe I met a woman I want to date seriously?"

"I've known you almost ten years, Garrett, and in all that time not once did you ever have a serious relationship. You're far too selfish."

Pamela was right, but that selfish streak had led him to where he was now. He didn't miss the irony. Some might go so far as saying he was too selfish for his own good.

"Who's the lucky girl? Anyone I know?"

"No one you know," he assured her. Of course she knew *of* Louisa, but they had certainly never inhabited the same social circles.

"Well, I guess all I can say is good luck," Pamela said.

He said his goodbyes, hung up, then permanently deleted her number from his phone. He was about to set it down on the table beside him when it rang again.

This time it was Louisa, and he caught himself smiling. "I was just thinking about calling you," he said.

"Were you?" There was a distinct note of happiness in her voice.

"I wondered if you'd heard the results from Melissa's tests." As soon as the words left his mouth, he knew they were not entirely true. If he had called, it would have been just to talk to her. To hear her voice.

"How sweet of you," she responded, buying his fib without question. "She got the results just a bit ago and unfortunately the babies' lungs need at least a few more weeks to develop. They've started her on steroids to get things moving along. On the bright side, she hasn't had any more contractions."

"That's good news."

"Do you know why I called you?" she asked.

"Why?"

"I was lying in bed thinking about our kiss today and I just wanted to hear your voice."

Eight

Garrett found himself envying Louisa's unrelenting honesty. Why was he so incapable of expressing his feelings? Or maybe in her case, his discretion was the kindest thing he had to offer. Was it fair to lead her on when the emotions he was feeling now were driven by curiosity and fleeting at best?

He didn't think so.

"I'm starting to feel like I'll go crazy if we don't get some time alone soon," she said.

He could relate. If Chris hadn't stepped in the room when he did, things might have gotten out of hand. "I know what you mean."

"I think about it a lot," she admitted.

"Think about what?"

"Sex."

He sat up a little straighter in his chair. "You do?"

"I fantasize *all* the time."

"About what?"

"You. What it will be like when we're finally alone. How you'll touch me, and what it will feel like to touch you. Sometimes I get myself so worked up thinking about it that I have to...well, you know."

She couldn't possibly be saying what he thought she was saying. "You have to what?"

"*Touch* myself."

Bloody hell. He formed a mental picture of that and just about swallowed his tongue.

"I've been doing a lot of reading on the Internet, too," she said.

"What kind of reading?"

"Erotic short stories mostly. My favorites are the romantic ones, but there are a few with a bondage theme I thought were kind of fun."

Bloody hell. Now would be an excellent time to change the subject, but his brain just wasn't cooperating. Probably because all the blood in his body was pooling in the vicinity of his crotch. He was so hard he had to unfasten the button fly on his jeans.

"Nothing too extreme, of course. But I think I'd be willing to try silk scarves and feathers."

He resisted the visual representation, but it popped into his head anyway.

He was so stiff he was aching, and he was seriously considering asking what her feelings were on phone sex, but if he and Louisa were going to be intimate, he'd be damned if he was going to do it from across town.

"Are you trying to drive me insane?" he asked, and she laughed.

"Maybe. Is it working?"

"I'm in agony."

"You wouldn't believe all of the different things I could do to help you with that."

And, of course, a dozen or so instantly came to mind. "If you say another word, I swear to God I'm hanging up."

She laughed. "Okay, I promise I'll stop."

"All those rumors I've heard that you're inexperienced and pure—I'm not buying it."

"I hate to disappoint you, but the rumors are true."

"How is that even possible?"

"I was very sheltered. I wasn't even allowed to start dating until I was eighteen and when I did there was always a chaperone. I never had the chance to experiment, although not for lack of trying. Unfortunately, the more I tried, the tighter my family pulled back on the reins. It was as if everyone was determined to keep me unspoiled and pure. Eventually I got tired of fighting them and I just sort of, I don't know...lost interest, I guess."

"You seem interested now," he said.

"It was the Internet. I stumbled across a site full of stories and it opened up a whole new world to me. I finally started to realize what I've been missing all this time. It all just seemed so natural and...beautiful. I wanted to try everything. Well," she amended, "*almost* everything. When it comes to sex, people do some weird things."

"For the record, I'm not into weird."

"I'm glad," she said, sounding a little relieved.

"If you're so...interested, why don't you date more?"

"Because most men I meet are more interested in my wealth or my title than me."

How would she feel if she knew he was one of those men? That would remain his and Wes's secret.

"I find so many men, especially the ones close to my age, far too arrogant and entitled. So, here I am now, twenty-seven and still unspoiled, but dying to be corrupted. And don't ask me how, but when you took me in your arms on the dance floor, I just knew you were the one."

Though it made no sense at all, he felt honored that she had chosen him. "I can't say that I've ever corrupted anyone before, but I'd certainly be willing to give it a go. I'm free right now, in fact."

"Even with Chris and my parents gone, inviting you over at 11:30 p.m. might be pushing the envelope. But the time will come when we're completely alone, and I know it will be worth the wait. I just hope it's sooner rather than later."

"Me, too." What healthy heterosexual male didn't wish he had, at his disposal, a young, beautiful and sexy virgin willing to—in her own words—try practically everything? Men would pay exorbitant sums of money to trade places with him. And to think that he once believed he would have to take the sexual aspect of their courtship painfully slow. How completely wrong he'd been. This was working out far better than he ever could have imagined.

So why, somewhere deep down, did he feel so damned guilty?

The King had all the necessary adjustments performed on his heart pump Wednesday and the reinsertion after the capacity test went off without a hitch. Unfortunately, the news was not what they had hoped. Though some areas of the heart showed signs of healing, there had been little improvement in his overall heart function.

Everyone was disappointed, but Louisa refused to let the news get her down. As far as she was concerned, this was just a minor setback. His heart was just taking a little longer to heal, that's all.

Anne was still in England with their parents, so Louisa sat in a visitor's chair in Melissa's hospital room with Aaron, Liv, Chris, and of course Melissa, discussing how the setback would affect the family.

Chris sat on the edge of the bed with his wife. "Obviously I'll continue to perform Father's duties, and Aaron will cover my duties."

Liv leaned beside Aaron against the wall by the door. "But who will take over for Aaron when he starts school?" she asked, clearly concerned that his plans would be pushed aside yet another semester.

"I have a backup plan," Chris told her.

Aaron regarded him curiously. "Since when?"

"Recently," Chris said, glancing Louisa's way. "I'm considering offering a position to Garrett Sutherland."

Suddenly all eyes were on Louisa.

"What you mean is, if Louisa marries him," Melissa clarified.

Chris nodded. "Of course."

"He is more than qualified," Aaron confirmed.

"I agree," Melissa said. "But is it fair to put that kind of pressure on Louisa?"

"We're all under pressure," Chris told her. "Besides, she's always asking for more responsibility."

Louisa hated when they talked about her as though she wasn't sitting right there. Why did they insist on treating her like a child?

It was a moot point anyway. Their father was going to recover and resume his duties, then everything would go back to normal. These last couple years would be nothing more than a bad memory.

"What do *you* think, Louisa?" Liv asked.

Finally, she was part of the conversation. "I think you're blowing this way out of proportion. This is just a minor setback. Father will be fine."

She could tell by their expressions that they thought she was being naive, and she pitied them for their cynicism. This would be so much easier for all of them if they would just have faith.

No one scolded or tried to reason with her, and she was grateful for that, but she felt as though, if she didn't get out of there soon, she would lose her mind. Even though she wasn't supposed to see Garrett until tomorrow evening, that was one day too long as far as she was concerned.

She grabbed her purse and rose from her chair. "If the family discussion is over, I'm leaving."

"Where are you going?" Chris asked.

"Garrett is working from home today so I thought I would stop in and see him. If that's not a problem."

Chris and Aaron exchanged a look. Louisa honestly expected them to tell her no. In fact, she sort of hoped they would as she was itching for a fight. To her surprise though, Chris nodded and said, "Be sure to take a full detail with you. And you leave the vehicle only after the area has been secured."

"I know the rules," she snapped, and everyone looked surprised by her sharp tone. Did they think there was no limit to the flack she would take from them? That she was immune to their condescension?

"Remember that Anne is flying home and we're having dinner together here at the hospital," Chris told her, and there was an unspoken warning of *be there or else* in his tone. "Seven sharp."

If there was any way she could get out of it, she would, but for Melissa, who was desperate for company, Louisa couldn't say no. "I'll be here," she said and pulled the door open. Her bodyguards Gordon and Jack were waiting for her in the hall. She gestured to them and said, "We're leaving, gentlemen."

On the way to the car, Jack received a call on his cell. Chris, she was assuming, because when they got in the Bentley and she instructed Jack to take her to Garrett's town house he didn't bat an eyelash. It was a good thing she once again failed to mention the new e-mail she had gotten from the Gingerbread Man the day before. She would have mentioned it if there had been any direct threats or even an undertone of danger. All it had said was, Louisa and Garrett sitting in a tree K-I-S-S-I-N-G...

It was just his way of letting her know that he was keeping tabs on them. Par for the course.

When they got to Garrett's place, Louisa wasn't the least bit surprised to see that a team of security agents were already on the premises. Considering his net worth, she was a bit surprised he didn't live in a lavish home in a gated community. Not that his townhome wasn't very attractive, and very large, but he could afford much more. Although, she liked that he wasn't pretentious. Definitely not the kind of man interested in money and power.

It seemed to take forever before Gordon opened the car door and led her up the walk.

"You men will wait outside," she told him. Demanded

was more like it, even though she and Gordon both knew that he was obligated to do whatever Chris ordered. But he nodded and stepped to the side of the door where he had a clear view of the street. Louisa rang the bell, nearly buzzing with excitement at the idea of her and Garrett finally having some time to themselves.

It took him almost a full minute to answer the door, and when he did he was dressed more casually than she'd ever seen him, in lightweight jogging pants and a polo shirt with the emblem of the local yacht club embroidered over his left pec. The casual clothes for some reason seemed to accentuate his size. The thickness of his arms and the width of his shoulders. His lean waist and muscular thighs.

She expected a smile when he saw her standing there, maybe a hug and a kiss, but he just looked confused.

"Louisa? How did you…what are you doing here?"

It was true that Garrett hadn't technically invited her there, but she had been sure he wouldn't mind if she stopped by. How could he when they would get some much needed time alone? Wasn't that all they had been talking about? And why else would he mention, during their phone conversation Tuesday, that he would be working from home if he didn't want her to come over?

Now she wasn't so sure. Maybe the implied invitation hadn't been an invitation after all.

She pasted on a smile despite the sinking sensation in her belly. "I came to visit you."

"Chris let you?"

She nodded, keeping her smile bright. "I think he realized that if he forbid it, I might rebel." Garrett didn't say anything so she asked, "Aren't you going to invite me in?"

He looked behind him, into the town house, then back to her. "Um, sure, come on in."

He stepped aside to let her pass, but he was definitely edgy about something. He kept looking down a hallway that led to the rear of the unit. Behind him to the left was a staircase to the second floor.

She gazed around what was clearly a professionally decorated foyer and living room. It was undeniably male, but tastefully so. "This is nice."

He shrugged. "It suits my needs."

Why didn't he smile? Or take her into his arms and kiss her? Just a few nights ago he'd been dying to get his hands on her.

There was a brief, awkward silence, so she said brightly, "Aren't you going to offer me a tour?"

He shot another furtive glance behind him, and she began to wonder if he was with someone else. Maybe, despite his assurances that he was finished playing the field, he had another woman in his life. Her heart sank so hard and fast she could swear she felt it knocking around by her knees.

Please don't let him be like the others, she begged silently. He *had* to be the one. If not, her family would never let her live it down.

Garrett cleared his throat. "It's just that now isn't the best time."

Aware that her hands were shaking, she clasped them into fists, lifted her chin and asked him point blank, "Is there something you're not telling me?"

"Nothing that has anything to do with us. I promise. It's…complicated."

From down the hallway Louisa heard movement, then the timbre of a male voice called out, "Who is it, Garrett?"

It wasn't another woman, she thought with a relief that left her knees weak. Then it occurred to her, just because it was a man, it didn't mean Garrett wasn't… *involved* with him. Anne had dated a fellow for several months before she realized he was more interested in her bodyguard Gunter than her.

But Garrett was so masculine and virile.

Before she could work up the nerve to ask him, the owner of the voice appeared at the end of the hallway. His face was bruised and swollen and he leaned on a pair of crutches to take the weight off a leg that was encased in plaster from foot to midthigh. It was his friend from the hospital, she realized. The one who had been in the accident.

He walked toward them, the agony of each measured step clear on his poor battered face.

"Bloody hell, Ian!" Garrett barked in a tone Louisa had never heard him use. Like a father chastising a disobedient child. The way Chris had often spoken to her when she was younger. And sometimes still did. "The doctor said to stay off your feet as much as possible."

"Had to use the loo," the Ian person said with a wry smile, then he turned his attention to Louisa and opened his mouth to speak, but he must have recognized her because his jaw fell instead. He looked at Garrett and said, "Damn, that's the *Princess*."

Garrett cursed and shook his head, and when Ian just stood there gaping, he kicked him in his good leg and said, "Bow, you jackass."

"Sorry." He bowed his head, wearing a humble grin,

and said, "Must be all the pain medication they've pumped in me."

"Oh, it's all right," she assured him and offered a hand to shake. "Princess Louisa Josephine Elisabeth Alexander."

Balancing on one crutch, he took her hand, enfolding it in his rough, callused one and said, "I'm Ian. Ian Sutherland."

Nine

"Sutherland?" Louisa repeated, looking to Garrett, clearly confused. And why wouldn't she be when he'd told her this was an acquaintance who'd been in the accident. "You're related?"

Garrett cursed under his breath. Could this day possibly get any worse? He'd hoped to get Ian settled then leave him in the nurse's care and lock himself in his office for the rest of the day, but due to a scheduling snafu, the nurse wouldn't be coming until tomorrow morning.

And now, to top it all off, he had no choice but to tell Louisa the truth. "Ian is my brother."

"There's actually an uncanny family resemblance, when my face isn't all bruised and swollen," Ian told her. "Although I am the better looking one."

Louisa turned to Garrett, brow furrowed. "But you said—"

"I know. I lied."

This would normally be the time when Ian would jump in and say or do something to make Garrett look like even more of an ass, but instead he actually defended him. It was the least selfish thing Garrett had ever seen him do. "Compared to someone like me, Garrett here is a Boy Scout, Your Highness. If he did lie, I know he had a damned good reason."

She looked between Ian and Garrett as though she wasn't sure what to believe.

Though Ian would usually stick around for the fireworks, he yawned and said, "If you'll both excuse me, I'm feeling woozy from the pain medication. I think it's time for my afternoon nap. But I hope we'll get the chance to talk again, Your Highness."

"I'd like that," Louisa said with a smile, and as Ian limped back down the hall she turned to Garrett with a questioning look, as if to say, *Okay, what's the deal?*

"I know I owe you an explanation." He gestured to the staircase. "Let's go to my office, where we can talk in private."

She nodded and followed him up the stairs, but as they passed his bedroom, she stopped.

"This is your room?"

He nodded.

Without asking his permission, she stepped inside. She inhaled deeply and said, "Hmm, it smells like you."

He leaned in and sniffed, but to him it smelled the same way it always did. Just like the rest of the house.

He waited by the door for her to come out. Instead she dropped her purse on the floor, hoisted herself onto his bed and leaned back on her elbows, making herself comfortable. God, did she look sexy. She wore a sleeveless pink blouse and conservative white skirt, with her hair flowing loose and soft on her back. Maybe it was his imagination but it seemed the longer he knew her, the more attractive he found her.

She patted the mattress beside her, signaling him to sit down. Apparently they were having their talk right here.

He closed the door and crossed to the bed, taking a seat to her left. "Let me say first that I'm sorry I lied to you."

"When you first let me in and you looked so nervous, I thought maybe you were seeing another woman. Then I heard Ian's voice and for a second I thought maybe you were seeing a man."

The things that came out of her mouth never ceased to amaze him. "I told you before, Louisa, there's only you. And for the record, only *women*."

"Why didn't you tell me it was your brother in the accident?"

"Because I knew you would want to meet him."

"Is that such a bad thing?"

"Yes. Because he's a liar and a thief and I didn't want to expose you to someone like that. The only reason he came to see me is because my parents and my brothers have all written him off."

She frowned. "That's so sad."

"No, it isn't," he said, and told her some of the things Ian had done to the family, how he'd cheated and lied and stolen from them. And how Garrett was stuck with him now, until his leg healed. "He keeps telling me that he'll really change this time, but I've heard the story a hundred times before. People like that never change."

"But maybe this time he *really* means it."

"Do you know how he got into the accident? I told him I wouldn't give him money, so he stole my car instead."

"Are you sure he wasn't just borrowing it?"

"He admitted to stealing it, not to mention a dozen bottles of my best liquor. Then he tried to make me believe he'd had second thoughts and was bringing it back. But I know better. He left and had no intention of ever coming back."

"Yet you're letting him stay here," she said. "You must still care at least a little."

"I had no choice. He had nowhere else to go."

"If you really didn't care at all, that wouldn't have made a difference."

Though he hated to admit it, she had a point. But he didn't want her to be right. He wanted to hate Ian for all that he'd done. It was so much easier that way.

He groaned and flopped down on his back beside her.

"Stressed out?" she asked.

"Does it show?"

An impish smile curled her lips and he instantly knew she was up to no good. "You know what they say is supposed to be good for stress."

He had a few suggestions, but he was much more interested in her ideas. "Why don't you show me?"

She leaned over and brushed a soft, lingering kiss against his lips, then sat back and asked, "Better?"

Suppressing a smile, he shrugged and said, "A little, I guess."

Looking thoughtful, she said, "Hmm, maybe I'm just not trying hard enough."

She leaned over to give it another go, but he had a sudden revelation. "Hey, wait a minute."

She stopped abruptly and sat up. "What's wrong?"

"Something is missing."

She frowned. "What?"

He rose up on his elbows, looking around the room. "Security."

"Oh, they're here. They're outside, guarding the doors."

"Outside? As in, not inside?"

She looked at him funny. "Yes."

"And there's no chance of them possibly barging in and say, coming upstairs to this room?"

He could see by the slow smile creeping across her face that she knew where he was going with this. "Only if I ask them to. But what about your brother? Is there any reason he would come up here?"

"He's taking a nap. Besides, he can hardly walk, much less climb the stairs."

"You know what that means," she said.

They both smiled and said in unison, "We're finally alone."

Louisa was suddenly so excited her hands were trembling. "I have to be back to the hospital by seven for dinner."

He looked at his watch. "That gives us a little over two hours."

She thought of all the things they could do in two hours.

"Why don't you lie back against the pillows," Garrett said, and he had this look in his eyes, one that said, I'm going to eat you alive.

She realized that the dynamics had suddenly changed. A minute ago, when she was kissing Garrett, she had been the one in control. Now Garrett was clearly calling the shots, and though it scared her a little, it also thrilled her to the depths of her soul.

So why was she just sitting there wasting precious time?

Garrett regarded her curiously, "You're not getting cold feet, are you?"

She reached up and laid a hand on his cheek. "No! I want this, more than anything. It's all I've thought of for weeks. Maybe *too* much."

He leaned in and brushed a kiss against her lips and she could swear she felt it all the way down to her toes. "There's no such thing as too much."

"And that's the problem. Here we are alone, with no reason to stop if things start to go too far."

"How far is too far?"

"I know it's archaic and silly, but I want to be a virgin on my wedding night. I just think it will make it more special."

"It's not silly. It's an honorable decision, and knowing your wishes, I would never let things go too far."

His gaze was so earnest, she wanted to believe him, but who's to say he wouldn't get too carried away? "What if you can't stop?"

He grinned, his dimple winking at her. "Contrary to what you may have read, not all men are sex-starved fiends. You have my word that we won't go any further than we should."

She believed him, because she knew Garrett would never lie to her. At least, not about something so important. And when he had lied about Ian, he'd done it to protect her.

She sat up and scooted backward, laying her head on the pillow. Garrett lay down beside her and propped himself up on one elbow. He studied her face, softly tracing her features with his index finger. "Have I ever told you how beautiful you are?"

"Probably. But feel free to tell me again."

He kissed her instead. So tender and sweet—at first anyway. He kissed her lips and her chin and the side of her neck. He nibbled her earlobes and found a sensitive little spot behind her ear that made her shiver.

Her hesitance a memory now, she wrapped her arms around his neck, threaded her fingers through his hair, breathing in the scent of his skin and his hair. Feeding off his kisses.

Garrett cupped the side of her face, caressed her cheek with his thumb, but gradually his hand slipped lower, first down her throat and neck, then to her shoulder, but he stopped there.

A little voice inside of her was begging, *Keep going, please keep touching me*. Her breasts or even between her legs, anywhere that might relieve the ache building inside of her. It would be okay if he did, because he'd promised not to let this go too far, and she trusted him.

Maybe she was thinking loud enough for him to hear, because his hand started to move again, drifting slowly until it covered her breast. The ache between her thighs became a raging inferno, and her breasts felt swollen and tender. For a minute he just held his hand there, as though he worried she might be afraid—or he was trying to drive her mad. Louisa held her breath, anticipating his next move, and when he squeezed softly the sensation was so intense she gasped.

He stopped kissing her and gazed down with lust-filled eyes. "Too much?"

"No!" she said in a voice so husky with desire she barely recognized it as her own. "Not enough."

Wearing a sexy grin, he stroked one breast, then the other. When he took one nipple between his fingers and gently pinched, she whimpered. Men had touched her breasts before, but never had it felt this good. This... erotic.

Then he *stopped*. She opened her mouth to protest, but he started unbuttoning her blouse and the words died in her throat.

"I've been wondering something," he said, popping each button open with the flick of his skilled fingers. She watched as the last button gave way and he eased the sides back, exposing her pink lace bra. She wasn't particularly large, a modest B cup, but what she lacked in size, she made up for in quality.

"What were you wondering?" she asked.

"How inexperienced are you? I mean, you must have some experience."

"Some heavy petting, but always on top of the clothes. And kissing, of course."

"What kind of kissing?" he asked.

What kind? How many kinds were there?

Confused, she said, "Just regular kissing, I guess."

He flashed her an impish grin and she knew instantly that he was up to something.

"Anyone ever kiss you like this?" He dipped his head, brushing his lips on her breast at the very edge of the lace cup and Louisa could barely suppress the moan building in her throat. He kissed one, then the other, then he lifted his head to look at her.

"No," she answered in an unsteady voice. "Never like that."

"How about like this?" Using his tongue, he drew a damp path down the swell of one breast then up its mate. Then he looked at her and grinned.

Technically that wasn't a kiss, but this was no time to be splitting hairs. Kiss or not, she was so turned on she felt like crawling out of her own skin. "I'm going to have to say no. In fact, pretty much anything you do at this point will be new territory for me." And she could hardly wait to see where and how he touched her next. Fortunately she didn't have to wait long.

Garrett nudged the cup of her bra aside, and for a second all he did was look at her. Her nipple was small and pink and pulled tight with arousal.

"You have the most beautiful breasts I've ever seen," he said. She knew she should be polite and thank him, but he leaned forward and touched the very tip with his tongue and her brain went into shutdown mode. She didn't think anything could feel more erotic…until he drew her nipple into his mouth and sucked. Hard. She threw her head back and moaned, arching closer to his mouth.

He leaned back to look at his handiwork. Her nipple was damp and tinted deep red from the suction. She expected him to do the same to the other breast, but instead he gazed down at her, his expression serious, and said, "We should probably stop for now."

Wait, what? Was he serious? *"Stop?"*

"So things don't go too far."

She must have looked absolutely crestfallen, because he laughed and said, "Louisa, I'm teasing."

"Bloody hell, don't joke about a thing like that!" she scolded, expelling a relieved breath.

"We are running a little short on time."

She looked at his watch and couldn't believe how much time had passed already. And all they had done was kiss and touch. But she wanted more, and she wanted it now. If she was a little late for dinner, so be it. "Then let's not waste any more time."

She tugged on the hem of his shirt, and he helped her pull it over his head. His body was the most amazing she had ever seen and not just because his chest was wide and muscular, his abdomen hard and defined. She loved it because it belonged to him. She raised her hands and laid them on his chest, surprised by how hot his skin felt. Without his shirt to cover it, she could see his erection clearly against the loose jogging pants. So clearly that she realized he must not be wearing briefs or even boxers.

Garrett frowned and pressed one of his hands over hers. "You're shaking. Are you afraid?"

She shook her head. "Not at all. Just excited."

And fed up with going so slow.

She pushed Garrett onto his back, then sat up and straddled him, her skirt riding up all the way to the tops of her thighs. She shrugged out of her shirt then reached behind her and unclasped her bra, feeling an almost excruciating need to press her body to his, to rub her breasts against his chest. Garrett must have read her mind, because he seemed to know exactly what to do. As soon as her bra was off, he pulled her down to him, wrapping his arms around her. Their lips met in what was more of a mutual devouring than an actual kiss. They fed off one another, and if she could have eaten him alive, she would have.

Garrett's hands seemed to be everywhere at once. Up and down her back and arms, kneading her breasts, tangling in her hair. But when he reached under her skirt and cupped her behind in his big, warm hands, the ache between her legs became unbearable.

He rolled her onto her back, and it felt so good, the weight of his body on hers, lying chest to chest, stomach to stomach. She wrapped her legs around his waist, unaware until that very second that his erection had become pinned between them, centered perfectly in line with the crotch of her panties.

Louisa gasped with surprise and Garrett groaned, then they both went still, Garrett wearing an expression that suggested this time, they may have gone too far.

Technically this was her fault. Had she been more experienced, she would have anticipated this, and she knew they were tempting fate lying like this, with barely more than a thin layer of nylon and a swatch of lace to prevent this from going any further.

But it felt *so* good.

For several seconds they just stared at one another, as if neither was sure what to do next. She didn't relax her vise grip on his waist, and he didn't try to pull loose.

Then it happened. With his eyes locked on hers, Garrett rocked back then inched slowly forward, stroking her with the entire length of his erection. Louisa felt it like an electric charge that started between her thighs and raced outward. She shuddered involuntarily and all the fine hairs on her body shivered to life.

He did it again, but this time she arched up to meet

him and every inch of her skin, every cell in her body overflowed with pleasure, even though they still had their clothes on.

Garrett rocked into her, over and over, with the same slow, measured thrusts and her body moved naturally with him. She kissed his lips and his throat, bit his earlobes and raked her nails across his back and shoulders. She wanted to eat him up, brand him with her teeth and her nails. Not the way a proper princess should behave. But she didn't care. She felt naughty and sexy and half out of her mind with lust, his every thrust driving her closer and closer to ecstasy.

So close.

She looked up at Garrett. His eyes were closed, his breath ragged and sweat beaded his forehead. For some reason she'd thought he was doing this just to make her feel good, but in that instant she realized that he was going to climax, and that was all it took to drive her past the point of no return. Everything locked and a shudder that started in her center rippled out to encompass her entire being. She would have moaned but she couldn't breathe, couldn't even think past the numbing pleasure.

Feeling her climax must have done Garrett in. He groaned from deep within his chest then went rigid, hissing out a breath as he gave one final thrust then dropped beside her.

Ten

Louisa lay beside Garrett in his bed, limp and trying to catch her breath, and suddenly, for no reason, Garrett started to laugh. A deep throaty laugh, as though he found something about the situation profoundly amusing.

"What's so funny?" she asked.

He gazed up at the ceiling, shaking his head. "I can't believe we just did that."

She frowned. "Was it…bad?"

He rolled onto his side, rising up on one elbow to look at her. "No, not at all. It was…fantastic."

She was confused. "So why are you laughing?"

"Because the last time I did it that way I was fifteen. It's a bit like wet dreams. After a certain age, you just don't have them."

She nodded thoughtfully. "I guess that makes sense."

"What do you mean?"

"Well, despite all the stories I've read, I've never seen any mention of what we just did."

He grinned. "You would if they were written by adolescent boys."

"So what we did was…unusual?"

"Very. It usually takes actual intercourse for me to climax."

"Why is that, do you think?"

He shrugged. "I guess, once you start having sex, the novelty gradually wears off. But you turn me on so much, it's like being a kid again. Starting from the beginning."

That might have been one of the sweetest things a man had ever said to her. She grinned and said, "Think we could do it again?"

"Have you looked at the time?"

She read the display on his watch. Damn! It was already half past six. But if she hurried she could make it on time for dinner. "I'm sorry. I do have to go."

"I understand."

He looked so sexy lying there with no shirt on, wearing that adorable smile. She didn't want to leave. She wanted to curl into his chest and cuddle with him. She wanted to fall asleep in his bed and wake in his arms, but she knew that her family was expecting her. And if she didn't show, those guards who were waiting patiently outside might just break down the door to fetch her.

She rolled out of bed and grabbed her clothes.

Garrett lay there and watched her dress. "I have a grueling day at the office tomorrow, but maybe I could see you in the evening."

"Oh, I can't. I forgot to tell you, I'm filling in for

Chris at some executive dinner. Now that he's finally taking me seriously, I couldn't refuse. What about the night after that?"

"Friday? I have a dinner meeting."

"Do you have work to do Saturday?"

"If I do, it will have to wait. What would you like to do?"

Did he even have to ask?

Well, for propriety's sake she could at least *pretend* they weren't getting together just to ravish each other. "It might be difficult going out on an actual date," she reminded him. "With all the security issues."

"True," he agreed thoughtfully. "I suppose we could just stay indoors."

"I'm sure we could figure out *something* to keep us occupied."

He smiled that sexy smile and asked, with a voice full of sexual innuendo, "Your place or mine?"

They decided to meet at his place, since here they would have the least interruption, then Garrett walked Louisa to the door. She called her bodyguard to let him know she was ready, and through the front window Garrett could see that there was a slew of vehicles parked in the street in front of his town house.

"The media circus has begun," he told her.

She peered around him to see. "It sort of comes with the territory. But you get used to it. Once they have their photos and press releases, the hype will die down."

He hoped so. He preferred to keep his life low profile—one more thing he would sacrifice as Louisa's husband. Though he had a feeling, for a while at least, she would make up for it in *other* ways. And right now she looked so damned adorable, all rumpled and sexy, he wanted to drag her back upstairs.

There was a knock on the door and Garrett opened it to find two hulking bodyguards on his porch, the same ones from the hospital. Garrett was a big man, but these guys were giants, and he had little doubt Louisa would be quite safe in their care.

"We're ready, Your Highness," the one on the left said.

Louisa turned to Garrett, rose up on her toes and pressed a kiss to his lips, then she smiled and said, "See you Saturday."

As soon as her foot hit the step, he heard the dull roar of camera shutters firing away and reporters shouting questions from the street. Even knowing he would be tomorrow's fodder for the tabloids, he stood there and watched as she was helped in the car. She waved as the car pulled away and he waved back, watching until they rounded the corner at the end of the block. Then he heard from behind him, "My big brother, shagging a princess."

He closed the door and turned to find Ian standing a few feet away, at the end of the hallway.

"Who I 'shag' is none of your concern. And for the record, I'm not."

"Maybe, but you will be, because you always get what you want." Ian shook his head and laughed. "Leave it to Garrett the overachiever to set his sights on the royal family."

Garrett glared at him and walked past Ian to the kitchen to get himself a beer. If Ian hadn't cleaned him out already, that is.

Ian followed him.

Surprisingly, there was the same number of bottles as the night before. Garrett took one out and twisted off the cap.

"Aren't you going to offer me some?" Ian asked.

"Pain pills and alcohol. Smashing combination." He closed the refrigerator.

Ian leaned back against the counter and propped his crutches in the corner. "I knew you were a power hound, but I never imagined you had the stones to bag a princess. What do you think Mum and Dad would say?"

"Since they're not talking to me, I don't imagine they would say much of anything."

"I thought families were supposed to have only one black sheep," Ian said with a wry smile, but Garrett could swear he saw regret lurking behind his eyes.

Was it possible that he had a conscience after all? That he really did want to change?

Garrett washed the possibility away with a swallow of ale. If he let himself get his hopes up, he would only be disappointed later.

"He's jealous, you know," Ian said.

"Who?"

"Our father."

Garrett frowned. "Jealous of whom?"

"You."

He had no idea what Ian was talking about. His father had made it very clear that he wanted nothing to do with Garrett or his money. "That's ridiculous."

"It's true. He was never what you would call a pleasant man, we both have the scars to prove that, but after you left for university things were bad."

Garrett automatically reached up to touch the small scar at the corner of his mouth. From a crack in the jaw he'd received for staying late at school to finish a project when he should have been home doing his chores. "How bad?"

"His temper became even more volatile. I had never seen him so angry. He and Mum were fighting all the time. But you know Mum, she would take it all. I was just a kid, but even I knew that wasn't right. I asked her one day why he hated us so much."

Garrett couldn't help but ask, "What did she say?"

"That he was an unhappy man. That he had dreams of going to university and doing more with his life, but being the oldest, it was his responsibility to take over the farm when his father retired. And he did it, because that was what was expected of him. He married and became a farmer, just like he was supposed to. He settled. Then you came along, knowing exactly what you wanted and not letting a single thing get in your way. He envied you, Garrett, maybe even hated you for it, because that's the kind of man he was. And he convinced everyone else that what you'd done was some sort of slight against the family."

And here Garrett had always believed his father had been content as a farmer, that he was happy with the simple life he'd chosen. "He never once said a word about wanting anything different."

Ian shrugged. "It wasn't his way."

"Even if I knew, it wouldn't have changed anything. I still would have left."

"I'm not blaming you, Garrett. I just thought you should know why he's such a bastard. I mean, at least I *deserve* the family's hatred. You haven't done anything wrong."

"A father should want better for his sons. He should

want them to strive for more. Instead he was always trying to hold me back."

"That's his problem, not yours."

So why did Garrett still feel like it was his fault? Like he'd done something wrong? Parents were supposed to love their kids unconditionally. Push them to succeed. And it wasn't just his father at fault. His mum bore just as much blame. She should have defended Garrett, should have been his advocate, not her husband's enabler.

Like Ian said, it wasn't Garrett's fault. But he couldn't decide if this new information was a relief or only made him feel worse.

How many times had he told himself that he'd stopped caring? That nothing they could say or do could hurt him, even if that meant them not saying or doing anything at all? Somewhere deep down, did he still care?

He took a long swallow, draining the bottle, then said, "Shouldn't you be lying down resting or something?"

"I'm bored," Ian said. "She's really nice by the way."

"Who?"

"*Who?*" Ian laughed. "The *Princess*. Your girlfriend. The one you aren't shagging. Who did you think I meant?"

His brother had just informed him that everything he knew about his life was untrue, so it was natural for Garrett to be a bit confused. "Yes, she is."

"I'll bet she's a handful though."

He narrowed his eyes at his brother. "Why would you say that?"

"Mischief recognizes mischief. And honestly, I think that's exactly the kind of woman you need. One who won't give you the chance to be bored."

It surprised Garrett how well Ian knew him. Ian had been so young when Garrett left. So carefree. Maybe there was more going on in his head than people realized.

Garrett had left his phone on the counter and it began to ring. Before he could reach for it, Ian grabbed it. Rather than hand it to Garrett, he answered himself. He greeted the caller just the way Garrett would, then for several seconds just listened. At first Garrett thought it might be some sort of automated call, then Ian said, "Sorry, I think it's Garrett you want to speak to." With another wry smile he handed the phone to Garrett. "It's a fellow named Wes. He called to say that he saw you on the news just now and it looks as though the situation with the Princess is going just as planned."

Bloody hell. Ian knew. Not specifically what, but he knew Garrett was up to something. And he wouldn't hesitate to hold it against him.

Garrett took the phone. "Wes?"

"Christ, Garrett, was that Ian? He sounds just like you."

"Yes, it was."

"I'm sorry. If I had known…"

"Don't worry about it."

"I called to tell you that I just saw footage on the telly of her leaving your place."

That was quick. "It was something of a media frenzy outside."

"Well, you certainly gave them fodder to chew on."

Garrett frowned. "What do you mean?"

Wes told him about the footage he'd seen and Garrett groaned. Suddenly what Ian did or didn't know was inconsequential.

"I take it that wasn't deliberate," Wes said.

No, and he had the feeling he would be hearing from Chris regarding the matter, if the family hadn't banished him from the castle, from Louisa's life, already.

"I'm here!" Louisa called cheerily as she breezed into Melissa's hospital room at seven on the nose…and was met by total silence.

Melissa reclined in bed and Chris stood beside her, arms crossed over his chest. Aaron and Liv sat in chairs across the room by the window, and Anne was seated across from them. And they all just stared at her.

Did they know what she'd been up to?

Of course not. She had looked a bit rumpled when she left Garrett's town house but she'd fixed her makeup and hair in the car. "What? Why are you looking at me like that?"

"We saw you on the telly," Anne remarked with a smirk.

Was *that* all? They were always on television for some reason or another. It's not as though her relationship with Garrett was some kind of secret.

She shrugged and asked, "So?"

Everyone exchanged a look, then Melissa said, "You looked a little…disheveled."

Yes, she probably should have fixed up herself before she left, but it wasn't that big of a deal. "So my hair wasn't perfect. Is it really the end of the world?"

"Well," Liv began, looking pained. "There was your shirt, too."

"What about it?" she asked, and Liv gestured for her to see for herself.

Louisa looked down and her heart sank. She must

have been in quite a rush when she dressed because she'd fastened the buttons on her blouse cockeyed.

"Oops." She turned away and swiftly fixed it.

"I guess this means you blew that vow to be a virgin on your wedding night," Anne snipped, and Louisa spun to face her. That was supposed to be private, a secret shared between sisters.

"What's your problem?" Louisa said, so tired of Anne dumping on her that she wanted to scream.

Anne just sneered. "Should we expect a shotgun wedding, or were you smart enough to use a condom?"

"Anne!" Chris cut in sharply.

"I wish you would do something to kill the bug that has crawled up your you-know-where, so I could have my sister back," Louisa retorted. "And not that it's yours or anyone else's business, but I am still pure as the driven snow." More or less.

"That may be true," Aaron said, "but it looked as though you'd spent the afternoon shagging."

She could understand why people might get that impression, and why Chris looked so disappointed in her. "It was an accident," she told him.

"Yes, well, it's not the kind of thing that someone would do on purpose. All that tells me is that you were being careless."

"I was in a hurry. I was running late and wanted to get here on time. If I had taken the time to fix myself up, I would have been late and you would have chastised me for that." No matter what she did, she couldn't win.

"Then you should have taken that into consideration and stopped whatever it was you were doing earlier to give yourself extra time. With everything else we have to worry about, this is the last thing the family needs, Louisa. It reflects badly on me."

Him? "How did this become about *you?*"

"Because it is my responsibility to hold this family together in our father's absence. How do you think he and Mother will feel when they see this on the news? Who do you think they'll blame?"

She hadn't thought about it like that. She bit her lip and lowered her eyes, suddenly filled with shame. "I'm sorry."

Sometimes she forgot how much pressure Chris must be under. First taking over their father's duties, and now having Melissa in the hospital and his children's health at risk. He was right. She was being irresponsible and selfish.

"I'm sending Anne to speak for me tomorrow," he told her, twisting the knife in a little deeper. Prince Chris giveth, then he taketh away.

She nodded, unable to meet his eyes. "I understand."

Not only had she let him and the rest of the family down, but the way Anne had been acting lately, she would take satisfaction rubbing this in Louisa's face.

"You *will* be more careful next time," he said, and she went limp with relief. At least he wasn't going to put her on house arrest, or insist she stop seeing Garrett. He was giving her another chance.

"I will," she told him. "I promise."

Her cell phone started to ring and she practically dove into her purse to grab it. It was Garrett's number. "I need to get this," she told Chris.

He nodded, signaling what she hoped was the end of

the tongue-lashing. At least for now, but God forbid she screw up again. Chris wouldn't be so lenient. He might do something drastic, like lock her in a tower and never let her out.

Eleven

Louisa escaped into the waiting room and answered her phone. "Hi."

"Did I get you at a bad time?" Garrett asked.

"No, your timing was perfect. Chris just finished chastising me to within an inch of my life," she said, and could swear she felt him cringe.

"I take it they saw the news clip."

"Yeah. Did you?"

"Yeah. A friend called to tell me so I put the television on. It's been on practically every channel, so it was hard to miss."

She tensed up. "Aaron said I looked like I spent the afternoon shagging."

"Yeah, you did. I'm sorry."

"Why are you apologizing?"

"Because I never should have let you leave my house. As you were getting ready to walk out the door I was thinking to myself how mussed you looked, but I just thought it was sexy as hell. It never occurred to me that the press would notice, too."

"What about my blouse?"

"That I honestly didn't notice or I would have told you." He paused then asked, "Chris was angry?"

"It was more of an I'm-not-angry-I'm-disappointed speech. And to be honest, anger would have been a lot easier to stomach. I feel terrible. I promised him that next time I would be more careful."

"Does that mean we're still on for Saturday?"

"Definitely. Although there was a point when I worried he might stick me on permanent house arrest. And coincidentally, I'm also free Thursday, as well. Chris asked Anne to sit in for him instead. I guess he doesn't trust me."

"Well, I made plans with my friend Wes to golf that evening, but I could cancel."

She shelved her disappointment. "No, don't do that. I don't want to be *that girl*."

"What girl?"

"The one who makes her boyfriend drop all of his friends and monopolizes his every waking moment. Go golfing and have fun. I'll see you Saturday."

The hospital room door opened and Anne stepped through. She shot a quick, nervous glance at Louisa then walked to the ladies' room. What was her deal?

"Are you sure? Because I know he would understand."

"I'm sure. I have plenty to keep me busy." She loved the idea that he wanted to be with her, but she needed to let him have some normalcy before things got too serious between them, because eventually he was bound to become a target for the Gingerbread Man and security would become an issue for him, as well. He should enjoy his freedom while he still could. "Maybe you could call me before you go to bed," she suggested.

"Eleven too late?"

"I'll keep the phone beside me just in case I drift off." Maybe they could even give that phone sex thing a try. She was about to mention it when she heard what sounded like retching from the ladies' room. Was Anne sick?

"Garrett, I have to let you go," she said. "I'll talk to you tomorrow."

They said their goodbyes and she walked over to the door to listen. It was quiet for a minute, then she heard the unmistakable sound echoing off the tile walls. She knocked on the door. "Anne, are you okay?"

"I'm fine," she called back, but immediately the vomiting started again. It sounded violent and painful, and Louisa started to actually worry something was seriously wrong.

"Do you need anything?" she asked.

"No. Go away."

She sighed. She was trying to help and Anne was still copping an attitude. "Would you stop being such a bitch and let me in? For reasons I cannot begin to comprehend, I'm worried about you!"

A few seconds passed and she heard the toilet flush, then the lock on the door snapped and Anne yelled, "You can come in."

She opened the door, taken aback by what she found. Anne was sitting on the floor near the commode, her cheek resting against the tile wall. A sheen of sweat dampened her face, and aside from two bright red patches on her cheeks, all the color had leeched from her skin.

Alarmed, Louisa stepped inside and shut the door. "What's wrong? Are you sick?"

She shook her head. "I'm fine."

"You are *not* fine." She reached down to feel her forehead, but Anne batted her hand away.

"I don't have a fever."

"If you're sick, you shouldn't be anywhere near Melissa."

"I told you I'm not sick."

Then what other explanation—

"Oh my God, are you bulimic?"

Anne laughed weakly. "Louisa, bulimics vomit *after* they eat. Not before."

"If you're not sick and you're not bulimic, what's going on? Healthy people don't throw up like that."

"Some healthy *women* do," Anne said.

It took a minute, but the meaning of her words finally sank in and Louisa gasped. "Oh my God," she hissed in a loud whisper. "Are you *pregnant?*"

"You can't tell *anyone*," Anne said.

"Oh my God," she said again, hardly able to believe it.

"Imagine how I felt when I took the pregnancy tests," Anne joked weakly.

"You took more than one?"

"I took five. I wanted to be sure."

That would definitely do it. "How far along are you?

"Just a few weeks."

"How did this happen?"

Anne raised a brow at her.

Louisa rolled her eyes. "Of course I know *how,* but when, and with whom? I didn't even know you were seeing anyone."

"I'm not. And the father is out of the picture. He doesn't want the baby or me."

"Are you sure?"

"*Very* sure."

"Oh, Anne, I'm so sorry." She sat down on the floor beside her sister and took her hand. She half expected her to pull away, but she didn't. At least this explained why Anne had been so cranky lately. Her hormones must have been raging, and to top it off, having the father reject her and the baby? She must have been devastated.

"Who is it, Anne?"

"It's not important."

"Yes, it is. Someone needs to make him own up to his responsibility."

"I'm not even sure what *I'm* going to do yet."

Louisa's heart skipped. "You don't mean…?"

"What I mean is, I haven't decided if I'm going to keep it, or give it up for adoption. If I choose adoption, I figure I can hold out until it's impossible to hide, then take an extended vacation. No one will have to know a thing."

That would be tough enough for an average woman to pull off, but a princess? Someone was bound to figure it out. "You don't want to have children?"

"Not like this. Besides, look how everyone reacted to you leaving your boyfriend's house looking a little untidy. Can you imagine how they would take the news of me having a child out of wedlock? I'm not sure Daddy could take the stress of a huge scandal right now."

She hadn't heard Anne call him "Daddy" in years. "He'll be okay."

Anne shook her head, looking troubled. "He doesn't look good, Louisa. He's lost so much weight and he has so little energy now. You should have seen the look on his face when the doctor said there was so little improvement. He was devastated. And Mum is a total wreck. I think she sees the same thing I do."

"What's that?"

"I think he's giving up."

Louisa shook her head. "He would never do that. He's strong."

"He's been so sick and in and out of hospitals for so long. I think he's just tired."

"I can't accept that."

"I know you love him. We all do, and I think right now he's holding on for us. But there is going to come a time when we have to let go. We have to let him know that it's okay to stop fighting."

She knew she was being selfish, but she didn't *want* him to stop fighting. He was going to walk her down the aisle at her wedding and be there to play with her children. She simply could not imagine her life without him in it. "How do you know he's ready to quit? Did he tell you?"

"He didn't have to. I just knew. I think you will, too. When you're ready."

She didn't know if she would *ever* be ready for that.

There was a soft rap at the door, startling them both.

"Come in," Anne called.

The door opened a crack and Liv stuck her head in, she looked around, then her gaze dropped and she frowned. "Oh, there you are. We thought maybe you'd left. Why are you sitting on the floor?"

"Hot flashes," Anne said. "Damned PMS. I thought it would be cooler down here."

It was the dumbest excuse Louisa had ever heard, but Liv didn't question it.

"Oh. Well, dinner is getting cold."

Louisa smiled. "Thanks, we'll be right in."

Liv shot them one last odd look that suggested her sisters-in-law were both a few beakers short of a complete lab, then disappeared. It probably did look odd, the two of them alone in the bathroom sitting on the floor and holding hands no less.

"I really like her," Anne said, "but she's way too uptight. Maybe she just needs a good shag."

"That's definitely not the problem," Louisa said, and to Anne's how-do-*you*-know look, she added, "My room is right down the hall, and suffice it to say they aren't exactly quiet. And for the record, I really didn't sleep with Garrett. I want to though. I'm not sure I can wait until my wedding night."

"I'm sorry for what I said, Louisa. About your virginity. That was rotten of me. And I'm sorry I've been such a bitch lately."

"Under the circumstances I guess I can cut you some slack." She looked at Anne and smiled. "I'm just glad to have my sister back."

Anne gave her hand a squeeze. "I think I'm just jealous that you found someone you care about. I should be happy for you, not trying to drag you down."

"You don't still think he's using me?"

She shrugged. "What the hell do I know? If I was so

damned smart I wouldn't have gotten myself into this mess."

"It'll be okay, Annie," she assured her, using the nickname from their childhood. Anne was Annie, and Louisa was Lulu. She wondered when they had stopped that, when they felt they were too mature or too refined for silly names. They used to be silly a lot back then, and Louisa missed that. Sometimes she wished they could go back to those days when things were so simple and uncomplicated.

Or maybe it was all relative. Problems that seemed enormous back then were, in retrospect, not such a big deal now.

"You ready?" Anne asked.

She nodded and asked, "You?"

Balancing on the wall, she pushed herself to her feet. "May as well get this over with."

Louisa followed her out, thinking that maybe the trick was going back over all the experiences she'd had up until this point—the good times and bad times, the hurts and the happiness—and starting fresh.

Of course, going back would mean leaving Garrett forever, and that wasn't something she would ever do.

The headline of the morning paper was brutal. Clever, but brutal.

"Has Snow White Drifted?"

The photo beneath it was even worse. It was a shot of her being ushered to the car, her hair messy, her makeup all but gone. And of course there was the sloppily buttoned shirt, which the paper had conveniently circled for their readers' viewing ease. Under that was a smaller photo of Garrett standing at his front doorway in bare feet, his hair a mess and his clothes wrinkled.

"We *do* look like we've been shagging," she told Garrett.

"It's not *that* bad. For all the press knows, we could have been out for a run."

She tossed the paper off the bed and switched the phone to her other ear. "Yes, I often run in a skirt and sandals."

"My point is, no one can know for sure *what* we were doing. Besides us, of course. Now if we'd made a sex tape that was leaked to the press…"

"Bite your tongue," she said and he laughed.

"Don't worry. It'll blow over."

She wondered how his family was reacting to the press. But he'd already told her that he no longer spoke to them.

"When was the last time you talked to your father?" she asked.

Her question seemed to surprise him. "Where did that come from?"

"I've been thinking about family a lot lately. I was just curious."

"I haven't spoken to him since the day I purchased his land."

"You bought his farm?"

"It was the first piece of property I ever owned. They were in trouble. They had a bad crop, and with their debt, he wasn't able to pay his taxes. The land was about to be seized and put up for auction. I bought it, thinking that I would present it to him as a gift. He and my mum could live there until the day he died and never have to worry about money again."

"He must have been so grateful."

"He tore the deed in half and threw it back in my face. He told me that I was no longer his son."

Louisa gasped. "He didn't!"

"He said he didn't want my charity."

The idea that he would do that to his son made Louisa's heart ache. And all Garrett had done was try to help. "You must have felt horrible."

"My father was always a proud man, but I admit I never expected that reaction. I thought he would finally see that my choice to go to college had paid off. That I'd made the right decision. He always told me that the land would someday be mine. I guess that only applied if I became a farmer like him. Instead he preferred that it be purchased off the auction block by some stranger rather than by his own flesh and blood."

Tears shimmered in her eyes. "I can't imagine how much that must have hurt you."

"It was a feeling of resignation more than anything. And maybe in a way a relief. He had drawn his line in the sand. I could finally stop trying to please him."

"You at least tried to talk to him, didn't you?"

"There wasn't much point. He made his feelings clear."

"But…he's your father. I'm sure he still loves you."

"Well, it's too late now."

"It's never too late, Garrett. If you don't at least try to heal the rift between you and he dies, it will haunt you for the rest of your life."

"Why this sudden interest in my family?"

"Anne told me something about our father the other day, and…" Tears welled up in her eyes again and she swallowed back a sob.

"Is something wrong?" he asked.

"It's not looking good." She told Garrett what Anne had said, and it took every ounce of energy she had not to fall apart.

Garrett figured he would be relishing the news of the King's permanent vacation from the throne. Because even if he didn't die, it sounded as though he would never be healthy enough to rule again. Which meant that Garrett was a shoo-in for that position Louisa had mentioned. At the very least, Garrett should have been relieved that finally all of his hard work was going to reap benefits.

Instead he felt like a piece of garbage.

He used to see the royal family as nothing more than an obstacle. A united front made up of faceless individuals he was determined to conquer. That attitude had suited him just fine—until he'd gotten to know them. Now everything had changed, and the idea that he could have been so greedy and shallow, so manipulative, disturbed him deeper than he could have imagined. He used to be a good person. He used to have principles, used to care about people.

He was revolted by the man he had become.

But he couldn't deny that he was really starting to care about Louisa. When she told him about the situation with her father, her voice so full of grief and fear, Garrett would have moved heaven and earth to take away her pain. To make it better. And quite frankly, it scared the hell out of him.

He didn't have time for attachments like that, time to worry himself with other people's baggage. He preferred to keep his life simple and uncomplicated.

And by choosing Louisa, that was what he believed he was getting. A sweet, demure, shell of a woman who would be easily manipulated and more or less trained to be exactly the kind of wife he wanted. The less seen and heard, the better.

Instead he got a feisty, passionate and independent woman. One who was about as likely to follow his "rules" as he was to don a tutu and become a ballerina.

Maybe she was his punishment for all his selfishness, his ruthless attitude. The thing is, she didn't *feel* like a punishment. Was it possible that she might actually be a blessing in disguise?

Twelve

Louisa lay in bed most of the night, tossing and turning, her mind working a million miles an hour. The idea of losing their father, and the possibility of Anne giving up her baby, was almost too much for her to bear. There was nothing much she could do for her father but be there to support him. And she could only do the same for Anne.

Early the following morning, she went to Anne's room to check on her. Louisa knocked, and when Anne answered she looked like death warmed over.

"Feeling sick?"

"Does it show?" Anne asked wryly, letting her in, then she crawled back into bed and burrowed under the covers.

"Is there anything I can do?"

She shook her head. "What's up?"

"I was wondering if you had decided what to do."

"About the baby, you mean?"

Louisa nodded and sat on the edge of the bed.

"Not definitively, but I'm leaning toward adoption. I'm just…I'm not ready to do this. Not this way. Besides, I would be a terrible single mother. I'm pessimistic and difficult. The baby would be much better off with someone else. Someone more…maternal. I'm just not cut out to be a mother."

"Of course you are! You would be a wonderful mother."

Anne shook her head. "Not now. Not like this."

Louisa wished there was something she could say to change her mind, but who was she to tell her sister how to live?

"What happened to this family, Anne? How did everything get all screwed up and turned around?"

"It just…happens. Things can't stay the same forever."

But she wanted them to. She wanted everything to go back to the way it used to be, when they were all healthy and happy and safe. Now it was just so…confusing. It seemed that the only really good thing in her life right now was Garrett. He made her happy. But it was a sort of happy she had never experienced before. Not with a man, anyway. When she was with him, she felt excited and hopeful and content all at once.

"Just for the record," Anne said, "I actually think you and Garrett will be really happy together."

"I think…I think I love him."

Anne regarded her curiously. "You sound surprised. From the second you met him, you've been so sure he was the one."

"I know, but that was different."

"Different how?"

"Let's face it, I've said I 'loved' at least a dozen other men before him. And yes, when I met Garrett I was convinced it was love at first sight. He was so dark and mysterious and sexy. But now that I've gotten to know him, the *real* him, I realize how immature and shallow those feelings really were. He's so much more than what I expected. And what I feel for him now is so much bigger than anything I've felt before. Complex and confusing and…wonderful."

"That's a good thing, right?"

"I hope so. A week ago I was absolutely certain that we were perfect for each other, that it was destiny. But what if I was wrong? What if I fell in love with him, but he doesn't love me back?"

"And what if he does?"

That would be wonderful, of course. "You know, the great thing about being naive is that you don't think about stuff like this. It's so much easier existing in a bubble, convinced life is wonderful and everything will work out."

"Yeah, but you can't live like that forever. Eventually the bubble will burst."

Maybe that was what had happened to her. Maybe her bubble had finally burst, because for the first time in her life she didn't have all the answers. She didn't believe that everything would be okay.

"By the way, as soon as I can manage to crawl out of bed, I'm telling Chris that I can't fill in for him anymore. Last night was miserable. Not only did I feel as though any second I would toss all over the podium, but when it comes to public speaking, you're just better than me.

You're in your element when you're interacting with people, and let's face it, I'm not."

"What if he says no?"

"I won't give him a choice. It's you or Aaron, and we both know Aaron won't want to do it."

After so many years of wanting her family to take her more seriously, to give her more responsibility, suddenly she was afraid. What if she wasn't good enough? What if she made another mistake?

She'd spent so much time whining and complaining and never had the slightest clue how easy she had it.

Technically she had been an adult for nine years, but until recently, she hadn't really grown up. She felt as though now it was finally time. But to grow up she would have to face one of her biggest fears. The one thing she'd been stalwartly avoiding.

"I have to go call Garrett," she told Anne.

"Is everything okay? You look...I don't know, like you're up to something." She frowned suddenly then asked, "You're not going to do something drastic are you?"

Drastic for Louisa maybe. "Everything is fine," she promised. Or at least, as close to fine as it could be under the circumstances.

Louisa dialed Garrett's home number, but he didn't answer.

She was about to try his cell when Geoffrey knocked on her door. "You have a visitor, Your Highness."

A visitor? This early? Then she realized it could be only one person. She raced to the door and flung it open. Garrett stood on the other side. He was dressed for work, a shy grin on his face. He looked delicious.

"Surprise," he said.

"Thank you, Geoffrey," Louisa said, grabbing Garrett's hand and tugging him into her room. The instant the door was closed she was in his arms. She must have looked a fright, still in her pajamas with her hair mussed, but she was so happy to see him she didn't care.

"I know it's early. I hope I didn't wake you."

"No, I've been up awhile." She pressed her cheek to his suit jacket, breathed in the scent of his aftershave. "And even if I had been asleep, I couldn't think of a better way to wake up."

He kissed the top of her head. "I've missed you, Princess."

Her heart overflowed with happiness. "I've missed you, too. But how did you get Geoffrey to bring you up here?"

"I lied and said you were expecting me. I know I'll see you tonight, but I didn't want to wait that long."

She really didn't want to do this, but she had to. "I was wondering if you would be upset if I cancelled our date."

"I guess that would depend on why you want to cancel it."

"I keep thinking about what Anne said, about our father. If she's right, I may not have a lot of time left with him. Not only that, but I think I need to see him for myself, but he's going to be in England for at least another week. Maybe longer. I'm thinking I should go stay with him. Just a few days."

"I think that's a good idea," he said.

She looked up at him. "You do?"

He touched her cheek. "Louisa, he's your father. Of course he should come first."

"I would leave this afternoon and fly back either Wednesday or Thursday."

"Take all the time you need. I'll still be here when you get back."

"You promise?"

He smiled. "I promise."

"Have I told you how wonderful you are?"

"Yeah, but you can tell me again." There was a smile in his voice, and it made her smile, too. "I suppose this means our trip to Cabo will have to wait awhile?"

"Are you angry?"

"Of course not."

She got up on her toes to press a kiss to his lips. "You're wonderful, and I'm going to miss you."

"You won't be on a different planet. We can still talk on the phone."

"I'd like that. In fact, if it's as bad as Anne has led me to believe, I might just need someone to talk to."

"In that case, I promise I'll call you every night."

"I'm terrified of what I'm going to find when I get there."

"Whatever it is, you'll deal with it. You're stronger than you give yourself credit for, you know."

She hoped so. "It would be so much harder going through this alone. I'm glad I met you, Garrett."

"You wouldn't be alone. You have your family."

"Yes, but they don't see me the way you do. They don't really listen to me, or take me seriously. But I know that you really care how I feel. I don't know what I would do without you."

"You never have to worry about that," he said.

She wondered if that was his way of saying that he wanted to marry her without actually saying it. But the truth was, right now she didn't care what it meant. She was just thankful to have him.

"How much time have you got?" she asked him.

He glanced at his watch. "A few minutes. Why?"

She slid her hands under his jacket and up his chest. "Well, since we won't see each other for several days, I thought we could spend some quality time together."

He grinned. "Oh, did you?"

"But if you only have a few minutes…"

He looped his arms around her and walked her backward toward the bed. "I'll make time," he growled, his eyes dark with desire.

Though he did eventually make it to work, he was very late.

Garrett did call her, just as he'd promised, and thank goodness she had him to talk to. Because things weren't as bad as Anne described. They were worse.

In the week he had been gone, it seemed as if her father had aged a decade. He was thin and sallow, as though the life had been sucked out of him, and when she embraced him, he felt frail. Gone was the strong and vibrant king. The leader. And in that instant she knew, without a shadow of a doubt, that he would never be coming back. Anne had been right. He'd lost his will to fight. His desire to live. It was a matter of time now.

Oddly enough, the person she felt more sorry for was her mother. She looked utterly exhausted and so brittle that with the slightest agitation, she could easily shatter.

"So, tell me about this new man of yours," her father

said, trying to sound jovial, but his voice was thready and weak.

"He's wonderful. He's handsome and smart and fun."

"Sounds like me," he said with a wink. "I'm anxious to meet him. I've heard good things from your brother."

It was odd, because this courtship hadn't been at all what she had imagined. She had expected it to be like a dream, like a fairy tale come true. Garrett would ride in like a knight in shining armor and whisk her away to a fantasy land. He would wine and dine her and take her on exotic trips. But thanks to security, they hadn't even had an actual date! And he hadn't showered her with lavish gifts and attention, like other men. He hadn't treated her like royalty at all. He'd treated her like…a person. And the strange thing was, she liked it. By acting the opposite of what she had expected, he'd won her heart.

"I know I've said this before about other men, but I really think he's the one. I…I like the way I feel when I'm with him. I like who I am."

"And who is that?" her mother asked.

"*Me*. And he seems to appreciate me for who I am."

"Are you saying I might finally get to walk one of my daughters down the aisle?" her father asked.

"It looks that way," she said, and oh, how she hoped he could. But if he couldn't be there physically, she knew he would be there in spirit. In her heart. "He hasn't actually asked yet, but I have this feeling it might be soon."

"You'll let us know the minute he does?" her mother prompted.

"I promise."

They chatted for a while, her parents carrying on as if everything was fine. They asked how Melissa was feeling, and how Chris was adjusting to having her away from home. They asked about Liv's research and if Aaron was still assisting her in the lab. They even asked about Muffin, who Louisa had left in the care of Elise, one of the maids. She had small children who loved to play with and pamper him, and an elderly mother who adored him. Of course Muffin, being a total attention hound, was in his glory. He needed someone who had more time to devote to him. Louisa confessed to her parents that as much as she loved him, in light of everything that was happening lately, she might let Elise keep him permanently.

After a while her father drifted off to sleep and her mother motioned her out into the private waiting room next door. As soon as they were there, she pulled her mother into her arms and gave her a big hug.

"What's this for?" she asked.

"Because you look like you need it."

"Oh, I'm fine," she said, waving Louisa's concerns away with the flip of her wrist. "I'm just a little tired. And homesick."

"And worried about Father?"

"Nothing to worry about," she said brightly, but Louisa could hear the undertone of strain in her voice, like guitar strings stretched too taut. "His cardiologist was in yesterday and he's still confident the heart pump will do its job and your father will be back on his feet in no time. We just have to be patient."

A week ago Louisa probably would have believed her, despite all the evidence to the contrary. She would have believed it because it was what she wanted to hear. Now the blinders were off and she was ready to view the world from all sides.

"That's a nice fantasy," Louisa told her. "Now, why don't you tell me what he really said."

She gave her mother credit. She managed to hold it together for a good ten seconds, but then everything in her seemed to let go and she crumbled before Louisa's eyes. In the past that might have scared Louisa to death, but now she just took her mother into her arms and held her while she sobbed her heart out. She stroked her hair and rubbed her back, the way her mother had for Louisa when she was little. When the downpour finally ceased, Louisa handed her a tissue, and as she dabbed her eyes, it seemed as though some of the stress she'd been carrying around had lifted.

"I'm sorry I fell apart like that," she said. "I must look a fright."

"We all need a good cry every now and then. And you look beautiful, as always."

"It's just been a long few weeks. A long few *years,* actually."

"It's not working, is it?" Louisa said. "The pump."

Her mother shook her head. "There should have been a much more drastic improvement since the last time they checked. They could leave him on it, but the longer he stays on, the odds of infection increase. In his weakened state it could be fatal."

"And without the pump?"

"He could live as long as a few years."

But they both knew he probably wouldn't. He didn't have the strength left. Or the will.

"What are the chances he would have another heart attack?" Louisa asked.

"Very likely."

"And the odds he would survive?"

"Slim to none. There's just too much damage already."

"How did he take the news?"

"You know, I think in a way he was…relieved. He's fought so hard. Maybe he feels he finally has an excuse to surrender without letting us down."

"He could never let me down," Louisa told her. Maybe it was partially due to the seed that Anne had planted in her brain, but after seeing his condition and talking with him, she honestly believed that he was ready to let go. It was his time.

The pain she felt when she thought of losing him was indescribable. Like a thousand arrows straight through the heart, yet knowing that he had made peace with the idea of dying was a deep comfort.

She was surprisingly calm when she talked to Garrett that night and explained the situation. Not that she wasn't sad or upset, but crying wouldn't help anyone at this point.

"If you need me, I can be on the next flight to London," Garrett told her more than once. "Just say the word and I'll be there."

It was so tempting to say yes, but she needed to do this alone. To know that she *could*. Because if she could handle this, she figured she could handle just about anything.

After they hung up, she booted up her laptop to research any information she could find about her father's condition. What they could expect to happen near the end. Waiting for her in her mailbox was another message from her pal the Gingerbread Man. It read, Send the old man my regards.

Thirteen

A well of emotions crashed down on Louisa like a tidal wave and she was suddenly so filled with rage, her first instinct was to lob her computer out the window and watch it smash onto the London streets below. She couldn't recall a time in her life when she had ever felt so angry at another human being.

So he knew where she was, *big bloody deal*. These childish little games he was playing were just plain ridiculous. He needed to grow a pair and confront her face-to-face.

Though they had been strictly forbidden from answering his e-mails for fear that it would provoke him, she'd had enough. Maybe they *should* provoke him, draw him out into the open where he could be identified and captured.

She wrote back, You're a coward.

She clicked the send button and it felt good. It gave her a sense of power.

Barely a minute later another e-mail appeared from him. It said, Careful, Lulu. Or Daddy won't be the only one to shuffle loose the mortal coil.

Seeing him use her nickname and what was a very direct threat gave her such a serious case of the creeps that she slammed the computer shut. Maybe replying to him hadn't been such a good idea after all. What if he did lash out? What if someone was hurt? Then it would be completely her fault.

Damn! If only she would think before she acted. She had to stop being so selfish. So quick to fly off the handle.

At the risk of further restricting her already limited freedom, she opened her computer back up and forwarded the e-mail to the head of security at the palace, then she called Chris to give him a heads-up.

"He's a persistent son of a bitch," Chris noted. "How many e-mails is it now, Louisa? Four or five in the past two weeks?"

"But…how did you—"

"I had the feeling you might be less than honest, so I've been monitoring your e-mail."

"My *private* e-mail?"

"Don't worry, security is under strict orders to read only the messages that come from him."

She wanted to scream at him, tell him that he had no right to violate her privacy, but how could she be angry when he was right? She *had* lied to him. And by doing so, she could have been putting everyone in danger. "I can't seem to stop letting you down, can I?" she lamented.

"I noticed that, too."

"I've been so selfish."

"Yes, you have. Although it probably hasn't helped that we've spent the last twenty-seven years sheltering and spoiling you."

"I don't want to be that person anymore, Chris. I'm tired of her. I want to grow up. I want to be responsible."

"I think we would all appreciate that."

She thought about what she had just done and frowned. "However…there is one last really stupid and irresponsible thing I have to confess to first."

"Oh God, what did you do?"

She told him about the e-mail that she sent to the Gingerbread Man.

"That *was* stupid. You know what they said about provoking him. What's the point of keeping all of this security around if we don't bother to listen?"

"Maybe this time they're wrong. What if we *should* be antagonizing him? Maybe we should draw him out so they can catch him."

"You know that's too dangerous."

"I'm beginning to wonder if it might be worth the risk. I mean, how much longer can we live like this, Chris? Constantly on high alert? Somebody has to *do* something."

"We're *all* frustrated, Louisa, but finding him isn't worth risking anyone's safety. You just have to be patient."

But she was tired of being patient. Sweet, patient, obedient—for the most part anyway—Princess Louisa. She was sick to death of her.

All the time they wasted worrying about their stalker

and what he *might* do was time they should spend living life to the fullest.

And from now on, living her life was exactly what she intended to do.

Garrett was bloody exhausted by the time he trudged up the steps and opened his front door Tuesday night. It had been another long, grueling day and all he wanted to do now was change out of his suit, collapse into bed and call Louisa. Hearing her voice had become the highlight of his day. But he looked forward to tomorrow evening, when she would finally return home. That phrase about absence making the heart grow fonder seemed to have some truth to it.

He let himself inside, dropped his briefcase at the foot of the stairs and headed to the kitchen for a drink. From the hallway he could see the light was on, and since the nurse had left more than an hour ago, that meant Ian was still up.

As odd as it was, Garrett had grown a bit fond of not coming home to an empty house. He didn't resent Ian's presence nearly as much as he thought he would. He no longer had the feeling that any second the other shoe was going to fall, or that he would arrive home from work and his house would be cleaned out. In fact, there were times when he actually enjoyed Ian's company.

But tonight, as he stepped into the kitchen, Ian wasn't alone.

"Louisa?"

Grinning brightly, she sat across from Ian at the kitchen table, a half-finished bottle of beer in front of her on the table. "Surprised to see me?"

Without even thinking about what he was doing, he

rounded the table and scooped up Louisa from her chair. She threw her arms around his neck and hugged him, and the stress of the entire day seemed to evaporate into thin air. He set her down and breathed in the scent of her hair and her skin, relished the feel of her body pressed against him. If Ian hadn't been sitting right there, he and Louisa would have been doing a lot more than just embracing.

Louisa on the other hand didn't seem to care that his brother was in the room. She rose up on her toes and pressed her lips to his. It wasn't a passionate kiss, but it wasn't exactly chaste, either. He considered her more of a champagne and caviar kind of woman, but he had to admit that the flavor of the ale on her lips was a major turn-on.

"I thought you weren't coming home until tomorrow," he said.

She grinned up at him. "I missed you. And I thought it would be fun to surprise you. I even made my security detail hide so you wouldn't see them."

They were apparently good at it, because he hadn't had a clue that they were there. "I'm definitely surprised. Have you been here long?"

"Only an hour or so."

"If I had known I would have left work earlier."

"That's okay." She looked over at Ian and smiled. "Your brother and I have been having a very nice chat."

Garrett regarded him curiously. "Oh, have you?"

Ian grinned. "Don't worry, I didn't tell her anything *too* embarrassing."

Or anything having to do with Garrett's ulterior

motives, he hoped. Of course, if he had, Garrett doubted Louisa would be so happy to see him.

Is this the way it would be from now on? Garrett always paranoid that something might slip and she would learn the truth? *And how would she take it?* he wondered. As far as he was concerned, the only thing that mattered was the way he felt about her right here. Right now.

"How long can you stay?"

"I told Chris that I wouldn't be home tonight." She gestured down the hall and said, "Can we talk upstairs?" Her expression gave him the feeling something might be wrong. Maybe Ian had said something.

"Of course."

He shot Ian a questioning look. Ian shrugged, as if to say, *Don't ask me.*

Louisa smiled at Ian. "It was really nice talking with you, Ian."

"You, too," Ian said.

"I know everything will work out."

Ian smiled and nodded.

Garrett wondered what that was about, but he was more concerned with what was on Louisa's mind. There was something about her tonight. Something… different.

Maybe it was her clothes. Clothes that for her, he suddenly noticed as she preceded him up the stairs, could almost be considered racy. She wore a sleeveless, fitted top made from a gauzy, pale pink fabric that was so sheer, he could see the faintest outline of her bra underneath. She also wore a fitted skirt in a deep fuchsia that ended at least six inches above her knee, and a pair of strappy white sandals with a modest heel.

What had happened in London?

"How is your father?" he asked when they reached the top of the stairs.

"He's very…peaceful."

"That's good, right?"

She nodded and followed him into his bedroom. He closed and locked the door, then turned to ask what she wanted to talk about, but before he could she was back in his arms, hugging herself close to him. Because she seemed to need it, he hugged her back.

"I missed you so much," she said. She nuzzled her face against his shirt, her hair catching in the stubble on his chin.

"I missed you, too."

"I did a lot of thinking while I was gone, about us and our future. I used to be so sure about everything, but now everything has changed. I've changed."

"I felt it. The second I saw you I knew something was different."

"I think I grew up."

"When you say everything has changed, do you mean us?"

"I know I said I want to wait until I'm married to make love, but now I'm thinking, maybe I shouldn't."

Making love to Louisa was pretty much all he'd been able to think of lately, but pushing her into something she wasn't ready for would be a mistake. "I thought waiting was important to you."

"It was. It *is*. But what if I was waiting for the wrong thing? What if it's not about the marriage vows?"

"What *is* it about?"

"The way I feel about you. Right now. I'm pretty sure

I love you, Garrett. In fact, I *know* I do. And I want you to be the first."

"I just don't want you to do something you'll regret later." Maybe, in a way, he didn't feel worthy. He didn't deserve something so special.

"Garrett, if we never made love, then something happened and things didn't work out, I would regret it the rest of my life."

"What makes you think it won't work out?"

"The way things have been going in my life lately, I'd be wise not to take anything for granted."

"I want to," he said. "You have no idea how much I want to. But it feels like we're just jumping into this."

"On the contrary, it's all I've been thinking about. This is not a hasty decision on my part."

"Well, maybe *I* need more time."

A quirky grin curled her lips.

"What?" he asked.

"It's just funny. I'm the virgin, and *you* need time. Most men would jump at the chance to defile me."

She was right. And a couple weeks ago, he might have been one of them. But he wasn't that man anymore. And he had her to thank for that. Being with her had forced him to take a good hard look at his life.

He shrugged and remarked, "I guess I'm just not most men."

"And that," she said, reaching up to stroke his cheek, "is why I want to make love to *you*."

"How about a compromise? Right now we don't say yes or no. We just let things progress naturally, and if it happens, it happens."

"I would be willing to compromise," she said. "If it happens, it happens."

Something in her expression, in the impish smile she was wearing, led him to believe it would be happening sooner rather than later.

"Until then there are other things we could do," she continued as she shoved his suit jacket off his shoulders and let it drop to the floor.

"What things?"

"Kissing." She tugged his tie loose and pulled it from around his neck. "And touching."

She unfastened the buttons on his shirt and it hit the floor in seconds flat.

"Are you in some kind of hurry?" he asked.

"I've just been dying to get my hands on you," she admitted. "And this time I want to touch *everything*."

She wasn't going to get an argument from him. He just hoped she understood that she would have to play fair. A tit for a tat—pardon the expression. Or more appropriately, you can touch mine if I can touch yours.

She jerked the hem of his undershirt from the waist of his slacks and he helped her pull it over his head. She looked at his bare chest as though she had been fasting and he was her first meal in months.

"I love your chest," she said, laying her hands on him. "I love all of you, but I think this is my favorite."

She leaned forward and kissed one nipple, then the other, then she licked him. It was hot as hell, but what really turned him on was the look of pure ecstasy on her face as she did it. She looked halfway there already and he hadn't even touched her yet.

She slid her hands down his chest and across his stomach to the waist of his slacks. She undid the button, pulled the zipper down, then hooked her thumbs under the waistband and eased them down, leaving only his boxers resting low on his hips. He was so hard it seemed they barely contained him.

He waited for her to take those off, too, but instead she said, "Why don't you lie down?"

He climbed into bed and reclined with his head against the pillows. He expected her to climb in with him, but instead she pulled her shirt over her head, then reached behind her and unhooked her bra. As soon as that hit the floor, she tugged the skirt, which must have been made of some sort of stretchy material, down her hips and let it drop to the floor. When the score was even, both of them in only their underwear, she climbed on the bed and knelt beside him.

Suddenly Louisa wasn't admiring his chest anymore. Her eyes were glued to his crotch.

"It looks...*big*," she said.

"Why don't you touch me and find out for yourself?"

Looking excited and nervous all at once, she reached over and laid her hand on him. After a second or two she slid her hand back and forth, up and down the entire length of him. He couldn't begin to count how many women had touched him like this, but he couldn't recall it ever feeling this fantastic. He usually preferred a woman who knew her way around a man's body. At least, he used to. But watching Louisa touch him, knowing she had never touched a man this way before, was one of the hottest things he had ever seen.

"Feels pretty big to me," she confirmed, her eyes, and her hand, never straying from his hard-on. "But just to be sure that I'm making an accurate estimation, maybe I should take off your boxers."

"You're probably right," he agreed.

Looking as though she were about to unwrap a Christmas gift, she took hold of the waistband of his boxers and eased them down. He lifted his hips to help and when she got them to his feet, he kicked them away.

She made a soft sighing sound, as though she liked what she was seeing. For several seconds she just looked, then reached out and tentatively touched him.

"It's not going to bite," he said.

With a wry smile she repeated the question he'd asked only a few minutes ago. "Are you in some kind of hurry?"

Yes and no.

She wrapped her hand around him and squeezed, and Garrett inhaled sharply. Then she started stroking him and he was in ecstasy.

"Is this right?" she asked.

He groaned his approval and his eyes drifted shut.

"I think I was wrong. This is my favorite part of your body."

In that case, he could think of several ways she could show her appreciation, the majority using her mouth. But he knew that would be pushing too far, too fast. It could be weeks, or even months before she was ready for that, or maybe never. Some women just didn't get off on that sort of thing.

No sooner had the thought formed when Louisa leaned over, the ends of her hair tickling his stomach. He thought, *No way, not even possible.* He felt her breath, warm and moist. Then, starting at the base of his erection, with the flat of her tongue, she licked him, moving slowly upward, and when she reached the tip, the sensation was so intense he jerked.

Louisa lifted her head and shot him a curious look.

In a gravelly voice he said, "Sorry. I just wasn't expecting that."

"Should I stop?"

"No!" he said, a bit too forcefully, then added in a much calmer tone, "Not if you don't want to."

She answered him by doing it again, only this time when she reached the tip, she took him into her mouth. Garrett groaned and tangled his fingers through her hair.

Granted, it took a few tries to get the angle and the rhythm right and she got him with her teeth a couple times, but that didn't seem to matter because within minutes he was barely hanging on.

"If you don't stop, you're going to get more than you bargained for," he warned her, and either she didn't know what he meant, or she didn't care, because instead of stopping, she took him deeper in her mouth.

So damned deep that he instantly lost it.

If there was a world record for the fastest, most intense orgasm, Garrett was pretty sure he'd just broken it. When he opened his eyes, Louisa was still on her knees beside him, grinning.

"I've read that there are women who don't like doing that, but I can't imagine why. I thought it was awesome."

He closed his eyes and said a silent prayer of thanks.

"I'm sorry if I was a little awkward," she said.

He couldn't believe she was *apologizing*. Watching Louisa take him in her mouth, knowing he was the first, just might have been the single most erotic experience of his adult life. Although he was sure that eventually she would manage to top that, too.

"I guess there are some things you just can't learn from a book," she said thoughtfully. "Although I'm sure with practice I'll get better."

He honestly didn't think it could get much better, but he wasn't going to argue. "Feel free to practice on me as often as you like."

"Like right now?" she said, an eager gleam in her eyes. He realized she was serious. She would do it again. Right here, right now. As tempted as he was to say yes, he could never be that selfish.

The only thing he wanted right now was to make *her* feel good.

Fourteen

"Let's try something different instead," Garrett told Louisa, and she was disappointed—right up until the instant he put his hand on her knee then slid it up her inner thigh.

"Why don't we switch places," he suggested, so she took his spot against the pillow and he knelt beside her.

He stroked her thighs, starting low, then moving higher each time, until he was barely grazing the edge of her panties with each pass.

"Has anyone ever touched you like this before?" he asked.

"Does it count if I had clothes on?"

"Nope."

"Then I guess not."

"Then I guess no one ever did this, either." He brushed his fingers against the crotch of her panties and it felt so good Louisa moaned and spread her thighs farther apart. She didn't have to feel it to know that she was so wet, she'd soaked right through the lace.

He slipped his fingers under the edge of her panties and Louisa shuddered. He looked up at her and asked, "You shave?"

"Wax, actually."

"Everything?"

She nodded. "I read that some men like that."

He grinned. "I think I'm going to need a better look before I form a definitive conclusion."

So they were going to play *this* game again. "Do what you must."

Still grinning he hooked his fingers under the edge and slowly pulled the panties down and off her feet, then he tossed them over his shoulder and across the room. Was he worried she might try to put them back on? He knelt between her legs, spreading her thighs apart—*far apart*—then he just looked at her, and as he did, he started getting hard again. It excited and thrilled her to know that he was turned on simply by looking at her.

"Well?" she asked.

He shrugged apologetically. "Still not sure."

His erection said otherwise, but okay, she would play along.

"It might help if you touched me," she said, keeping with the script.

His smile turned feral and there was something wicked behind his eyes. "You're right," he conceded. "That would probably work." He scooted closer, then, instead of using his hands, he leaned forward and brushed his lips against her bare mound. It was so not what she expected, so exciting, Louisa gasped and fisted the sheet.

He had strayed from the script by totally reworking the touching scene.

Garrett looked up at her, wearing a mischievous grin.

"You cheated."

"Just keeping things exciting. Did you want me to stop?"

She glared at him.

He shrugged and said, "Just asking."

He leaned forward and kissed her again, then he licked her and she nearly vaulted off the bed.

He shot her another look and opened his mouth to speak and she said, "Ask me if I want to stop and I'll *hurt* you."

She could tell by his grin that she was right, and this time when he lowered his head, she tangled her fingers through his hair, just in case he got the idea that he would stop again.

But this time he didn't stop. He kissed and nibbled, teased her with his tongue, everywhere but the one place that needed to be kissed and nibbled and teased the most. He drove her to the point of mindless frustration, every muscle coiled so blasted tight she felt like a spring ready to snap.

She shifted her hips, trying to align his mouth just right, but went left when he would go right, and he ended up on the complete opposite side from where he was supposed to be. He got fed up with all of her wiggling and used his weight to pin her against the mattress. She realized the only way to get her point across was to just come right out and tell him.

She opened her mouth to give him a gentle pointer, when suddenly he found her center, and the word she'd been forming came out like a garbled moan. He took her into his mouth and the spring gave its final stretch then snapped like a dry twig, then it sparked and ignited, and burst into flames.

Louisa was still gasping for breath when Garrett flopped down next to her on his side and said, "I'm sorry if I was a little awkward."

She laughed weakly and gave him a playful shove. "You're making fun of me."

He smiled and pushed back a lock of hair that had fallen across her cheek. "Yep."

"What you really need is a geography lesson."

He frowned. "Geography of what?"

"The female anatomy."

He looked confused, then he realized what she meant and laughed. "Is that what all that squirming was for?"

"I was trying to help. You kept missing the target. Though for the life of me, I don't know how. It's right there in the middle."

"Did it ever occur to you that I might have been missing it for a reason?"

"To do what? *Torture* me?"

His grin said that was exactly what he was doing. "You can't tell me you didn't enjoy it."

She could, but it would be a lie.

"I guess I see your point." She rolled close and snuggled up against him, laying her head on his chest, touching him. She just couldn't seem to get close enough, get enough of her hands on his skin. It just felt so…good. But she still wanted more.

She used to hear girls talk about saving themselves

for marriage, and a month or two later admit that they'd given in and slept with their boyfriend. She never got why they didn't just wait. But now, for the first time in her life, she understood. All the kissing and touching and orgasms in the world wouldn't satiate this yearning to be closer to him. To be connected in a way she never had been before.

"I can hardly believe that I'm twenty-seven and I've never been in bed with a naked man before," she said.

"Well, technically, neither have I. But you don't hear me bragging about it."

She laughed and tickled his ribs, making him squirm.

He batted her hand away. "Don't do that."

"Why, are you ticklish?"

He frowned. "I refuse to answer that on the grounds that it might incriminate me."

She waited a minute or two, then did a sneak attack on his belly and he nearly jumped out of his skin. There was nothing more adorable than a big, tough man who was ticklish.

His tone stern, he said, "*Don't*, Louisa."

Two minutes ago didn't he admit to deliberately torturing her? And he thought she would cut him any slack?

She dove for his armpit, but he was too quick. He captured her wrists and rolled her onto her back, pinning her to the mattress with the weight of his body, and just like that, they were back in the position they had been in the other day, his erection cradled between her legs, only this time there were no clothes to get in the way. This time it was just skin against skin.

Just like before they both went completely still and Garrett got that *what-have-I-done* look.

"If it happens, it happens," she reminded him, but they both seemed to realize that, ready or not, it was happening.

In an odd way, she sort of felt as if she was the veteran and he was the virgin, which certainly put an interesting spin on things.

She pulled free of his grasp, wrapped her arms around his neck and kissed him. For a while that was all they did…kissed and touched, and it was really…*sweet*. But she didn't want sweet. She wanted sexy and crazy and out of control. Grinding and thrusting and writhing in ecstasy. She was *aching* for it. But every time she tried to move things along, he shut her down. If she tried to touch his erection, he would intercept her hand and put it on his chest instead. If she tried to kiss his throat or nibble his ear, he would duck out of the way. It was almost as if, the instant he realized where this was going, he'd switched off emotionally. Now she was feeling more frustrated than aroused.

She slipped her hand down from his shoulder, and when she hit the fleshy part just below his underarm, she gave it a good, hard pinch.

"Ow!" He jerked his arm away and looked at the red mark she'd created. "What was that for?"

"I thought you might enjoy actually feeling something."

His expression softened. "Louisa, what are you talking about? Of course I feel something."

She shrugged. "I couldn't tell."

"I'm just taking it slow."

"I noticed." At the rate he was going, she would be

eighty before they finally made love. "I have an idea. Let's pretend I'm not a virgin. Make love to me like you would if this wasn't my first time."

"But it is, and I don't want to hurt you."

"Maybe I want you to hurt me. I'd rather feel pain than feel *nothing!*"

Anger sparked in his eyes and she thought, *good, at least he's feeling something.* Now that she had her foot in the door, rather than back down, she stoked the fire.

"Do you even want this, Garrett?"

"You know that I do," he growled.

"Then bloody well act like it or stop wasting my time!"

Garrett stared down at Louisa, his temper blazing, unable to believe what he'd just heard her say. What had happened to his sweet, innocent princess?

Good riddance to her, he thought. He liked this Louisa better anyway. She had spunk and passion. This Louisa, the one who was now unflinchingly meeting his eye, unwilling to back down until he realized what an ass he was being, would never bore him.

She was right, he was trying like hell not to feel this, because he knew deep down that once he made love to her, once he accepted the gift that she offered with no question or reserve, every one of his defenses would crumble. He might be taking her virginity, but in exchange she would be taking from him something even more remarkable. The love in a heart he believed he had locked away for good.

If passion was what she wanted, that's what he would give her.

He wrapped a hand under the back of her neck,

lifted her head right off the pillow and crushed his lips to hers. If he startled her, she didn't let it show. She moaned against his lips and wrapped herself around him, pressing her body to his.

Everything they had done up to now, all the kissing and touching, had been child's play. Right here, right now, this was the real thing. He held nothing back, and neither did she. Her ability to give herself so freely, with no shame or hesitation, never ceased to amaze him.

Her body language said she was more than ready, and he could only endure so much of her writhing around underneath him. He was considering warning her first, so she could prepare herself before he took the plunge, but he never got the chance. He rocked against her and as he did, she arched up, by some fluke of nature creating the perfect angle, and the next thing he knew, he was inside her.

Louisa's eyes went wide and she gasped softly, her mouth forming a perfect *O,* and he imagined he was wearing a similar expression.

"Did you mean to do that?" she asked.

He shook his head. "It just…happened."

Was it fate? She had talked about that often during their phone conversations while she was in London, how she used to believe in it, but now she wasn't so sure. He never believed in things like fate and Karma, but the ease of their bodies coming together in what seemed to be perfect sync, could that really be an accident? *Everything* about their relationship seemed somehow… predisposed.

"You're all the way in, right?" Louisa asked.

"As far as I can go." And she was tight. Tight and wet and warm. And wonderful.

She blinked, looking adorably confused, and asked, "When is it going to hurt?"

"Actually, if it was going to, I think it would have already." *Now can we please get on with it?*

"But it's *supposed* to," she insisted.

Well, that had to be a first, a virgin who *wanted* sex to hurt.

"I don't know what to tell you," he said.

She opened her mouth to say something, and before she got a word out, he covered her lips with his and kissed her. Not so easy for her to talk with his tongue in her mouth.

He started to move inside her, slow and easy, savoring the sensation of slippery walls hugging him so tightly, knowing that at this rate he would be lucky to last five minutes.

Louisa sighed against his lips, tunneled her fingers through his hair, looking as though she was in pure ecstasy. It took all of his concentration, and a little extra he didn't even know he had, to keep up the slow, steady pace.

Louisa pushed at his chest, saying, "I want to see."

He leaned back and braced himself up on his arms, increasing the friction and giving all new meaning to the word *torture*. He could barely watch as Louisa rose up on her elbows, spreading her legs wide so to gaze at the place where their bodies were joined.

"That's us," she whispered, her face flushed, her eyes glazed and full of wonder. "You're inside me, Garrett."

If she was going to give him a play-by-play, he wouldn't last five seconds. He was barely hanging on as it was, then Louisa's head rolled back and her body began to tremble with release, clamping down around him, squeezing and contracting until he lost it, too, riding out the crest of the wave with her.

Louisa was no longer a virgin.

She always thought that afterward she would feel different somehow, that anyone who looked at her would just *know*. But as she and Garrett lay wrapped around each other, arms and legs entwined, she didn't really feel any different. There was something else she didn't feel, either. Regret.

Wait a minute…had they…?

"Garrett?"

"Hmm," he mumbled sleepily.

"Did we…*forget* something?" she asked. "When we made love?"

"If we did, it's going to have to wait, because I need to sleep for a while."

"Garrett, did we use birth control?"

He was quiet for a minute, like he was scanning the memory banks, then he mumbled a curse.

She cringed. "Should I take that as a no?"

"Maybe I was thinking you had it covered, or maybe I just *wasn't* thinking. I don't know."

"My period is due any second, so odds are that I'm not fertile, but there's no guarantee."

He nodded and yawned. "Okay."

She untangled herself from him and sat up. "You're not worried?"

He pried one eye open and peered up at her. "Didn't you just tell me not to be?"

"I also said there's no guarantee."

He shrugged. "So we'll wait and see."

"That's it?"

"I don't see what you're so worried about," he grumbled. "Aren't you the one who said you want sixteen kids?"

"I didn't say sixteen, I said *six*. And yes, of course I want kids. But I also don't want to get you stuck in a situation you don't want to be in."

"You won't."

"How can you know that?"

"Because I know."

"But *how?*"

Garrett pushed himself up on his elbows and rubbed his eyes with his thumb and forefinger. "Okay, I was going to wait and do this right, with a nice candlelit dinner and maybe some soft music playing. But if it'll ease your mind, and you don't mind that I haven't gotten the ring yet, or the fact that I'm too bloody tired to get on one knee, I could ask you to marry me right now."

She bit her lip, to hold back the huge smile that was just dying to get out. He wanted to *marry* her.

"No, that's okay," she said. "I can wait."

"Does that mean I can sleep now?"

"Of course."

He collapsed back down and closed his eyes. Unfortunately, she wasn't the least bit tired. She had just lost her virginity and Garrett had more or less proposed to her. How could she even think of sleeping? Not to mention that there was the slightest possibility that she could be *pregnant!* If she was, her baby would be close in age to the triplets. Who could be born very soon.

"Garrett?" she said softly.

He groaned.

"Sorry. I just wondered if you would mind me using your computer. I wanted to look online for some gifts for the babies, since getting out to shop these days is complicated, to say the least."

He nodded and grumbled something incoherent.

"Thanks!" She pressed a kiss to his cheek and rolled out of bed. Since she didn't feel like getting dressed, she found a robe hanging on the back of his closet door and slipped it on. She thought about going downstairs and making herself a cup of tea, but Ian was camped out on the family-room couch and she didn't want to disturb him.

Garrett's office was across the hall at the opposite end, and typically male. Lots of glass and steel and hundreds of books. She'd never realized what an avid reader he must be. But she had pulled a few strings and discovered that he had graduated at the top of his class at both primary school and university. She hoped their children would inherit his intelligence. Not that she was a dummy. Louisa had done all right in school. Her problem was that she just didn't care.

Louisa doesn't work to her potential became her slogan for the better part of her childhood.

She made herself comfortable in Garrett's chair and when she touched the mouse, the computer screen flashed to life. His e-mail program was open and she was about to click it closed when she saw a list of e-mails with the subject: Princess Louisa. They had been sent back and forth between Garrett and someone named Weston. She noticed the oldest one dated back to the weekend of the charity ball. Had it really been less than three weeks ago? It felt as though she had known him forever.

Garrett probably wrote about meeting her, and how

magical it had been. Not that he would have used the term *magical,* but something equivalent in guy speak.

Louisa knew firsthand what it was like to have someone shuffling through her personal messages, and realized how wrong it would be to invade his privacy, but she was *dying* to know what he'd said about her.

Maybe if she just took a quick peek. Just the first one, and that was it.

She clicked it open, and as she expected, it was about her. But the more she read, she realized it had nothing to do with meeting her at the ball, and the things he'd written were never meant for her eyes. And as she clicked open one message after the other, it only got worse. She felt sick to her stomach and sick in her heart, and she finally had to face the realization that her family had been right about her all along. It was as though destiny had painted a target on her back that announced: *Use me! I'm dense and naive!*

A lot of men had taken aim and missed, but Garrett, the man she thought she would spend the rest of her life with, had hit the target dead on. He had her totally duped. And if she'd only been paying attention, if she'd bothered to look hard enough, maybe she would have noticed the arrow planted in her back.

Fifteen

Garrett jerked out of a sound sleep and bolted up in bed. He reached over to feel for Louisa, but the sheets were cold.

He'd been dreaming about his computer, about Louisa asking to use it. Or had that really happened?

They had talked about birth control, then he'd started dozing....

Yes. She'd asked to use it to shop for baby things.

Then he realized why he'd been jolted awake. He had closed his e-mail program, hadn't he?

He flung back the covers and groped around the floor for his slacks. If not, would she have noticed the e-mails with her name in the subject? And if she noticed them, would she have read them?

He yanked his pants on and was out the bedroom door before he even got them fastened. He half ran down the hall to his office and burst through the door, but he knew the second he saw her sitting there, her face ashen, that not only had she seen the e-mails, she'd read them, too.

Bloody goddamn hell.

Why hadn't he just erased them? Why leave evidence? Unless he actually wanted to get caught. Was living with the guilt of the way he had planned to use her too much to bear? And it was all there, every gruesome detail.

For what felt like an eternity he just stood there, at a loss for what to say. At a time like this, *I'm sorry* didn't even begin to cover it.

Finally she looked up at him and said in a very calm voice, "Everything my family has said, about me being too trusting and naive, I guess they were right."

"Louisa—"

"You and this Weston fellow must have had a good laugh at my expense. I mean, I fell for it, hook, line and sinker, didn't I? You had me totally duped."

"If you would just let me explain—"

"Explain what?" She gestured to the screen. "It's all right here. I've read each one at least a dozen times, so I'll never forget how stupid I've been."

The idea that she could believe he was that man, the one who had been so selfishly obsessed, made him sick. Why didn't she scream at him and call him names? Instead she sounded so…disappointed.

Anger he could handle, but this? This was…*awful*. It was heart wrenching and painful. It wasn't the first time he'd let someone down, but Louisa didn't deserve this.

"That's not me," he said. "Not anymore. I don't even recognize that man."

"People don't change, isn't that what you told me? You can't have it both ways."

She was using his own words against him. And could he blame her? He'd painted himself into this corner.

"I was an ass, I admit it. I was greedy and selfish, and yes, I used you, and I will never be able to adequately express how sorry I am for that. But then everything... changed. The money and the power, none of that matters to me now. *You* are the only thing that matters."

"I don't believe you. This is all just a game to you. I think you're just sorry that you lost, and you would do or say anything to get what you want." She shrugged and said, "What the hell, I should be thanking you. You've given me a gift, Garrett. You've finally made me see things clearly. See people for who they are. My family spent all those years sheltering me, but you gave me what I really needed. You've taught me how not to trust."

Her honesty, her ability to trust people enough to always say exactly what was on her mind, was what made her special and different from everyone else. And what she was telling him now was that he had killed that. He'd made her less than whole.

The idea that he had done that to her was almost too much to comprehend. No man should have that kind of power over another human being. Especially a man like him. And he would do anything, *anything* it took to turn the clock back, but there was no way to fix this. No way to repair the damage he'd done.

"I should go now," she said rising to her feet, wearing his robe. She walked past him to the door, but stopped halfway through and looked back. "Just so you know,

I don't regret that we made love. It doesn't make sense, but despite everything, I'm still glad it was you."

If she would hit him or cry or show some sort of emotion, he wouldn't feel so rotten. He would at least know that she cared. And as long as she cared there was still a chance. But her eyes looked…dead. The spark was gone.

He stood there listening as she dressed and gathered her things from his room and walked down the stairs. He heard the front door open, and hushed conversation between Louisa and her bodyguards. Then, when he heard it close, he had to fight to keep from going after her.

He wanted to beg her to stay. He wanted to tell her that without her in it, his life meant nothing.

But maybe without him around to poison her soul she would recover. Maybe someday she would be herself again.

It was no longer about what he wanted or needed. This was about Louisa. And the kindest thing he could do for her now was let her go.

On autopilot, Garrett walked down to the kitchen and made himself a cup of tea, then sat at the table, cupping the steaming mug in his hands, trying to chase away the chill that had settled in his bones.

He was still sitting there when Ian hobbled in, hours after the tea had gone cold.

Ian saw Garrett's wrinkled pants and robe, and with one brow lifted said, "Must have been some night. You're usually off to the gym by now."

"What time is it?" Garrett asked, but his voice was so rusty he had to clear his throat.

"After eight. Louisa still sleeping?"

"She left last night."

Ian limped to the stove and put the kettle on. "Sorry to hear that. She mentioned something about making crepes for breakfast. Maybe another time."

"There won't be another time."

Ian turned to him, frowning. "What do you mean?"

"I messed up. I lost her."

Ian turned the kettle off and crossed the kitchen, easing into the chair across from Garrett. "Give her a day or two to cool down. It's probably not as bad as it seems."

If only it were that simple. "No, it's pretty bad."

"Something to do with that plan your mate Wes mentioned?"

Since Garrett no longer had to worry about the truth getting out, he told Ian the entire grisly tale, right up to the confrontation in his office.

Ian winced. "Ah, you gotta hate it when they lay on the guilt. Women do love their drama."

"Louisa doesn't have a manipulative bone in her body."

"Don't misunderstand. I'm not suggesting she's doing it on purpose. Women just open their mouths and out it comes. They don't even realize it's happening."

"You didn't see her face. Her eyes. I think she honestly has no feelings left for me whatsoever."

"Take it from someone who's been in his share of relationships—she does. Besides, I've seen the way she looks at you. That woman loves you."

"Even if she does, I don't think I deserve her. Even if I could get her back, which seems bloody unlikely at this point, I'd always worry that I might screw up and disappoint her again."

"And you will. But so will she."

Somehow he couldn't imagine Louisa ever making a mistake. Other than trusting him.

"You love her, don't you?" Ian asked, and Garrett nodded. "Did you tell her?"

"I couldn't."

"Why the hell not?"

"Because she wouldn't have believed me. She would have thought I was saying it to try to win her back."

Ian nodded grimly. "Good point. It's confusing as hell, isn't it? Being in love. It's like you lose a part of yourself, but at the same time, you gain so much back."

"You sound as though you're speaking from experience."

Ian rubbed his palms together, his brow wrinkled. "I guess now is as good a time as any to tell you."

"Tell me what?"

"Though I appreciate all you've done for me, I'm going to be leaving soon."

"Where are you going?"

"Remember the girl I told you about? Maggie?"

"The farmer's daughter?" Garrett asked, and Ian nodded.

"Well, her father has offered to make me a partner in his cattle business. I've just been waiting for my leg to stabilize enough to travel."

"Why would he do that?"

"Because I'm going to be the father of his grandchild."

Garrett's jaw fell. He tried to come up with an appropriate response, but he was too flabbergasted to speak.

"Hard to believe, I know. *Me,* someone's papa."

"How long have you known?"

"A while. We found out a few weeks before her father chased me off. Maggie and I have been communicating behind her father's back ever since I left. We've been planning to run away together, but we needed money. That's why I took your car. I was going to sell it. But as I was driving away, I felt so damned guilty. Which of course was an odd sensation for me, seeing as how I never feel guilty. I really was bringing it back. I was going to tell you the truth and ask for your help. I was going to beg you for a job and maybe a small parcel of land to get started. A loan I could pay back over time."

"So why didn't you tell me the truth?"

"After the accident, I knew you would never believe me. I knew I would have to prove myself to you. As soon as I was able to work, I was going to get Maggie and bring her back here, but her parents found out she was pregnant and now they want me to come live with them instead." He leaned forward. "I know changing won't be easy, but I'm determined to try. I want to do right by my child. I won't make the mistakes our father made."

Garrett clasped his brother's hand. "Then you'll be a damned fine father. And a good man."

Ian gave his hand a squeeze then quickly turned away, but not before Garrett saw what looked like a tear spill from his eye. Ian got up from his chair and hobbled over to the stove to put on the kettle. "Might as well get comfortable. We have work to do."

"What kind of work?"

Ian turned to him and grinned. "We're going to figure out a way to get your princess back."

Louisa wanted to cry, but the tears wouldn't come. She wanted to scream and throw things, but she couldn't work up the will to feel angry. She wanted to hate Garrett for being so cold and calculating, for lying to her, but she couldn't make herself hate him.

The only emotion she had been able to feel was disgust. Disgust in herself, for letting this happen. For being so unsuspecting and so blind.

She'd come home from Garrett's in a daze and had gone straight to her room. She stood there for several minutes, looking around, really seeing it. The frilly pink curtains and canopy bed, the doll collection lining the wall. She was twenty-seven years old and she was living in a little girl's room.

Disgusted with herself, she shoved it all into trash bags. First thing the next morning, she picked up the phone and called a decorator. She didn't tell anyone or ask anyone's permission. She just did it, and surprisingly, no one seemed to care.

"You can't stay like this," Anne told her a few days later. She was the only one Louisa had confided in. She just couldn't bear facing the rest of them yet, knowing how disappointed they would be in her and how all this time they had been right.

"Stay like what?" she asked Anne.

"So unhappy. Without you to cheer me up and your

glass-half-full mentality, I could very possibly sink into a bottomless pit of negativity."

Louisa didn't want the responsibility any longer. She was sick of trying to convince herself and everyone else that everything was roses and sunshine. She wanted to start living in the real world. She even wondered, since she had never actually experienced real, soul-deep grief before, if this funk she had slipped into, this abyss of nothingness, was just her peculiar way of coping. She'd even stopped caring about the Gingerbread Man, who it would seem had slipped under the radar.

Five days after she and Garrett had split up, Louisa was in a meeting with her decorator finalizing the plans for her new room when Chris popped his head in. He was usually at the hospital with Melissa, so it was a pleasant surprise to see him. "Is this a bad time?"

"Not at all—we're just finishing up."

"In that case, why don't you come to the study? There's someone I want you to meet."

"Who?"

"A friend."

Curious as to who this mystery friend could be, she said goodbye to the decorator and followed Chris down the hall to the study. She followed him in, and when she saw the man standing by the window, dressed in jeans, a polo shirt and Docksiders, she froze.

"Louisa, this is a good friend of mine, Garrett Sutherland, and Garrett, meet my sister Princess Louisa."

Garrett walked slowly toward her, one hand tucked into his pants pockets, the other holding a thick legal-size manila envelope, and for the first time in days she finally felt something.

Confusion.

It must have shown on her face, because Garrett said, "I thought we should be reintroduced, since the man you met the first time, at the ball, wasn't really me."

Louisa looked at Chris, who didn't seem to find it the least bit unusual that he was reintroducing her to the man who, as far as he knew, she was planning to marry.

"He knows everything," Garrett explained. "I figured it would be best to come clean with everyone."

"Well, I've done my part," Chris told Garrett. "I'll leave you to it."

The idea of being alone with Garrett made Louisa's heart jump into her throat. "Leave you to what?"

"Win you back," Garrett declared, looking so confident it was unsettling. That night when he'd found her reading the e-mails, he had looked so beside himself, so at a loss for what to do or say, it had been empowering. It had given her the strength to do what she had to. She wasn't feeling quite so confident now.

"You can't have me," she told him.

"If you're so sure about that, then what's the harm in hearing me out?" He paused then added, "Unless you're afraid."

She wasn't afraid—she was *terrified*. But she couldn't let it show, because men like him fed off fear. "Fine," she said, walking to the sofa, remembering halfway there that it was where they had sat together his first time here, so she changed course for the chair instead. She sat primly on the edge, arms folded over her chest. "Say what you have to say. Even though it will be a waste of time."

"First," he began, taking a seat on the sofa and setting the envelope beside him, "I want to thank you."

Thank her? "For what?"

"For reading those e-mails. You needed to know the truth, and God knows I never would have had the guts to tell you myself. The fear of you someday finding out and of what it would do to us would have haunted me for the rest of my life."

She didn't know what to say to that, but he didn't seem to expect her to say anything.

"Second, for the record, as far as lies go, I only lied to you twice. And before you go saying that a lie by omission is still a lie," he continued, which was exactly what she'd been about to do, "you have to admit that it's at the very least a slippery slope, because *no one* says everything they're thinking one hundred percent of the time. And while I may not have always been forthcoming about my intentions, I was always honest. Except those two times."

"One was about your brother, right?"

"Right."

"So what was the other one?"

"No man, especially one with my past dating habits, forgets to use a condom."

Her jaw dropped. "You did that on *purpose?* Why? So I would *have* to marry you? And isn't it typically the woman who traps the man?"

He grinned, his dimple winking at her, and her knees went soft. "It had nothing to do with trapping you. It was more of a base instinct thing. My way of branding you or possessing you or something."

She frowned. "I'm pretty sure the last man to act on that particular instinct wore animal skins and carried a club."

"Nope. Men still do it. And if they don't, they want to. It's nature."

She didn't know if she was buying that.

"And, quite frankly, it feels better," he admitted, and she thought that sounded like a much more plausible excuse.

"But back to my original point. I lied twice. That's it."

Okay, fine, so he wasn't a liar. That didn't mean he wasn't a lot of other awful things that she wanted nothing to do with.

"Okay, third," he said, "for all the times in my life that I told myself I didn't give a damn what my father thought of me, I was still trying to impress him. To show him that he was wrong about me. And unfortunately, that desire manifested itself in an overdeveloped sense of greed and entitlement. Coincidentally, all the things you claimed to hate in men. I guess I was just good at hiding it."

"So, Daddy made you do it?" she snapped, and instantly felt guilty for the heartless comment. She was just no good at being snarky.

But Garrett didn't look wounded. "Don't misunderstand. It's not an excuse. What I did was wrong and inexcusable. It's only an explanation of why I acted that way."

"Do you still care?"

"What my father thinks?" He regarded her curiously, as though he'd never really considered it before. "I suppose I'll always care somewhere deep down, or at the very least, wish things were different. The difference is, now I know that the things my father said and did were his problem. They had nothing to do with me."

So, unresolved past family issues were always a nuisance, and she was glad that he'd finally made peace with it, but it had nothing to do with her. And it certainly didn't mean she could trust him.

"Okay, fourth, and this one is important so you need to really pay attention. You are *not* stupid or naive. In fact, you're one of the smartest, most resourceful people I know." He leaned forward, meeting her eye. "When I met you, Louisa, I was in a dark place. I had sunk about as low as I could go, but despite that, you saw the good in me. The *real* me that was trapped underneath all the lies. By putting your trust in me, you drew me back out into the light. You *saved* me. You also made me realize what's important." He picked up the envelope. "And it isn't this."

He held it out to her, and only when she took it did she realize her hands were trembling. Her heart was pounding, too. So hard it felt as if it might beat right through her chest.

"What's in here?" she asked.

"The deed to every parcel of land I own on both Thomas and Morgan Isle. Everything I own. Except my father's land. That one I want to keep."

He was going to sell his land?

"Of course, the names will have to be legally transferred," he explained. "But as far as I'm concerned, they're yours now."

"*Mine?* You're *giving* it to me?"

"Consider it an early wedding gift."

"But what if I won't marry you?"

He shrugged. "Then just consider it a gift."

"But…Garrett, this is your livelihood. Everything you've worked so hard for. You can't just give it away."

"I just did."

"But—"

"Louisa, I would rather be penniless than *ever* be that man again."

"But…what will you do?"

He shrugged. "Who knows, maybe I'll try farming."

God, he was serious. He was going to give up everything for her. But not just for her, for himself. *Everything.*

This was crazy.

No, this was Garrett. The real Garrett. The one she had fallen in love with. And *still* loved.

"Well," he said, rising from the couch, "that was pretty much all I came here to say. I won't take up any more of your time."

He made a move toward the door, and Louisa launched herself at him. She didn't even know she was going to do it until she was on her feet. But she knew, deep down to the depths of her soul, that she couldn't let him go. Not ever. And when his arms went around her and he held her close, all the emotions she thought might have shut down forever came rushing back at the same time.

It was a little overwhelming, and even a little scary, but it was wonderful.

Garrett buried his face in her hair, nuzzled her neck. "I love you so much, Louisa."

"I love you, too."

"As long as we both shall live?"

She squeezed him tighter. "Definitely. Even longer."

"I have a ring in my pocket with your name on it, and if you would let go for a second, I'll even get down on one knee."

Instead of letting go, she held him tighter. "The ring can wait. This can't."

For a long time they just held each other, and Louisa thought about marriage and babies and loving only him for the rest of her life, and she started having another feeling, one she was sure both she and Garrett would be feeling a lot from now on.

Happy.

* * * * *

And the ROYAL SEDUCTIONS *continue
with Anne's story,*
Expectant Princess, Unexpected Affair,
*coming next month
from Mills & Boon® Desire™.*

He let himself look at her, really look at her.

A man could lose himself in those eyes. She seemed utterly sincere, but given what he knew, how could he take what she said at face value?

He wanted her. And he despised himself for the weakness. She was like a bright, beautiful butterfly, dancing on the wind. But if he reached out and grabbed for what he wanted, would the beauty be smashed into powder in his hand? Would he destroy Bryn? Himself?

He put his hands on her shoulders and the world stood still. Her eyes were wide.

A wave of lust and yearning and exultation swept over him. She was his. She had always been his.

THE SECRET CHILD
& THE COWBOY CEO

BY
JANICE MAYNARD

Published in Great Britain 2011
by Mills & Boon, an imprint of Harlequin (UK) Limited,
Eton House, 18-24 Paradise Road, Richmond, Surrey TW9 1SR

© Janice Maynard 2010

ISBN: 978 0 263 88310 7

51-0711

Harlequin (UK) policy is to use papers that are natural, renewable and recyclable products and made from wood grown in sustainable forests. The logging and manufacturing processes conform to the legal environmental regulations of the country of origin.

Printed and bound in Spain
by Blackprint CPI, Barcelona

For Caroline and Anna,
who shared with us one wonderful Wyoming summer.
A van, an X-cargo and the open road…
six weeks of fun…memories to last a lifetime.

Janice Maynard came to writing early in life. When her short story *The Princess and the Robbers* won a red ribbon in her school arts fair, Janice was hooked. She holds a B.A. from Emory and Henry College and an M.A. from East Tennessee State University. In 2002 Janice left a fifteen-year career as a primary teacher to pursue writing full-time. Her first love is creating sexy, character-driven, contemporary romance. She has written for Kensington and NAL, and now is so very happy to also be part of the Mills & Boon/Harlequin/ Silhouette family—a lifelong dream, by the way!

Janice and her husband live in beautiful east Tennessee in the shadow of the Great Smoky Mountains. She loves to travel and enjoys using those experiences as settings for books.

Hearing from readers is one of the best perks of the job! Visit her website at www.janicemaynard.com or e-mail her at JESM13@aol.com. Snail mail is PO Box 4611, Johnson City, TN 37602, USA. And of course, don't forget Facebook (www.facebook.com/janiceSmaynard) and MySpace (www.myspace.com/janicemaynard).

Dear Reader,

The Grand Teton Mountains in Wyoming offer some of the most beautiful scenery in the world. Famed photographer Ansel Adams surely thought so! The pricey real estate in the valley of Jackson Hole has become a playground for the rich and famous who want to get away from it all.

My husband and I have visited the Tetons several times. On one particular trip, I was lucky enough to run into Harrison Ford and his wife on the street in the small, charming town of Jackson! He was quiet and reserved, but he signed an autograph for me. (This was pre-Calista days.) During the entire encounter, which lasted all of three minutes, my husband stood ten feet away with a video camera and *never* turned it on. Men!

I have the autograph displayed with a color movie still from one of the Indiana Jones movies where "Harry" is wearing his famous leather hat. The whole thing is framed in weathered barn wood and is one of my prized possessions.

I've always wanted to set a book in Wyoming because I am fascinated by men like Harrison Ford and my hero, Trent. These are tough, macho guys who are perfectly comfortable doing hard, dirty manual labor on a ranch, and yet can move seamlessly into the glittering world of wealth and privilege as they wear their tuxes and make female hearts swoon.

My heroine, Bryn, has suffered a few hard knocks in her short life—who hasn't? But for her young son, she is strong enough and brave enough to face the man who broke her heart and who still has the power to hurt her all over again.

I hope you enjoy their story, and I hope your travels may one day take you to Jackson Hole and the Tetons.

Happy reading,

Janice

One

A half-dozen years… One look from those fabulous eyes and she could still make him act like a foolish kid.

Trent felt his heart slug hard in his chest. Oxygen backed up in his lungs. *Dear God, Bryn.*

He dragged the remnants of his self-control together and cleared his throat, pretending to ignore the woman standing beside his father's bed.

Her presence in the room made him sweat. The lust, loathing and sharp anger teeming in his gut made it impossible to act naturally, particularly since he wasn't sure if the anger was self-directed or not.

His father, Mac, watched them both with avid curiosity, giving his son a canny, calculating look. "Aren't you going to say something to Bryn?"

Trent tossed aside the damp towel he'd been using to dry his hair when he walked into the room. He folded his arms across his bare chest, then changed his mind and slid his hands into his back pockets. He turned toward the silent woman with what he hoped like hell was an impassive expression. "Hello, Bryn. Long time no see."

The insolence in his tone caused a visible wince to mark her otherwise serene expression, but she recovered rapidly. Her eyes were as cool as a crisp Wyoming morning. "Trent." She inclined her head stiffly in a semblance of courtesy.

For the first time in weeks, Trent saw anticipation on his father's face. The old man was pale and weak, but his voice was strong. "Bryn's here to keep me company for the next month. Surely she won't aggravate me like all those other cows. I can't stand strangers poking and prodding at me...." His voice trailed off, slurring the last few words.

Trent frowned in concern. "I thought you said you didn't need a nurse anymore. And the doctor agreed."

Mac grunted. "I don't. Can't a man invite an old friend without getting cross-examined? Last time I checked, this was *my* ranch."

Trent smothered a small, reluctant grin. His father was a grouch on his best days, and recently, he'd turned into Attila the Hun. Three nurses had quit, and Mac had fired two more. Physically, the Sinclair patriarch might be on the mend, but he was still mentally fragile.

It was a comfort to Trent that, although exhaustion marked Mac's face, he was as ornery as ever. The heart attack he'd suffered two months ago, when his youngest son was found dead of a heroin overdose, had nearly cost the family *two* lives.

Bryn Matthews spoke up. "I was happy to come when Mac contacted me. I've missed you all."

Trent's spine stiffened. Was that a taunt in her perfectly polite words?

He forced himself to look at her. When she was barely eighteen, her beauty had tugged at him like a raw ache. But he'd been on the fast track already, an ambitious twenty-three-year-old with no time for a young wife.

She had matured into a lovely woman. Her skin was the same sun-kissed ivory. Her delicate features were framed by a thick fall of shiny black hair. And her almost-violet eyes gazed at him warily. She didn't appear unduly surprised to see him, but he was shocked right down to his bare toes. His heart was beating so hard, he was afraid she'd be able to see the evidence with her own eyes.

She was dressed more formally than he had ever seen her, in a dark pantsuit with a prim white blouse beneath. Her waist was narrow, her hips curvy. The no-nonsense cut of her jacket disguised her breasts, but his imagination filled in the details.

Bitterness choked him. Bryn was here to cause trouble. He knew it. And all he could think about was how badly he wanted her in his bed.

He ground his teeth together and lowered his voice. "Step into the hall with me." He didn't phrase it as a request.

Bryn preceded him from the room and turned to

face him across the narrow space. They were so close he could see a pulse beating in the side of her throat. And he caught a whiff of her familiar, floral-scented perfume. Delicate…like she was. The top of her head barely came up to his chin.

He ignored the arousal jittering through his veins. "What in the hell are you doing here?"

Her eyes flared in shock. "You know why. Your father asked me to come."

Trent growled low in his throat, wanting to pound a hole in the wall. "If he did, it was because you manipulated him into thinking it was his idea. My brother Jesse's not even cold in his grave and yet here you are, ready to see what you can get."

Her eyes flashed, reminding him she had never lacked for gumption. "You're a self-righteous ass," she hissed.

"Never mind." He cut her off, swamped with a wave of self-loathing. She was a liar. And she had tried to blame Jesse for another man's sins. But that didn't stop Trent from wanting her.

He firmed his jaw. "Apparently you couldn't be bothered to make it to the funeral?"

Her lips trembled briefly. "No one let me know that Jesse had died until it was too late."

"Convenient." He sneered. Only by whipping up his anger could he keep his hands off her.

The hurt that flickered in her gaze made him feel as if he was kicking a defenseless puppy. At one time he and Bryn had been good friends. And later—well… there had been a tantalizing hint of something more.

Something that might have developed into a physical relationship, if he hadn't screwed things up.

Bryn had been innocent, not-quite-eighteen, and Trent had freaked out over his reaction to her. He had rejected her clumsily when she asked him to be her date for the senior prom, and she was heartbroken. A few weeks later, she and Jesse started dating.

Had Bryn done it to hurt him?

Trent couldn't blame Jesse. Jesse and Bryn were the same age and had a lot in common.

Bryn's face was pale. Her body language said she wanted to be anywhere other than in this hallway with him.

Well, that was too damn bad.

He leaned forward to tuck a strand of her hair behind her ear, whispering softly, "If you think I'll let you take advantage of a sick old man, you're an idiot." He couldn't stop himself.

Bryn's chin lifted and she stepped sideways. "I don't care what you think about me, Trent. I'm here to help Mac. That's all you need to know. And I'm sure you'll be on your way back to Denver very soon…right?" In another situation the naked hope on her face would have amused him. But at the moment, he couldn't escape the irony.

He cocked his head, wishing he could discern the truth. Why had she really come back to Wyoming?

He shrugged. "Tough luck, Bryn. I'm here for the foreseeable future.… I got tapped to take a turn running the place until the old man is back on his feet. So you're stuck with me, sweetheart."

Her cheeks flushed, and her air of sophistication vanished like mist in the morning sun. For the first time he saw a hint of the girl she had been at eighteen. Her agitation made him want to soothe her when what he should be doing was showing her the door.

But his good sense was at odds with his libido. He wanted to crush her mouth beneath his, strip away the somber-looking jacket and find the curves he would map in detail.

The past beckoned, sharp and sweet.… He remembered one of the last times he and Bryn had been together before everything went so badly wrong. He had flown in for his dad's birthday party. Bryn had run to meet him, talking a mile a minute as soon as he got out of the car. She was all legs and slim energy. And she'd had a crush on him.

She would have been mortified if she'd realized he had known all along. So, on that long-ago day he had treated her with the same easy camaraderie that had always existed between them. And he'd done his best to ignore the tug of attraction he felt.

They were not a match in any way.

At least that's what he'd told himself.

Now, in this quiet hallway, he got lost for a moment, caught between the past and the present. He touched her cheek. It was soft…warm. Her eyes were the color of dried lavender, like the small bouquets his mother used to hang in the closets. "Bryn." He felt the muscles in his throat tighten.

Her gaze was guarded, her thoughts a mystery. No longer did he see naked adoration on her face. He didn't trust her momentary docility. She might be trying to play him for her own advantage. But she'd soon find that she was no match for him. He'd do anything to protect his father. Even if it meant bedding the enemy to learn her secrets.

Without thought or reason, his lips found hers. Their mouths clung, pressed, moved awkwardly. His hands found the ripe curves of her breasts and he caressed her gently. He thought she responded, but he couldn't be sure. He was caught up in some weird time warp. When sharp daggers of arousal made him breathless, he jerked back, drawing great gulps of air into his starving lungs.

He ran his hands through his hair. "No." He couldn't think of a follow-up explanation. Was he talking to her or himself?

Bryn's face was dead-white but for two spots of hectic color on her cheekbones. She wiped a shaky hand across her mouth and backed away from him.

Distress filled her eyes and embarrassment etched her face.

She turned and walked away, her gait jerky.

He watched her go, his gut a knot the size of Texas. If she had come again to try to convince them that Jesse had fathered her child, she would get short shrift. It would be in extremely bad taste to accuse a man who wasn't here to defend himself.

Remembering Jesse at this particular moment was a mistake. It brought back every single moment of torment Trent had experienced when his baby brother started dating the woman Trent wanted. The situation had been intolerable, and only by keeping himself in Denver, far away from temptation, had Trent been able to deal with it.

But in his heated fantasies, during the dead of night, it was Bryn, always Bryn. He'd told himself he was over her. He'd told himself he hated her.

But it was all a lie....

Bryn didn't have the luxury of locking herself in her room and giving way to the storm of emotions that tightened her throat and knotted the muscles between her shoulder blades. Why couldn't Mac's son Gage have been here...or Sloan? She loved both of them like brothers and would have been happy for a reunion. But Trent... Oh, God, had she given herself away? Did he know now she had never gotten over her fascination with him?

She couldn't allow herself to think about what had just happened...refused to acknowledge how she enjoyed the way his hard, naked chest felt beneath her hands. Had she pushed him away or leaned into him?

Don't be a fool, Bryn. Nothing can come of going down that road but more hurt.

When Bryn was sure Mac was napping, she went out to the car to retrieve her suitcase and carry-on. Trent had disappeared to do chores. Bryn was grateful for the respite from his presence.

She stood, arms upraised, and stretched for a moment, shaking off the stiffness from the long flight and subsequent drive. She had forgotten the clearness of the air, the pure blue of the Wyoming sky. In the distance, the Grand Tetons ripped at the heavens, their jagged peaks still snow-capped, even in mid-May.

Despite her stress and confusion, after six years of exile, the familiar Crooked S brand entwined prominently in the massive wrought-iron gates at the end of the driveway felt like a homecoming. The imposing metalwork arched skyward as if to remind importunate visitors, "You're nobody. Trespass at your own risk."

The four boys used to call it the "Crooked Ass Ranch." Mac hadn't thought the irreverence funny.

Before going back inside, Bryn studied the house with yearning eyes. Little had changed since she had been gone. The sprawling two-story structure of timber and stone had cost millions to build, even in the mid-seventies when Mac had constructed it for his young bride.

The house rested, like a conqueror, on the crest of a low hill. Everything about it reeked of money, from the enormous wraparound porch to the copper guttering that gleamed in the midday sun. The support beams for the porch were thick tree trunks stripped of bark. Flowering shrubs tucked at the base of the house gave a semblance of softness to the curb appeal, but Bryn wasn't fooled.

This was a house of powerful, arrogant men.

Back inside, she picked up her phone and dialed her aunt's number. Even though the Sinclair's ranch was in the middle of nowhere, Mac had long ago paid for a cell tower to be built near the house. With enough money, anything could be bought, including all the trappings of an electronic society.

When Aunt Beverly answered, Bryn felt immediately

soothed by the familiar voice. Six years ago her mother's older sister had taken in a scared, pregnant teenager and had not only helped Bryn enroll in community college and find a part-time job, but when the time came, she had also been a doting grandmother, in every sense of the word, to Allen.

Bryn chatted with a cheer she didn't feel, and then asked to speak to her son. Allen's tolerance for phone conversations was limited, but it comforted Bryn to hear his high-pitched voice. The family next door had two new puppies. Aunt Beverly was taking him to the neighborhood pool tomorrow. His favorite toy fire truck had lost a wheel. "Love you. Bye, Mommy."

And with that, he was gone.

Beverly came back on the line. "Are you sure everything is okay, sweetheart? He can't make you stay."

Bryn squeezed the bridge of her nose and cleared her throat. "I'm fine…honestly. Mac is weaker than I expected, and they're grieving for Jesse."

"What about you?"

Bryn paused, trying to sort through her chaotic feelings. "I'm still coming to terms with it. He didn't break my heart. What we had was more hormones than happily-ever-afters. But he nearly destroyed my world. I never forgave him for that, but I didn't want him dead." Her throat thickened, making it hard to speak.

Beverly's gentle words echoed her strength. "We've gotten by without the money all this time, Bryn. It's not worth losing your pride and your self-respect. If they give you trouble, promise me you'll leave."

Bryn smiled, though her aunt couldn't see her. "Allen deserves a share of the wealth. And I'll put it in a special account for his college education and whatever else he might need down the road. It will give him a secure future, and that's important. I'll be home in four weeks. Don't you worry about me."

They chitchatted a few more minutes, but then Allen demanded Aunt Beverly's attention. Bryn clicked the phone shut and blinked rapidly to stave off a wave of loneliness and heartache. She had never been away from her baby more than a night or two.

Allen would be fine. She knew that. But she felt like she'd been given a life sentence without parole.

She changed into comfortable jeans and a petal-pink sweater. It was time to check on Mac.

She tiptoed as she neared his room. He needed his rest desperately. Fortunately, this entire wing of the house was quiet as a tomb, so maybe he was still sleeping. Everything in his luxurious but masculine suite was designed for comfort, so as long as his medication was relieving any pain, he should be recovering on schedule.

But she knew as well as anyone that grief manifested itself in serious and complex ways.

Her foot was moving forward to enter the room when she realized Trent was sitting on the side of his father's bed. She caught her breath and drew back instinctively.

Trent murmured softly, the conversation one-sided as Mac slept. Bryn couldn't make out the words. Trent stroked his father's forehead, the gesture so gentle a huge lump strangled her throat.

The old man was feeble and frail in the large bed. His eldest son, in contrast, was virile, strong and healthy. Seeing Trent show such tenderness shocked her. He had always been a reserved man, self-contained and difficult to read. Striking and impressive, but a man of few smiles.

His steel-gray eyes and jet-black hair, dusted with premature silver at the temples, complemented a complexion tanned dark by the sun. Despite the years he'd been gone from Wyoming, he still retained the look of one who spent much of his time outdoors.

She swallowed hard and forced herself to enter the room. "When is his next doctor's appointment?"

Though her words were soft and low, Trent snatched back his hand and rose to his feet, his expression closed and forbidding. "Next Tuesday, I think. It's written on the kitchen calendar."

She nodded, her voice threatening to fail her. "Okay." She tried to step past him, but he put a hand on her arm.

Trent was raw with grief over the loss of his brother. He could barely contemplate the possibility of losing the old man so soon after Jesse's death. How could Bryn still turn him inside out? His grip tightened. Not enough to hurt her, but enough to let her know he wouldn't be a pushover.

He put his face close to hers, perhaps to prove to himself that kissing her was a temptation he could withstand. "Stay out of my way, Bryn Matthews. And we'll get along just fine."

This close he could see the almost imperceptible lines at the corners of her eyes. She was not a child anymore. She was a grown woman. And he saw in one brief instant that she had suffered, too.

But then she blinked and the tense moment was gone. "No problem," she said, her voice quiet so as not to wake her patient. "You won't even know I'm here."

Trent strode outdoors blindly, feeling suffocated and out of control. He needed physical exertion to clear his head. A half hour later, he slung a heavy saddle over the corral rail and wiped sweat from his forehead. Working out at the gym in Denver wasn't quite the same as doing ranch labor. The chores here were hard, hot and strangely cathartic. It had been a decade since Trent had played an active role in running the Crooked S. But the skills, rusty as they might be, were coming back to him.

He had repaired fences, mucked out stalls, hunted down stray calves and helped the vet deliver two new foals. Up until yesterday, his brothers, Gage and Sloan, had done their part, as well. But they were gone now—for at least a month—until one of them returned to relieve Trent.

A month seemed like a lifetime.

Trent's father employed an army of ranch hands, but in his old age, he'd become cantankerous and intolerant of strangers—reluctant to let outsiders know his business. He'd fired his foreman not long before Jesse's death.

The tragedy had taken a toll on all of them, but Mac had aged overnight.

Even now, eight weeks after Jesse's death, Trent was blindsided at least once a day by a poignant memory of his youngest brother. The coroner's report still made no sense. Cause of death: heroin overdose. It was ridiculous. Jesse had been an Eagle Scout, for God's sake. Had someone slipped him the drug without his knowledge?

Trent finished rubbing down the stallion and glanced at his watch. He'd fallen into the habit of checking on the old man at least once an hour, and with Bryn around, that routine was more important than ever. He didn't trust her one damn bit. Six years ago she had lied to weasel her way into the family. Now she was back to try again. The next few weeks were going to be hell.

Especially if he couldn't keep his traitorous body under control.

Two

When Trent stormed out of the room, albeit quietly, Bryn couldn't decide if she was disappointed or relieved. He made her furious, but at the same time, she felt so alive when he was around. Six years had not changed that.

She sat at Mac's bedside for a half hour, just watching the rise and fall of his chest. In some ways, it was as if no time had passed at all. This man had meant the world to her.

When he finally roused from his nap and shifted upright in the bed, she handed him a tumbler of water, which he drained thirstily and placed on the bedside table.

He stared at her, his expression sober. "Do you hate me, girl?"

She shrugged, opting for honesty. "I did for a long time. You broke your promise to me." When her parents, Mac's foreman and cook, died in a car accident years ago, Mac had sat a fourteen-year-old Bryn down in his study and promised her that she would always have a home on the huge Wyoming ranch where she had grown up.

But four years later that promise was worth less than nothing. Jesse, spoiled golden child and chillingly proficient liar, turned them all against her in one insane, surreal instant.

Mac shifted in the bed. "I did what I had to do." His words were sulky…pure, stubborn Mac. But knowing how much he had suffered softened Bryn's heart a little.

In spite of herself, forgiveness tightened her throat and squeezed her chest. Mac had made a mistake.… They all had made mistakes, Bryn included. But Mac had done his best to look out for her after her parents were gone. Until it all went to hell.

Then he'd sent her to Aunt Beverly. Punishment by exile. Bryn had been crushed. But six years was a long time to hold a grudge.

She sighed. "I'm sorry Jesse died, Mac. I know how much you loved him."

"I loved you, too," he said gruffly, not meeting her eyes.

His behavior bore that out. Mac hadn't forgotten her. For six years he'd sent birthday and Christmas presents like clockwork. But Bryn, hugging her injured pride like the baby she was, promptly sent them back every time.

Now shame choked her. Did Mac's one moment of weakness erase all the years he'd been like a grandfather to her?

She took a deep breath. "I came back to Wyoming because you asked me to. But even if you hadn't, I would have been here once I knew Jesse was gone. We have to talk about a lot of things, Mac." Like the fact that she wanted a paternity test to prove that Jesse was Allen's father. And that her son was entitled to his dead father's share of the Sinclair empire.

Mac's lips trembled, and he pulled the blanket to his chest. "There's time. Don't push it, girl." He slid back down in the bed and closed his eyes, effectively ending the conversation.

Bryn stepped into the hall, leaving the bedroom door open so she could hear him call out if he needed her. The study was only steps away. She couldn't help herself… she went in.

The room seemed benign now, not at all the way she remembered it in her nightmares. That dreadful day was etched in her memory by the sharp blades of hurt and disillusionment. She'd considered herself an honorary Sinclair, but they had sided with Jesse.

"What are you doing in here?"

Trent's sharp voice startled her so badly, she spun and almost lost her balance. She placed a steadying hand on the rolltop desk and bit her lip. "You scared me."

His scowl deepened. "I asked you a question, Bryn."

She licked her lips, her legs like jelly. "I wanted to send my son an e-mail."

Trent's face went blank, but she saw him clench his fists. "Don't mention your son in my presence," he said, his voice soft but deadly. "Not if you know what's good for you."

Bryn could take the knocks life dealt her, but no one was going to speak ill of her baby while there was breath in her body.

She squared her shoulders. "His name is Allen. And he's Jesse's son. I know it, and I think deep in your heart, you and Mac and Gage and Sloan know it, too. Why would I lie, for heaven's sake?"

Trent shrugged, his gaze watchful. "Women lie," he said, his words deliberately cutting, "all the time—to get what they want."

For the first time, she understood something that had never before been clear to her, especially not as an immature teenager. When Mac's flighty young wife abandoned her family years ago, the damage had run deep.

The Matthews family had come along to fill in the gaps. For more than a decade, Bryn and her mother had been the only females in an all-male enclave. And Bryn had assumed that trust was a two-way street. But when Jesse swore that he had never slept with Bryn, Mac and Trent had believed him. It was as simple as that.

Bryn chose her words carefully. "I don't lie. Maybe you've had bad luck with the women in your life, but I can't help that. I told the truth six years ago, and I'm telling the truth now."

He curled his lip. "Easy for you to say. With Jesse not here to defend himself."

She tamped down her anger, desperate to get through to him. "Jesse was a troubled boy who grew into a troubled man. You all spoiled him and babied him, and he used your love as a weapon. I have the scars to prove it. But Jesse's gone, and I'm still here. And so is my son. He deserves to know his birthright—his family."

Trent leaned back against his wall, the hard planes of his face showing no signs of remorse. "How much do you want?" he said bluntly. "How big a check do I have to write to make you leave and never come back?"

The bottom fell out of her stomach, and her jaw actually dropped. "Go to hell," she said, her lips trembling.

He grabbed her wrist as she headed for the door. "Maybe I'll take you with me," he muttered.

This time, there was no pretense of tenderness. He was angry and it showed in his kiss. Their mouths battled, his hands buried in her hair, hers clenched on his shoulders.

At eighteen she'd thought she understood sex and desire. After Jesse's betrayal, she'd understood that his love was an illusion. As was Mac's…and Trent's.

Now, with six years of celibacy to her credit and a heart that was being split wide open with the knowledge that she had never stopped loving Trent Sinclair, she was lost.

The kiss changed in one indefinable instant. She curled a hand behind his neck, stroking the short, soft hair that was never allowed to brush his collar. His skin was warm, so warm.

She went limp in his embrace, too tired to fight anymore. Her breasts were crushed against his hard chest. Her lips no longer struggled with his. She capitulated to the sweetness of being close to him again. A sweetness tainted with the knowledge that he thought she was a liar. That she had tried to manipulate them all.

Gradually, they stepped away from a dangerous point of no return. Trent's expression was closed, his body language defensive.

She nodded jerkily toward the desk. "I'll use the computer later. I'm sure you have work to do."

When he didn't respond at all, she fled.

Trent was not accustomed to second-guessing himself. Confidence and determination had propelled him to success in the cutting-edge, fast-paced world of solar and wind energy. When he'd received the call about his father's heart attack, Trent had been in the midst of an enormous deal that involved buying up a half-dozen smaller companies and incorporating them into the already well-respected business model that was Sinclair Synergies.

Except for some start-up cash that had long since been repaid, he'd never relied on his father's money. Trent was damned good at what he did. So why was the CEO of said company cooling his heels in Wyoming shoveling literal horseshit?

And why in the hell couldn't he read the truth in a

woman's eyes? A woman who had stayed in his heart all these years like a bad case of indigestion.

Had Jesse lied? And if so, why? Mac, Sloan, Gage and Trent had doted on the little boy who came along three years after his one-after-the-other siblings. Jesse had suffered from terrible bouts of asthma, and the entire family rallied whenever he was sick. So, yeah—maybe Bryn was right. Maybe they *had* catered to Jesse's whims, especially when their mother bailed on them. But that didn't mean Jesse was a bad person.

Heroin overdose. Trent shifted uneasily in Mac's office chair. Going through the books was proving to be more difficult than he'd anticipated. Jesse had never been a whiz at math, so God knows why Mac put him in charge of the finances. His youth alone should have been a red flag. And his inexperience.

Already, Trent was uneasy about some ways money had been shifted from one account to another. A heart-to-heart with Mac was in order, but until the old man was a little steadier on his emotional feet, Trent would hold off on the questions.

Which brought him back to Bryn. What was Mac thinking? Why had he brought Bryn back to Wyoming?

Trent shoved back from the desk and stood up to stretch, his eyes going automatically to the magnificent scene outside the window. Wyoming was his birthplace, his home. And he loved it. But it had not been able to hold him…or Gage or Sloan, either, for that matter.

Gage had developed a bad case of wanderlust at an early age…and Sloan—well—Sloan's brilliance was never going to be challenged by ranching. Had Jesse felt the need to be his father's heir apparent? It didn't fit what Trent knew of his baby brother's temperament, but what else could explain Jesse's role in running the ranch?

At one time the Crooked S had been the largest cattle operation in a six-state area…back when Mac was in his forties and had a brand-new twenty-year-old bride at his side. Now it was nothing more than acres of really valuable land.

What would become of the ranch when Mac was gone?

Trent waited until he heard Bryn talking on the phone in her bedroom before he went back in to check on his dad. Mac was sitting up in bed, and already his eyes seemed brighter, his skin a healthier shade. Had something as simple as bringing Bryn home wrought the change?

Trent sat down in a ladderback chair near the foot of the bed and hooked one ankle over the opposite knee. He put his hands behind his head and leaned back. "You're looking better."

Mac grunted. "I'll live." The two of them had never been much for sentimentality.

Trent smothered a smile. "Do you feel like going for a ride? I need to pick up a few things in town. Might do you good to get out for a couple of hours."

His father seemed to wilt suddenly, as though his burst of energy had come and gone in an instant. "Don't think I ought to try it yet. But maybe Bryn would like to go."

Trent stiffened. He wasn't ready to spend the hour and a half it would take to go into Jackson Hole and back cooped up in a car with the woman who was tying him in knots. "I'd say she's still tired from her trip. And I can be there and back in no time."

Mac's dark eyes, so much like his son's, held a calculating gleam. "Bryn promised to pick out a new blanket for my bed at the Pendleton store. You know how women are...always shopping for something. I don't want to disappoint her. And you can have dinner before you drive back. Julio and I are going to play poker tonight."

Julio was one of the ranch hands. Trent sighed. He knew when he'd been suckered. But he wasn't going to fight with his dad...not yet.

Moments later, Trent knocked on Bryn's door. It was slightly ajar, and he waited impatiently until she finished her phone conversation.

Bryn ground her teeth when she realized Trent was standing in the doorway. Maybe she should put a cow bell on him so he'd quit sneaking up on her. "What do you want?" The curt question was rude, but she was still stinging from their earlier encounter.

Trent's expression was no happier than hers. His lips twisted. "I'm supposed to take you into town with me to do some errands...a blanket my father mentioned? And he wants me to take you out to dinner."

She cocked her head, reading his discomfort in every taut muscle of his lean body. "And you'd rather wrestle with a rattlesnake...right?"

He shrugged, leaning against the door frame, his face impassive. "I'm here this month to make my father's life easier. And if that means allowing him to boss me around, I'm willing to do so."

"Such a dutiful son," she mocked.

His jaw hardened. "Be out front in twenty minutes."

Bryn fumed as he walked out on her, and she locked her door long enough to change from jeans into nice dress slacks and a spring sweater. She didn't understand Trent at all. But she read his hostility loud and clear. From now on, there would be no kissing, no reliving the past. She was here to right past wrongs, and Trent was no more than a minor inconvenience.

She managed to make herself believe that until she climbed into the passenger seat of a silver, high-end Mercedes and got a whiff of freshly showered male and expensive aftershave. *Oh, Lord.*

Her stomach flipped once…hard…and she clasped her hands in her lap, her feet planted on the floor and her spine plumb-line straight.

The atmosphere in the car was as frigid as a January Wyoming morning. Trent turned the satellite radio to a news station, and they managed to complete the entire journey in total silence.

He let her out in front of the Pendleton store. "I've got some business to attend to. Can you entertain yourself for an hour or so?"

She sketched a salute. "Yes, sir. I'll be right here at six o'clock."

His jaw went even harder than before, and his tires squealed as he pulled away from the curb.

Bryn's brief show of defiance drained away, and her bottom lip trembled. Why couldn't Trent let the past stay in the past? Why couldn't they start over as friends?

She picked out Mac's beautiful Native American–patterned blanket in no time, and visited a few more of the shops down the street, managing to select gifts for her aunt and for Allen. A friendly shopkeeper offered to stow Bryn's bulky packages until Trent returned, so Bryn took the opportunity to stretch her legs.

Back in Minnesota she and Beverly and Allen walked each evening when the weather was nice. The two women enjoyed the exercise, and it was good for Allen to use up some of his energy before bedtime.

Bryn missed her baby. He hated it when she called him that. He was five and would be starting kindergarten in the fall. She wasn't ready. Maybe because it pointed out the fact that he wouldn't always need her. He'd go off to college and meet some scary girl who would take him away for good.

She laughed softy at her own maudlin thoughts. She was twenty-four years old. She was two semesters away from finishing a degree in communications, and as soon as she was able to return home, she would fall back into her familiar, comfortable routine. She had her whole life ahead of her.

So why did she feel despondent?

The answer was simple. She wanted Trent to trust her. To ensure Allen's future, she had no choice but to insist on a paternity test. But everything inside her rebelled at that thought. She didn't want a litigious battle with the Sinclair family.

She wanted Mac, Trent, Gage and Sloan to admit that she was one of them, blood or not. She wanted an apology. She wanted to see more in Trent's face than suspicion and anger.

Her daddy used to say, "Men in prison want out." So what?

She was sitting on a bench, packages tucked beside her, when Trent returned. Without speaking, he got out, opened the trunk and waited for her to put her shopping spoils inside.

Then he faced her across the roof of the car, his expression stoic. "Where would you like to eat?"

Bryn's temper had a long fuse, but his manner was insulting. She glared at him. "There's a sandwich shop on the corner. We can grab something and eat on the way home…so we don't waste any time."

Her sarcasm hit the mark. He opened his mouth and shut it again, displeasure marking his patrician features. "Fine."

Twenty minutes later, they were on the road. Bryn chewed a turkey sandwich that felt like sand in her mouth. Finally, she gave up and wrapped most of it in the waxed paper and stuffed it in the bag.

Trent had finished his without fanfare and was sipping coffee and staring out the windshield in the dwindling light. Encountering large wildlife on the road was always a hazard, but Trent was a careful driver and Bryn felt perfectly safe with him.

She chewed her lip, wishing she could go back in time

and erase every stupid thing she'd ever done. Including the day she invited Trent to take her to the prom. Trent had said no, of course. Bryn had cried her eyes out behind the barn, and Jesse had come along to comfort her.

In retrospect, she suspected Jesse's motive, even from that first moment, had been troublemaking.

When the silence in the car became unbearably oppressive, Bryn put her hand on Trent's sleeve. "I'm really sorry about Jesse. I know you loved him very much." She felt the muscles in his forearm tense, so she took her hand away. Apparently even brief contact with her disgusted him.

Trent drummed his fingers on the steering wheel, his profile bleak. "I still can't believe it. He was such a good kid."

"You weren't around him much in the last several years, though. He changed a lot."

"What do you mean?" The words were sharp.

"Didn't you wonder why he never graduated from college?"

"Dad said he had trouble settling on a major. He was restless and confused. So he switched schools several times. Apparently he decided he wanted to get more involved with the ranch."

Bryn groaned inwardly. It was worse than she thought. Mac clearly must have known about Jesse's problems, but apparently he had done a bang-up job of keeping that information from his other three sons.

Did Bryn have the right to dispel the myths?

She thought of little Allen, and the answer was clear.

"Trent—" she sighed "—Jesse got kicked out of four universities for excessive drinking and drug use. Your father finally made him come home to keep an eye on him."

The car swerved, the brakes screeched and Bryn's seat belt cut into her chest as Trent slammed the car to a halt at the side of the road. He punched on the overhead light and turned to face her. "How dare you try to smear my brother's memory.… You have no right." His dark eyes flashed, and the curve of his sensual lips was tight.

She wouldn't back down, not now. "I'm sorry," she said softly. "I really am. But Mac has done you a disservice. Perhaps you could have helped if you had known."

Trent's laser gaze would have ripped her in half if she hadn't known in her heart she was doing the right thing. Pain etched his face, along with confusion and remorse, and a seldom-seen, heart-wrenching vulnerability—at least not by Bryn.

He ran a hand through his hair. "You're lying again. How would you know anything about Jesse?"

Denial was a normal stage of grief. But Bryn held firm. "I'm not lying," she said calmly. "Jesse called me a couple or three times a year. And every time it was the same. He was either drunk or high. He'd ramble on about how he wanted me to come back to Wyoming."

"If you're telling the truth, it's even worse. He might

have wanted to make a family with you and the baby, even if it wasn't his."

"Focus, Trent. He didn't know what he was saying half the time. If anything, he wanted to use me and Allen to win points with Mac…to help cover his ass after whatever new trouble he'd gotten himself into."

"Jesse loved children."

"Jesse offered me money to get an abortion," she said flatly. "He said he had big plans for his life and they didn't include a baby…or me for that matter. That's why I ran into Mac's study that day so upset. I thought Mac would talk some sense into him."

Trent's face was white. He didn't say a word.

"But instead," she said, grimacing at the quiver she heard in her own voice, "Mac put me on a plane to Minnesota."

Please, please, please believe me.

He shrugged. "With your talent for drama, you might have a career on the silver screen."

His flippant words hurt, but they were no more than she expected. He'd been fed a pack of lies, all right. But not by Bryn.

She sighed. "Ask Mac," she begged. "Make him tell you the truth."

Trent shook his head slowly. "My father nearly died. He's grieving over the loss of his son. No way in hell am I going to upset him with your wild accusations."

She slumped back in her seat and turned her head so he wouldn't see her cry. "Well, then—we're at an impasse. Take me home. I want to see how Mac is doing."

She didn't know what she expected from Trent. But he gave her nothing. Nothing at all. His face closed up. He started the engine.

Three

Trent was appalled by the picture Bryn painted of Jesse. The young brother Trent remembered was fun-loving, maybe a little immature for his age, but not amoral, not unprincipled.

Bryn had unwittingly touched on Trent's own personal guilt. He hadn't been much of a big brother in recent years. Other than Mac's birthday in the fall, and Thanksgiving and Christmas, Trent had seldom made the trip home from Colorado to Wyoming.

His company was wildly successful, and the atmosphere of cutthroat competition was consuming and addictive. He'd made obscene amounts of money in a very short time period, but it was the challenge that kept him going. He thrived on being the best.

But at what cost? Had he missed the signs that Jesse

was struggling? Or had the truth been kept from him deliberately? Gage wouldn't have known. He was usually halfway around the word on any given day. And Sloan was more attuned to the world of numbers and formulas than emotions and personalities. No…Trent should have been the one to see it, and he'd been too damned busy to help.

Of course, there was always the possibility that Bryn was exaggerating…or even inventing the entire scenario. That was the most palatable choice. But though he was far from being willing to trust her, the passionate sincerity in her eyes and in her words would be difficult to fabricate.

When they pulled up in front of the house, Bryn got out and retrieved her packages before he could help her. Her body language wasn't difficult to read. She was angry.

He took her arm before she walked away, registering the slender bones. "I don't want you talking to Mac about Jesse. Not for a while. God knows what you're hoping to get out of this sudden, compassionate visit, but I'll be watching you, so don't do anything to upset Mac or you'll have me to deal with."

She threw him a mocking smile as she walked toward the porch. "I love Mac. And your threats don't scare me. I think your original idea was the best.… I plan to stay out of your way."

Bryn saw little of Trent for three days, which was a good thing. She was still smarting from their most recent confrontation. He showed up in his dad's room several times a day to chat with him, and on those occasions, Bryn slipped away to give the men privacy.

Mac was aware of Trent's burdens and complained to Bryn. "Can't you slow him down? The boy works round the clock. If he's not on the ranch, he's holding conference calls with his staff and staying up half the night doing God knows what."

"How am I supposed to stop him? Your sons would do anything for you, Mac, but it must be terribly difficult for a man like Trent to put his life on hold for a month." Trent had built a highly successful company from the ground up, and his drive and intelligence had enabled him to amass his first million before he was twenty-five. Even without the financial largesse he would one day inherit from his father, Trent was a wealthy man.

Mac frowned stubbornly. "He would listen to you, Brynnie."

"I don't think so. You know he doesn't trust me. He's got lawyers flying in by helicopter almost every day with contracts to sign. He's an important, high-profile businessman. He and I might have been close at one time, but I don't even know him anymore." The older boy she remembered—the young man who had seemed like the most wonderful person in the world to her—was long gone. The Trent of today operated in an arena that was sophisticated, intimidating and completely foreign to her.

The change in the man she had once been so close to made her sad.

Bryn wouldn't have minded the distraction of helping out around the house, but with Mac's revolving staff of cooks and housekeepers, she might as well have been staying in a four-star hotel. Any dirty laundry disappeared as if by magic, and her luxurious bathroom and bedroom were kept spotless.

For someone accustomed to caring for a child, working part-time and keeping up with school, she found herself at loose ends when Mac was resting.

On the third night after the uneasy trip to Jackson Hole, Trent encountered her in the kitchen chatting with the cook.

His expression was brooding. "I thought I might see if Mac is up to having dinner at the table tonight. What do you think?"

She nodded slowly, wishing she didn't feel so awkward around Trent. "It's a great idea. It would do him good to get out of that room for a change." It was really more of a suite than a single room, but even the most luxurious surroundings could seem like a prison.

When the two men reappeared, Mac leaning on his son's arm, Bryn was helping set everything on the table. The menu, by doctor's orders, included as many heart healthy ingredients as possible, and the aroma was enough to tempt even the most uninspired appetite.

Mac picked at his food to start with, but finally dug in. Bryn watched, pleased, as he cleared his plate.

The conversation was stilted. But Bryn did her best. "So tomorrow's the doctor's appointment, right?"

Mac had his mouth full, so Trent answered. "Yes. At 11:00 a.m. I'll take Dad. You can stay here and have some time off the clock."

She frowned. He made it sound as if she were the hired help. "But I would be happy to go."

Trent shook his head, his calm demeanor hiding whatever he might be feeling. "No need."

And that was it. The oracle had spoken.

After dinner Mac and Trent played chess on a jade-and-onyx board that Gage had brought back from one of his trips to Asia. Bryn could tell by the quality of the workmanship that the set was expensive. And she wondered wryly what it must be like to never once have to worry about money.

She stood unnoticed in the doorway for several minutes, just watching the interplay between the two men. The Sinclair males had never been the type to wear their hearts on their sleeves, but Bryn knew they loved each other deeply. They were a tightly knit clan.

Unfortunately, she was still outside the circle.

The following morning, Bryn was shooed out of the sickroom so Trent could help his father get dressed and leave. Unbidden, her feet carried her upstairs to Jesse's room. It was as far from Mac's as it was possible to be in the rambling house. On purpose? Perhaps. Jesse would have wanted to avoid his father's watchful eye.

A thin layer of dust coated everything. Mac paid a weekly cleaning service to come in, but they must have been given instructions not to enter this room. Nothing had been touched since the day Jesse died. Even the bed was still unmade.

Though it made her stomach hurt, the first thing she

did was to gather a few items that could be used for testing…a comb that held stray hairs, a toothbrush, a razor. She couldn't afford to be squeamish. This was why she had come.

Bryn continued to straighten the mess as her mind whirled with unanswered questions. She had seen the coroner's report. Mac had laid it out in full view on the dresser in his bedroom. She suspected he wanted her to read it for herself so he wouldn't have to say the awful words out loud: *My son was a drug addict.*

What a waste of a young life. She picked up a neon blue iPod, plugged it into the dock, and flipped through the selections. Nostalgia and grief hit hard as she saw one familiar title, "Jessie's Girl." How many times had the two of them played that oldie at full volume, singing along, careening down a Wyoming road?

She had believed it with her whole heart. She had been Jesse's girl, and even though he wasn't Trent, he had made her feel special and wanted. She'd been happy mostly, relieved to know that she would forever be a part of the Sinclair clan.

But it had all been an illusion.

She opened the closet door and reached to put the sports equipment on a top shelf. As she did, she dislodged an old shoe box held together with a rubber band. It fell at her feet. Something about it made a cold chill slither down her spine.

She sat down on the double bed and took off the lid. She'd been expecting drugs, maybe a gun. Certainly not what she found.

The box held letters, maybe two dozen in all. As she

riffled through them, she saw that the earliest ones were dated the year Jesse turned sixteen. The return addresses were all the same…a single line that read *RRIF*. The postmarks were all Cheyenne.

Had no one at the house ever questioned Jesse about them, or were they spaced so far apart that no one took notice? Or had Mac known all along? The three older boys would have been in college when the first ones showed up in the mailbox.

Bryn opened one at random and began reading. Horrified, she went through them all. Her stomach clenched.

What kind of mother would poison the mind of her young son, a boy she had abandoned when he was six years old?

The damage was insidious. A child might have missed the venom behind the words. But what about Jesse? Had he been happy his mother contacted him? Happy enough to not to look beneath the surface? Or as a young adult, had he been able to see the subtext beneath the whining, manipulative words?

Jesse, you were always my favorite.

Jesse, Mac was a tyrant. I was so unhappy. He wouldn't let me take you.

Jesse, I miss you.

Jesse, Trent and Gage and Sloan never loved me the way they should.

Jesse, you have my brains. Brawn isn't everything.

Jesse, you deserve more.

Jesse…Jesse…Jesse…

Bryn couldn't imagine why Mac's wife would have

been so cruel. To punish her ex-husband? To bring discord into the family? Why? *She* had left them, not the other way around.

The later letters were the most damning. Etta Sinclair talked about her many boyfriends. She hinted that she'd had affairs while she was married to Mac. And she intimated that Mac might not be Jesse's father.

Bryn's legs went weak, so much so that she might have fallen if she hadn't been sitting down. It wouldn't matter if Trent and Mac ever believed that Jesse was Allen's father. Jesse might not be a Sinclair at all, and if *he* wasn't, then his young son was not, either.

Bryn gathered the letters with shaking hands, tucked them back in the box and went downstairs to her room.

Would there be any point in letting Mac see them? Best to hide them. Until she could decide what to do with them. Surely he had long since become immune to his wife's defection.

The more she thought about the letters, the more confused she became. She had seen pictures of Etta, though they were few and far between. Trent, Gage and Sloan were all carbon copies of their dad—big, strong men with dark coloring.

Jesse was blond and slender, the spitting image of his mother. Was it simply a quirk of DNA, or was there any truth in those letters?

By the time the men returned in the late afternoon, Bryn had almost made herself ill. She excused herself after dinner and hid in her room. After a shower and a long phone call with Aunt Beverly, she curled up in bed and read for hours until she fell into a restless sleep.

Trent's immediate anxieties were eased considerably by the doctor's glowing report on Mac's recovery. The heart attack had been a serious one, but Mac's overall health and fitness had mitigated some of the long-term damage. Mac Sinclair was a tough old bird.

Which emboldened Trent on the way home to press gently for some answers. He kept his voice casual. "Was it really necessary to invite Bryn to come out here? She's bound to cause trouble. You know what she did six years ago. I doubt she's changed."

Mac wrapped his arms across his chest, gazing pensively through the windshield. "I handled things all wrong back then. She deserves a fair hearing. That's why I asked her to come."

Trent was stunned. "But she lied."

Mac shrugged. "Maybe she did, maybe she didn't. But it still does my heart good to see her again."

Trent opened his mouth to protest, but choked back the words with effort. His tough father had never been prone to sentimentality. Trent feared that in this vulnerable state his father might be fooled by a woman who was beautiful, charming and had a not-so-secret agenda.

He spoke carefully. "It would be human nature if Bryn wanted a piece of the pie." Trent's job, like it or not, would be to ferret out the truth and protect his father from doing anything rash.

"Bryn is not a threat," Mac insisted. "She's the same girl she always was."

"That's what worries me. I can't forget what she tried to do to Jesse." Trent, too, felt the pull of Bryn's charisma, acknowledged the presence of nostalgic memories and emotions. But he was not so easily swayed by soft smiles and sweet words. He'd been in business long enough to know that people were not always what they seemed.

"Jesse played a part in what happened six years ago."

"All I'm asking, Dad, is that you don't promise her anything. Bryn might look like a dark-headed angel, but that doesn't mean she isn't out to get what she wants by fair means or foul." Trent would be wise to remember his own advice the next time he had an urge to taste those lush lips.

Mac moved restlessly in his seat, clearly exhausted by the outing. "You're paranoid, boy. Don't be so suspicious."

"I'll try, Dad. For your sake." Trent lived by the adage "Keep your friends close and your enemies closer." Whether or not Bryn was an enemy remained to be seen, but in the meantime, he'd keep an eye on her. She wasn't the only one who could put on an act. He would pretend to be the gracious host, and if she let down her guard, he'd be able to circumvent any mischief she might have in mind.

Tension and stress threatened to turn Bryn into an insomniac. After one particularly restless night, there was a knock at her bedroom door, and she realized with chagrin that the sun was shining brightly through a crack in the draperies.

She cleared her throat. "Come in." She expected the cleaning lady. But it was Trent.

The grimace that crossed his handsome face might almost have been a lopsided half smile. "I owe you a thank-you for coming so quickly when Mac called."

She sat up in bed, covers clutched to her chest, and scraped the hair from her face. Trent was clean shaven and his hair was still damp from his shower. In contrast, Bryn was decidedly rumpled.

He'd brought scrambled eggs and toast. It was all arranged on a tray with coffee, jam and a napkin.

He set it on the dresser and kept his distance.

She tried to clear her sleep-fogged throat. "Thank you."

His brooding gaze studied her. "One of Mac's old college buddies is coming to visit today. I thought you and I should make ourselves scarce. It's a beautiful day. We could take a hike…like we used to."

"A hike?" Her coffee-deprived brain was slow to catch up.

He nodded, still unsmiling. "We got off on the wrong foot this week, Bryn. I appreciate what you're doing for Mac."

"So this is an olive branch?" Her heart leaped in her chest.

He shrugged. "I wouldn't say that. But it bothers him when we're at each other's throats. We can at least put on a good front when we're around him. So maybe we need to clear the air."

The breakfast was delicious, but Bryn chewed and swallowed absently, still pondering Trent's final cryptic statement. He'd left her bedroom abruptly, and he didn't sound like a man who was suddenly convinced she was telling the truth. If anything, he wanted to brush the past under the rug.

She couldn't do that. She had Allen to consider.

She dressed rapidly in light hiking pants and a short-sleeved shirt. She hadn't brought her boots with her on the plane, because they were heavy, so a sturdy pair of sneakers would have to do.

Sunshine must be strong medicine, because she found Mac in good spirits. She smoothed his sheets absently. "Are you sure you'll be okay while we're gone?"

Mac nodded. "I'm fine. No need to hover. You've been in Minnesota a long time. Get out and enjoy the ranch."

Bryn and Trent left shortly thereafter, this time in one of the ranch Jeeps. Trent drove with the quiet confidence that was so characteristic of him.

Bryn wasn't entirely comfortable with his silence. "Where are we going?" she asked.

Trent shifted into low gear as they wound partway up the side of a steep hill. "Falcon Ridge."

There was no inflection in his voice, but Bryn felt a kick of excitement. Falcon Ridge was a family favorite. She and Mac's boys had spent many a happy afternoon there over the years.

Trent parked the Jeep and got out. He attached the quilt like a bedroll at the base of his high-tech pack and stuffed their picnic lunch inside.

"I can carry something," Bryn said.

His motions were quick and methodical. "I've got it."

The trail was only a mile long, but it went up, up, up. Trent led the way, his stride steady, his back straight. Bryn's leg muscles were burning and her lungs gasping for air when they reached the summit.

"Oh, Trent…I'd forgotten how beautiful it is up here."

The valley of Jackson Hole lay before them, breathtaking, magnificent, tucked against the backdrop of the Grand Tetons. A lone eagle soared on thermal currents overhead. Her throat tightened, and she wondered how she had stayed away so long.

"It's my favorite spot on the ranch." For a moment she saw vulnerability in his face and she wondered if he ever regretted moving away.

Trent spread the quilt, and they sat in silence, enjoying the view. Bryn was extremely conscious of him at her side, so close she could feel his body heat. He had leaned back on his elbows, and his flat stomach drew her attention. He was lean and fit and utterly masculine.

She had loved him one way or another for most of her life. When her parents died, it was nineteen-year-old Trent, more than anyone else, who had been able to comfort her. She had cried on his shoulder for hours, and finally, she had believed him when he said the hurt would get better.

If Trent said it, it must be so.

She tried to bridge the gulf between them, wanting some kind of peace. "You taught me to ride a horse… to drive a car. I always wanted you to give me my first kiss. But instead, it was Jesse."

Trent's expression was bleak. "That was a long time ago. Things change."

She pulled her knees to her chest and wrapped her arms around them. She was not the same scared, devastated girl who left the ranch six years ago. She had borne a child, gone back to school, learned to deal with life's disappointments.

But here on this mountaintop, she could feel the pull of emotion. And that was a recipe for disaster.

"What did the doctor say about Mac yesterday?"

Trent sat up, his shoulder momentarily brushing hers. "He was pleased with his physical progress. But he pulled me aside and said he's concerned about Mac's mental condition. There's no real reason Mac needs you or anyone to babysit him anymore. Mac seems to think he's more fragile than he really is. The doc says we need to coax him out of that damned bedroom and get him back to living."

She flipped an adventurous ant from the edge of the quilt. "They say that even for a normal heart-attack patient that can be hard. But on the heels of Jesse's death…" She trailed off. They both knew that Mac hadn't dealt with either the reality *or* the circumstances of Jesse's passing.

Finally, still without looking at her, Trent spoke. "I'm sorry I didn't take you to the prom."

She was surprised that he would bring it up after all this time. "I was a silly girl. You were a grown man. That was bound to end badly."

"Still," he said doggedly, "I could have handled it better."

What could she say to that?

At last he turned toward her. "I was attracted to you, Bryn. And that scared the hell out of me."

"You're just saying that to make me feel better." She couldn't meet his probing gaze. "I was so embarrassed. I wanted to crawl in a hole and die. Literally." Thinking about that long-ago afternoon made her cringe.

He brushed the back of his hand across her cheek. "I'm serious, Bryn. When you started dating Jesse, I hated it."

At last she found the courage to look at him. His eyes were sober, his expression unguarded. His small grin was self-deprecating. "He was my own baby brother, and I wanted to punch him in the face."

Her breath hitched in her throat. "I didn't mean for it to happen that way. I never should have asked you to take me to the prom. But then Jesse found me crying behind the barn and he promised to take me to the dance. He made me feel better."

"Because I had made you feel like nothing."

A jerky nod was all she could manage.

"I've asked myself a million times if things could have turned out differently. If *I'd* taken you to the damn dance instead of Jesse. We might have ended up together."

She rested her forehead on her bent knees. "*I've*

questioned a million times why he asked me to be his girlfriend. And in the end, I'm pretty sure it's because he knew I had a crush on *you*. And maybe he thought you had feelings for me. He wanted so badly to be like you and Gage and Sloan. He spent his whole life, I think, trying to measure up. But he was never big enough, tall enough, strong enough. He was always the scrawny baby brother, and he hated it."

"Did he hate *me?*" There was a world of pain in that question.

She reached out blindly and squeezed his hand. "Maybe. At times. But only because he loved you so much."

"Ah, hell, Bryn..." The choked emotion in those three ragged words made her ache for him, but she knew without looking that Trent would be dry-eyed. Stoic. He'd been the eldest, and as such, Mac had trained him in the art of keeping emotion under lock and key.

She turned to face him. "No one's to blame for Jesse's death. No one but Jesse. We make our own road in this world, Trent. He had every blessing, every opportunity."

His jawline could have chiseled stone. "This might have been an isolated event."

"Possibly," she said, trying to keep all judgment out of her voice. "But knowing what I know of Jesse, probably not. He had a dark side, Trent. You never saw it, because you never looked for it. He was your brother and you loved him. I understand that, I do. But Mac protected him and covered for him, and I think that only made things worse."

"You make him seem like a monster."

"Not a monster. But a pathological liar and a user. I know that sounds harsh. But Mac has done you no favors by hiding the trouble. You and Gage and Sloan should have known."

Trent felt the breeze on his hot face. He wanted badly to believe her, but what she was telling him was tough to swallow. Bryn had a young child to support. And she'd had six years to work on a story that would tug at all their heartstrings and open Mac's checkbook.

If Mac hadn't summoned her, she would have found another way to reinstall herself at the Crooked S. He was sure of that.

Suddenly, he wished his two brothers hadn't left already. Between the three of them they would have been able to determine if Bryn was telling the truth or not.

He let himself look at her, really look at her. A man could lose himself in those eyes. She seemed utterly sincere, but given what he knew, how could he take what she said at face value?

God, he wanted her. And he despised himself for the weakness. She was like a bright, beautiful butterfly, dancing on the wind. But if he reached out and grabbed for what he wanted, would the beauty be smashed into powder in his hand? Would he destroy Bryn? Himself? Mac?

He put his hands on her shoulders and the world stood still. Her eyes were wide. Shallow breaths lifted her chest, drawing his attention to the gentle curve of her breasts.

He laid her back on the quilt…slowly, so slowly. Her gaze never left his. And she didn't protest.

A wave of lust and yearning and exultation swept over him. She was his. She had always been his. Everything in the past was over and done with. There was no Jesse. No death. No suspicion. Only this fragile moment in time.

He shifted over her, resting on his hip and one elbow, leaving a hand free to trace the curve of her cheek, the slender column of her neck, the delicate line of her collarbone.

When his fingers went to the first button on her shirt, she didn't stop him. "Bryn." His voice was a hoarse croak in his own ears.

Finally, she moved. She linked her hands behind his neck and tugged. "Kiss me, Trent."

The invitation was unnecessary. Nothing short of an earthquake could have stopped him. His lips found hers, gentle, seeking. But when she responded, he lost his head.

He plundered the softness of her mouth, thrusting his tongue between her teeth desperately, shaking helplessly when she responded in kind. He was practically on top of her as he yanked her shirt from the waistband of her thin pants.

The skin of her flat belly was soft as silk. His hand moved upward, shoving aside her bra and cupping one bare breast. His head swam. His vision blurred. Her nipple peaked between his fingers, and when he tugged gently, Bryn cried out and arched closer.

Her response went to his head. He was so hard, he

ached from head to toe. Ached for her. For Bryn. He
hadn't been with a woman in several months…and
hadn't really noticed the omission. But now he was on
fire, out of control.

As she worked at his belt and found the zipper below,
her slight clumsiness tormented him. He groaned aloud
when her small fingers closed around his erection and
squeezed lightly. *God.* He was in danger of coming in
her hand.

What kind of man put sexual hunger ahead of loyalty
to his family? What kind of man betrayed the memory
of his brother? He panted, counting backward from a
hundred, anything to grab a toehold of control. In that
brief instant, his ardor chilled and his stomach pitched.
Bryn was either a sensual witch or a self-serving liar.
And all she had to do was smile at him and he was her
slave.

He lurched to his feet, sweating. She stared at him,
her cheeks flushed, a dawning misery on her face. With
dignity, she straightened her clothes and buttoned her
blouse.

She rose with more grace than he had managed and
faced him across the rumpled quilt.

He saw the muscles in her throat work as she
swallowed. "There's something you're not telling me,
Trent. Something important. Something significant. I
don't think you're the kind of man to be deliberately
cruel. Why start something with me and then back away
as if I'm about to infect you? For God's sake, Trent.
What is it?"

He told her what he should have said from the

beginning. The words felt like stones in his dry mouth. "On the day Mac put you on a plane to Minnesota, Jesse came to me and told me the truth. He said that you had been in his bedroom repeatedly…begging him to have sex with you to make me jealous. But he refused. He told me you probably slept with one of his friends until you were sure you were pregnant, and you planned all along to say it was Jesse's."

Bryn stared at him, frozen, her eyes blank with shock. She wet her lips. "That doesn't even make sense," she whispered.

He gazed at her bleakly. "The damned thing is, Bryn, it worked. I wanted you so much, I was sick with it. And if you had left Jesse alone, you and I might have ended up together. But you made that impossible. And then you tried to make Jesse take responsibility for another guy's kid. You disgust me."

She swayed, and he reached forward instinctively to catch her.

But she backed away, the look in her eyes difficult to see. He felt a lick of regret, a jolt of shame. It was partly his fault. If he had stayed away from her when she arrived in Wyoming, they could have avoided this unpleasant encounter.

She backed up again, her hand over her mouth. Suddenly, his pulse raced. She was too close to the edge of the drop-off.

"Bryn!" He reached for her again, urgently.

He was almost too late. Her foot hit the loose scree

at the edge of the steep hillside, her body bowed in a vain attempt to regain her balance, and she cried out as he grabbed for her.

Four

Trent cursed. In the bare seconds it had taken him to get to her, a dozen horrific scenarios filled his brain. But thank God she hadn't fallen. There would have been little to have stopped a precipitous descent—a small ledge here and there, a few low, scrubby bushes.

He held her tightly as sick relief flooded his chest. "You little fool. You could have killed yourself. What were you thinking?" He held her at arm's length. Her face was white and set. He was rigid, his stomach curling. "Are you okay? Tell me, dammit." The words came out more harshly than he had intended. She flinched, and then her expression went from vulnerable to stoic.

"I'm fine," she said. "No problem. Let me go. Get out of my way."

He ground his teeth. "Don't be stupid. You're standing on loose gravel. I'll help you."

"No." A single word. Two small letters. But the vehemence behind it made him feel like dirt.

Unfortunately, this was not a situation where he was willing to put her pride first. He didn't waste time arguing. He scooped her into his arms and took a deep breath. She went nuts, shrieking and struggling until her flailing knee nearly unmanned him.

"Bryn." His raised voice was the same one he used to put the fear of God into his employees when necessary. "Be still, damn it. Unless you want to kill us both."

She went limp in his arms, and he stepped backward carefully, keenly aware that one misstep on his part might send them hurtling down the mountain. When they were finally on firm, flat ground, he set her gently on her feet.

"C'mon," he said gruffly, grabbing up their belongings and stuffing them in his pack. "We're done here."

Bryn lifted her chin. "I'll find my own way back," she said. And she turned away and started down the mountain while he stood with his mouth open, watching, incredulous, as she did just that.

His temper boiled. He lunged after her, closing the distance in four long strides. He grabbed her arm, trying to keep a lid on his fury and losing the battle. "Don't be an idiot."

When she stopped dead, he had to pull up short to avoid knocking her over. He expected her eyes to be shooting sparks at him, but if she had been angry earlier, that emotion was long gone. Her eyes were dull. "Are you keeping count of those insults, Mr. Sinclair?" She jerked her elbow from his grasp and kept going.

They walked side by side, traversing the wide trail in silence. He noticed for the first time that she was limping slightly. No doubt the result of a blister from not having the proper footwear for the rough terrain. Stubborn woman. He ground to a halt and stopped her, as well, by the simple action of thrusting his body in front of hers. He put his hands on her shoulders, feeling her fragile bones. "You can't walk back to the house. It's almost five miles. You're not wearing hiking boots."

Her eyes were wet with unshed tears. "I don't care," she cried. "Leave me alone."

"I wish to God I could," he muttered. As they reached the Jeep, he reached in his pocket and extracted his handkerchief. "You've got some dirt on your face. Let's call a truce, Bryn. Please. For twenty minutes. That's how long it will take us to get home."

Bryn knew what it was like to have your heart broken. But the blow-up that happened six years ago paled in comparison to the utter despair now flooding her chest. Jesse's lies had been worse than she thought. He had poisoned his brother's mind so thoroughly, Bryn had no hope of making Trent see the truth.

While he maneuvered the vehicle over the rough trails, she ignored him. They completed the journey back to the house in silence. Without speaking, Trent dropped her by the front door before heading around back to the garage.

Bryn tried to slip inside unnoticed, but Mac caught

her sneaking down the hall past the kitchen. Julio had left, and Mac was fixing himself a cup of coffee.

His bushy eyebrows went up. "What in the hell happened to you, Brynnie? You look like something the cat dragged in."

Hearing the affectionate nickname stung her battered heart. She opened her mouth to explain, but was overtaken by a wave of grief. "Trent thinks I seduced Jesse," she said on a hiccupping half sob. "He'll never forgive me."

And then she broke down. Her body was sore, her feet rubbed raw, her emotions shredded. When Mac enfolded her in his big arms, she put her head on his shoulder and sighed. She hadn't realized until this very moment what a hole there had been in her life without his wise counsel and unconditional love.

He held her in silence for a few minutes, and then they went to his study and sat side by side on the oversize leather sofa.

Mac studied her face. "Talk to me, girl. Are you okay?"

Bryn managed a smile. "I'm fine…really. All I need is a shower and some clean clothes."

Then she bit her lip. "We're going to have to settle some things, Mac. I don't want to be away from Allen much longer. You're recovering on schedule. I know the grief is tough, but physically you're doing well. With lots of rest and healthy food, you'll be back to your old ornery self in no time. But I can't be here with Trent. It's an impossible situation." And with Jesse's parentage now in question her quest to secure Allen's future might be a moot point.

Mac leaned back, his arms folded across his chest. "It's my house," he said gruffly. "I invite whom I please."

She shook her head in desperation. "You don't understand what he thinks of me, Mac."

"He's wrong."

Her heart caught in her chest. Did he really believe her? After all this time? She hardly dared to hope.

Mac's expression was bleak. "I suspected as soon as you left six years ago that I had made a mistake. But bringing you back to marry Jesse would only have made things worse. You deserved far better. And Jesse needed...well, who knows what Jesse needed. So many things..."

"Did you and Jesse ever discuss me?"

He shrugged. "Not directly. But I think he knew I was suspicious of his take on the story."

"But you never put him on the spot and asked outright if he had lied?" That was what hurt so much.

The conversation had tired him. He was gray in the face suddenly and clearly exhausted.

Though it frustrated her, Bryn put her own feelings aside for the moment. She was here to help him, not make his life more upsetting. She took him by the hand. "Never mind," she said softly. "It can wait a few more days. Let's get you into bed for a nap."

He allowed her to lead him back to the bedroom, but he was still agitated. "You can't leave, Brynnie. Swear to me you'll stay."

She tucked him in and smoothed the covers. "We'll have to take it a day at a time, Mac. I can't promise more than that."

After settling Mac for his afternoon rest, Bryn retreated to her room. She had no desire to run into Trent. She was still aching from the knowledge that he believed she had seduced Jesse.

She spent part of the afternoon on the phone with Beverly.

Her aunt picked up on the tone in her voice. "What's wrong?"

"Well, Mac seems to have softened. I think he believes Allen is his grandson, but I haven't had the heart to press the paternity issue yet. Mac's really frail, and Trent is either hostile or suspicious or both."

"You'd think that Trent would want the test to prove that you're lying and let his family off the hook."

"I think he's afraid I'll manipulate Mac's emotions and get him to change the will regardless."

"I didn't get the impression that Mac was so gullible."

"He's not, definitely not. But the heart attack has changed him."

"It will all work out, honey."

"I hope so. But there's more. I found some letters that seem to indicate Jesse might not be Mac's son."

Dinner that evening was painfully uncomfortable. Mac's animated conversation was so out of character that Trent kept shooting him disbelieving glances. Trent never looked at Bryn at all.

Mac cleared his plate and finally dropped the "pleasant host" act. He glared at Trent. "Bryn's talking about going home. And I'm guessing it's your fault."

Trent snorted. "If Bryn wants to go home, she knows where the door is. I'm not stopping her."

Bryn's temper flared. "Charming." Trent Sinclair was a stubborn, arrogant beast.

He lifted an eyebrow and gazed at her coldly. "You can't blame me for wanting to protect my father."

Mac bristled. "I'm not feeble, dammit. Do you really think I'd let myself be manipulated by sentimentality?"

"It's not you I'm worried about." Trent scowled. "It's her."

Bryn felt her cheeks flush, especially because Mac watched the two of them with avid attention. In a flash, she was back on the mountaintop with Trent, his hand warm on her breast, his lips devouring hers. She cleared her throat. "I'm no threat to you or your father, Trent. And if you'd quit being an ass, you'd realize that." Her cutting reply might have been more impressive had her voice been less hoarse.

But remembering what had almost happened earlier that day made her knees weak with longing. The past and the present had melded for one brief, wonderful moment. But it hadn't lasted.

I wanted you so much, I was sick with it. The confession had been ripped from the depths of Trent's soul, and the self-disgust in his voice said more than words what he thought of her.

But fool that she was, despite Trent's obvious antipathy, she wanted him still. It was only sex. That's all. Surely she didn't really crave a relationship with a man who thought so little of her.

She stood up blindly. "Excuse me. I have phone calls to make."

Late that evening, Trent sat at the computer in the study, brooding. He could no longer ignore the evidence before him. Jesse had been stealing from the ranch. From Mac.

The knowledge made nausea churn in Trent's belly. Why? Mac would have given Jesse anything he wanted. The old man loved his youngest son dearly. There had been no need to steal.

Cause of death: heroin overdose. The coroner's report wasn't fabricated. Jesse had taken drugs at least once. The little brother Trent remembered would never have done such a thing. But Bryn was right…Trent hadn't been around much in the last few years. Mostly because of a demanding career, but in part because the ranch reminded him too much of Bryn. And the fact that she had slept with his brother, or lied, or both.

He groaned and shut down the computer. If Bryn was telling the truth about Jesse's drug habit, then Trent had not known his brother at all. But if Bryn was lying, why did Jesse die of an overdose? Neither option was at all palatable.

Bryn thought Mac had protected Jesse by covering

for him. Would Mac do that? Out of guilt perhaps…
because Etta Sinclair had left her young son when Jesse
was at such a vulnerable age?

Trent cursed beneath his breath and flung a paper clip
across the room, wishing it was something that would
shatter into a million pieces. He wanted answers, *needed*
them. Was Mac strong enough for a showdown? Trent
would never forgive himself if he caused his father to
relapse.

He got to his feet and went down the hall, treading
quietly. His father's door was open, but the room was
dim. Quiet snoring was the only sound. Mac slept like
the dead on a good day, and now that he was medicated,
he'd probably be out until morning.

Trent retreated carefully, only to find himself staring
at Bryn's bedroom door. A light shone from underneath.
It wasn't terribly late.…

Five

She was shocked to see him. It was written all over her face.

"I need to talk to you." He shut the door behind him and moved into the room.

Her nightgown lay on the bed but she was still dressed. The lingerie was a silky swathe of cream lace and mauve satin. He swallowed, dragging his gaze away from it and focusing on her face. "I have to leave in the morning."

"So soon?"

"Not for good," he said swiftly. "But I have to fly to Denver for a meeting that I can't handle over the phone. I'll be gone less than twenty-four hours."

Bryn nodded slowly. "I'll keep an eye on Mac. Despite what you think, Trent, I love him."

"Even though he sent you away?"

Her smile was wry. "I'm trying to let go of the past."

He prowled the small space between the door and the bed. "Some of us don't have that luxury."

She stood there staring at him with bare feet and a face washed clean of makeup. Young, vulnerable, sweetly sincere. "You can trust me, Trent. I swear."

His body hardened, and he groaned inwardly. How could he be sure of her when sex got in the way and clouded his judgment?

He shook his head to clear it. But when he looked at her again, she was more appealing to him than she had been mere moments before. His feet took him to her side. Her pull was inescapable.

She stiffened when he wrapped her in his arms. "I'm not playing this game with you, Trent."

The quaver in her voice hurt something deep in his chest. "I can assure you," he said roughly. "This is no game."

He kissed her because it was the only thing he could do. Because if he didn't, something inside him would shrivel and die. Because he was apparently weaker than he thought.

She was everything he had ever wanted and didn't know he needed. Her lips tasted like toothpaste and something else far more exotic. His past and his present woven into one complicated package.

She fit him perfectly, her head tucked against his shoulder, her arms wrapped loosely around his waist.

He slid a hand beneath her shirt and stroked the soft skin on her back.

When he tipped up her chin, their eyes met, his searching, hers filled with an emotion he shied away from. He wouldn't let her twist him in knots. This violent attraction was about sex, nothing more.

Slowly, waiting for her to protest, to escape his embrace, he bent his head. Their lips met easily, in perfect sync.

He moved his mouth over hers gently, dragging out the pleasure, making his own heart race with the effort to hold back. What had happened on the mountain only whetted his appetite for more. This had nothing to do with Jesse. This was about scratching an itch. Or at the very least, proving to himself how far she was willing to go. He wanted her.

Clothes drifted away in a sensual ballet. Skin heated. Voices hoarsened with desire. His and hers.

This time Bryn was the one to call a halt. Pale but calm, she slipped from the bed and donned her robe.

"I want you, Trent. But not like this. Not with mistrust between us."

Before he could summon a response, the shrill shriek of the smoke alarm sounded. For one crazed split second, he actually thought about dragging her down on the bed and saying to hell with it.

But the memory of his father jarred him to reality.

He rolled from the bed, groaning and cursing, and shoved his legs into his jeans. "This isn't over," he said.

* * *

Bryn knew her blood pressure must be through the roof. To go from desperate arousal to anxiety to fear so quickly made nausea swim in her stomach.

She found Trent and Mac in the kitchen. Trent was swearing a blue streak, and Mac presided over a ruined skillet than contained the charred remains of what must have been eggs.

Trent climbed on a chair to disable the smoke alarm. In the resultant silence, the three adults faced off in an uncomfortable triangle.

Bryn had the misfortune to giggle.

Trent glared and Mac chortled. Soon all three of them were laughing hysterically.

Trent was the first to regain control. "Good God, Dad. What in the hell were you doing? I thought you were sound asleep."

Mac's expression was sheepish. "I was hungry. And nobody will let me eat anything decent. So I was making an omelet…with whole eggs…and butter." He puffed out his chest and tried to face them down with bluster.

"I would have helped you," Bryn said mildly. She took the pan to the sink. "And since when do you know how to cook?"

"Since never. Hence the fire." Trent dropped into a chair.

Mac raked at the tufts of white hair standing in disarray all over his head. "It wasn't actually a fire," Mac muttered, sulking. "I went to the bathroom for just a second, and when I came back…"

"That one's a goner." Bryn gave up and tossed the ruined cookware in the trash bin.

Trent rubbed his forehead, where almost certainly a killer headache was attacking him. He'd not had the best half hour. Bryn felt his pain.

He looked up at both of them. "God knows I don't want to leave you two here alone, but please promise me you'll behave until I get back."

Bryn hugged Mac. "We'll be fine," she said, yawning suddenly. "Let's all get some sleep."

It didn't take a genius to figure out that any sexual overtures on Trent's part would not be repeated...at least not tonight.

There was an awkward moment in the hallway after Mac escaped to his quarters, but Bryn evaded Trent's gaze and slipped into her bedroom with a muttered good-night, closing the door behind her with a sigh of relief. Perhaps it was for the best. She didn't understand Trent's motives. And until she did, self-preservation was the order of the day.

Perhaps understandably, she overslept. She awakened to the sound of a car engine fading into the distance. Already it was clear to her that things were not the same. The house seemed empty with Trent gone. He'd always been a force to reckon with, and the world was oddly flat in his absence.

Instead of moping and trying to analyze the situation, she forced herself to get up and face the day. When Mac appeared in the kitchen, he was chipper and energetic in contrast to her aching head and troubled thoughts.

He ate his egg-white omelet and plain toast without

complaint. As Bryn picked at her oatmeal, he cocked his head. "I told Trent this morning to leave you alone so you would stay."

She felt her cheeks heat. Surely...

Mac went on. "I let him know that if he didn't have anything nice to say to you, he should keep his damn mouth shut."

Her pulse slowed to its normal pace, and she could breathe again. Mac didn't know about last night. How could he?

She twirled her spoon in the bowl. "I can handle Trent. Don't you worry. But we need to talk, Mac."

His bushy eyebrows went up. "Sounds ominous."

"Do you think Jesse's problems had anything to do with his mother's desertion?"

Mac's gaze shifted away from hers. His hands clenched. "Don't know what you mean."

"He was at a vulnerable age when she left. Sometimes kids blame themselves in situations like that."

Mac's complexion reddened alarmingly. "That was a long time ago. Jesse was a wild kid. Can't blame that on a woman who's been gone for almost twenty years."

"But what if she tried to contact him?" Did Mac know about the letters? Was that why he was getting upset?

"Forget his mother," Mac shouted. "I don't want to talk about her...ever."

The change was so dramatic, Bryn was blindsided. One minute Mac was the picture of health. And now...

He shoved back from the table and stood up so rapidly he knocked over his chair.

Bryn reached for him in alarm. "I'm sorry, Mac," she said urgently. "We'll drop it. I never should have said anything."

He backed toward the hallway. "Jesse's gone. Nothing's going to bring him back. End of story."

Mac's knees gave out beneath him. His eyes met hers, imploring, scared.

"Calm down, Mac. Everything's okay. Really." What had she done? But nothing was okay, not by a long shot.

Six

In that terrifying moment Bryn was desperately grateful that Sinclair wealth meant having access to a helicopter. A 911 call ensured that medical staff at the hospital would be waiting and ready.

Getting in touch with Trent was trickier, and she felt terrible that she was disrupting his important meeting, but she had no choice. She drove herself to the hospital and waited.

Mac was still in emergency when an ashen-faced Trent arrived. "What the hell happened? He was fine earlier. He drank his coffee while I had breakfast, and he was his old self."

Her eyes burned with tears. "I asked about Jesse's mother, and Mac went berserk."

Trent paled. "Dear God. Mac never speaks of her.

Surely you knew that. You lived here for most of your life. Etta's defection wasn't exactly dinner-table conversation. Are you *trying* to kill my father? Dammit, Bryn. What were you thinking?"

The accusation in his eyes was made all the worse by the knowledge that he was right. She should have waited.

"I'm sorry," she said. "But I wanted to get to the truth. This family has too many secrets."

In Trent's gaze, she saw not one whit of the man who had held her so intimately only hours before. He'd come straight from his meeting, and he was wearing an expensive dark suit, perfectly tailored to fit his tall, virile frame. His shoes were Italian leather. The thin gold watch on his wrist could have paid for several semesters of her schooling.

On the ranch, she had allowed herself to think of him as a normal man. But now he wore his wealth and power with a careless confidence that only underscored the gap between them.

She watched as Trent paced the drab waiting room like a caged lion. Her legs wouldn't hold her up. She picked a hard plastic chair in a far corner, sat down and stared blindly at her trembling fingers linked in her lap. Last night she had touched Trent intimately with those same hands. It seemed like a fairy tale now.

The wait was agonizing. What if Mac died? What would happen to all of them? Trent would never forgive her, much less admit that Allen was entitled to part of the estate, if indeed he was. And poor Trent...to lose his brother and father so close together. *Please, God. Let Mac be okay.*

When a young doctor came out, Bryn leaped to her feet, but Trent got there first. She had the impression he might have jerked the poor man to him by the collar if it hadn't been socially unacceptable.

Trent's hands were fisted at his sides instead. "How is he? Was it another heart attack?"

The doctor shook his head. "He's going to be fine. It was an anxiety attack. When his pulse rate skyrocketed, it probably scared him, which merely exacerbated the situation. A frightening cycle, but not life-threatening. Do you know what precipitated this?"

Bryn took a deep breath, trembling uncontrollably. "I asked him a question about his wife. She left the family eighteen years ago. I never dreamed it would still be such a sensitive subject." She stopped, choked up. "Has he suffered any lasting damage?"

The doc shook his head. "No. I want to keep him overnight for observation, but that's merely a precaution. We did a number of tests, and everything looks great. He's a strong old boy, and I predict he'll be around to aggravate you both for a long time. The two of you can go in to visit him now. Room 312."

The doctor excused himself. Trent glared at Bryn. "You stay here. I can't take the chance that seeing you will set him off again."

"But the doctor said—"

"No." He was implacable.

She waited until he took the elevator and then followed him up on the next one. Hovering in the hall, she listened anxiously to hear Mac's voice. Thankfully, he sounded a thousand times better.

Trent's deep, resonant voice was so tender and loving, she almost burst into tears.

"How are you feeling, Dad."

"Embarrassed." Mac's querulous reply might have made her smile if she hadn't been so fatigued and overwrought.

Trent spoke again. "I'll stay with you tonight. The doctor says he'll release you in the morning. Apparently you passed all the tests with flying colors. Your ticker's healing beautifully."

"Aren't you going to ask me what caused all this?"

There was a bite in Trent's reply. "No need. I already know."

"Bryn told you?"

"Yes."

"Where is she?"

"I wouldn't let her come in."

"Oh, for God's sake, boy. Don't be a complete ass. This wasn't Bryn's fault."

"It sure as hell was. If that's the kind of loving care she has to offer, we might as well go back to hiring strangers out of the phone book."

"You know the doctor said I don't really need anyone to take care of me anymore."

"So send her home."

Mac snorted. "You'd like that, wouldn't you? You're gonna have to face facts, Trent. I'm ninety-nine percent sure Jesse lied to us."

Trent's voice was icy. "Then we need to get the kid

out here, do a DNA test as soon as possible and find out once and for all."

A nurse, bustling to enter the room, jostled Bryn's shoulder and apologized swiftly. "I apologize, ma'am. I need to go in and take Mr. Sinclair's vitals."

Now Bryn would never know what Mac's reply might have been. The conversation at the bedside turned to medical details.

Bryn slipped away and pulled paper from her purse to jot a note to Trent. She passed it to the nurse's station. "Would you mind to give this to the visitor in 312 as he leaves? Thank you."

Outside, the fresh air was a welcome relief. She was appalled at her own lack of judgment when it came to Mac. Why couldn't she have left things alone?

She checked in to the small hotel around the corner from the hospital. Trent would know where she was. She'd left a note, after all. She wasn't running away.

With no luggage or toothbrush, settling into her standard issue room was a short process. After a long call home to talk to Beverly and Allen, she eyed the beds. She was running on adrenaline and about five hours of sleep total. Wearing only her blouse and underwear, she climbed into the closest clean, soft bed and was comatose in seconds.

Trent prowled the hallway while an orderly gave Mac a sponge bath. The old man was at full speed already, bossing everyone around, and cranky as hell. But the episode had scared Trent badly.

He owed Bryn an apology. In his fear and upset, he

had been harsher with her than she deserved. She had made a mistake. So what? It might have just as easily been Trent who blundered into a stressful conversation. He and his father butted heads often.

A nurse at the desk handed Trent a folded slip of paper. *I'm at the hotel. Bryn.* The doctor appeared at his side. "I'm going to give your father a light sedative so he'll rest this afternoon. Why don't you go get something to eat and come back around four? We'll call you if anything changes, but he's really doing very well, I promise."

Trent spent a few more minutes chatting with his father, but the medicine in the drip was already doing its job. When Mac's eyes fluttered shut, Trent exited the room and left the hospital.

In a small town like Jackson Hole, the long-timers all knew each other. The woman at the hotel desk was a classmate of Trent's. He gave her a tired smile. "Hey, Janine. Bryn checked in a little while ago, right? And she told you Dad's in the hospital?"

"She sure did. Poor thing looked beat. And you don't look so hot yourself."

He shrugged. "We're going to take turns sitting with him. If you'll give me another key to the room so I won't bother Bryn, and a take-out menu from anywhere—I'm not picky—I'll owe you."

He made his way down the hall and around the corner to the room Janine had indicated and swiped the key in the lock. The curtains in the room were closed, and in the dim light, he could see a Bryn-shaped lump in one of the beds. His body tightened. He was determined to have her, even if she had lied. But it would be on his terms. He would be in control. With a low curse for his own conflicted emotions, he kicked off his shoes, collapsed on top of the covers in the opposite bed and closed his eyes.

Bryn awoke to the smell of pepperoni pizza. Her stomach growled.

Her eyes snapped open when Trent's unmistakable voice sounded from close at hand. "The doctor said we could come back at four. I left you a few slices."

She sat up, carefully keeping the sheet at a decorous height, and brushed the hair out of her eyes, deeply regretting the fact that her pants were three feet away on a chair. The covers on the adjacent bed were rumpled, indicating that Trent had napped, as well.

Less than twenty-four hours ago, she had been naked and panting in this man's arms. Now she could scarcely meet his gaze.

She licked her lips, faint with hunger. She had only picked at her breakfast before Mac collapsed. "Close your eyes."

"No."

His answer took her by surprise and she looked at him head-on. Dark smudges under his eyes said he was in no better shape than she was, but he no longer looked furious.

She frowned. "Then hand me my pants."

"No." A faint grin accompanied the negative.

She crossed her arms over her chest, in no mood for a confrontation. "A gentleman would have gotten his own room. You're rich enough to buy the whole hotel. So why are you here?"

He leaned forward, elbows on his knees. "Because this is where you are." He paused and winced. "I have a temper, Bryn. You know that. But what happened with Dad this morning wasn't your fault. You acted swiftly and responsibly. No one could ask for more. I'm sorry I yelled at you."

His unprompted and uncharacteristically humble apology should have made her feel relieved. But she didn't deserve his absolution. "It *was* my fault," she said doggedly. "I never should have mentioned Etta." She had wanted to find out if Mac was aware of the letters. And she was as much in the dark now as before.

"What made you want to talk about our dearly departed mother?"

The macabre humor made her frown. Did anyone really know if Etta was dead or alive? "Well…" She cast about for an explanation that didn't involve the damning letters. She would have to share their contents with Trent, but not yet. "It occurred to me that some of Jesse's troubles could have stemmed from her leaving you all at such young ages. But you and Gage and Sloan turned out okay."

His expression hardened. "We were older. We understood what she had done and why. We didn't weave any fairy tales about her coming back. At least not after the first few days."

"You were *eleven*, Trent. An age when a boy still needs his mother."

He shrugged. "We had Dad. And if Etta cared so

little about her family that she could simply walk out, we didn't need her or want her."

Her heart bled for the stoic little child he had been. He wouldn't even refer to her as *Mother*. "And Jesse?"

"Jesse was different. He was only six. He cried every night for a month. We all took turns sleeping with him so that when he had nightmares, we'd be there to comfort him. He liked Gage the best. Gage would tell him stories about places all over the world...about the adventures the two of them would have one day. Jesse loved it."

"How long was it before he got over her leaving?"

"I don't know that he ever did. But he learned to man up and show he didn't need her to be happy."

But he did. Apparently Jesse had needed Etta a heck of a lot, and when he was a teenager, she wormed her way back into his life and drove him crazy. The thought gave her a shiver. She wanted so badly to unburden herself to Trent, to lean on his strength and counsel.

But with the specter that Jesse might not be a Sinclair, she didn't know what to do. It was naive to expect Trent to believe that Allen was Jesse's son without proof. She had wanted Trent to take her on faith, but *her* feelings were not as important as making sure Allen was taken care of.

Anything could happen to Bryn. And Aunt Beverly wouldn't always be around. Bryn had believed for six years that her son was a Sinclair, heir to a mighty empire that would make his life secure. The truth needed to come out. For all of them.

Once again, she eyed her distant jeans.

Trent stood, arms crossed over his chest, and grinned at her predicament.

"Aren't you being a little ridiculous, Brynnie? I've seen it all."

Her face flamed. "That was different."

"Different, how?"

"We were in the mood."

"I seem to always be in the mood around you."

His self-deprecating smile loosened the knot in her chest. A teasing Trent made her willpower evaporate. "We need to keep track of the time."

"We have all the time in the world."

He glanced at his watch, and her stomach flipped… hard.

He handed her the pizza box. "But never say I seduced you on an empty stomach."

"No seduction," she said primly as she gobbled a slice of pizza with unladylike fervor. "We have to go see Mac."

His eyes were like a watchful hawk. "It's only two-thirty. I can do a lot in an hour and a half."

Every atom of oxygen in the room evaporated as their eyes met. Hunger snapped its bounds and prowled between them. She trembled as each second of the heated moments in her bedroom unfolded in her imagination in Technicolor images complete with scent and sound.

The crust she held fell with a loud thud into the box. Trent took the cardboard container from her numb fingers and tossed it in the trash can. He sat beside her on the bed and twirled a strand of her hair around his finger. "We'll figure this all out, Bryn."

The knowledge that she was lying by omission choked her. "I don't know that we can. Some things can't be fixed."

He kissed her softly, then with more force. "I'll make it all right. You'll see."

She let him hold her, but her heart ached. Trent Sinclair was a man used to winning, to conquering, to molding the world to his specifications. But even the king occasionally had to admit defeat.

He nuzzled her neck. "Don't think so much. Just feel, Bryn. Let it happen."

Their lips met tentatively. Last night everything had seemed new and different. Now she knew the truth. Trent Sinclair was a hard-ass as far as the world was concerned. He kept his feelings under wraps. But beneath that proud, arrogant exterior, he was a man of great passion.

She kissed his chin, his nose, his eyelids. "I feel guilty. We should be at the hospital."

"He's sleeping. The doc said so. Hush and let me love you." He stroked her back as he magically made her reservations disappear.

She heard the four letter word and managed not to react. It was something men said when they wanted a woman. He didn't mean he loved her. She realized that. She was far too intelligent to delude herself.

Which meant that she had to be smart about this. She wanted Trent. Badly. But now was not the time.

"You nearly convinced me," she said, her heart aching for a multitude of reasons. "But one of us has to be sane.

I'll go sit with him. I'm sure you have some business calls you need to make."

Trent pondered what would have happened if they had not been interrupted last night. Today the mood was less mystical, more pragmatic. But she was as much a siren to him as she had been in the quiet intimacy of her bedroom. He reclined on his side, easing her down with him. Beneath her shirt, he traced the lace at the edge of her bra, feeling gooseflesh erupt everywhere his fingers passed.

Bryn studied him, big-eyed, her pupils dilated, her soft breathing ragged. Her chest rose and fell. She lay quiescent, passive. What was she thinking? He liked to believe he was a good judge of women, but Bryn was a conundrum wrapped in a puzzle. Young, but mature beyond her years. Inexperienced, but wildly passionate.

He reached for the tiny plastic hook at the middle that secured the two sides of the bra. As he unfastened it, her breasts fell free, lush, warm, soft as velvet. He pushed up her blouse and buried his face in them, inhaling the scent that was so evocatively Bryn. Her hands played with his hair, sending heat down his spine and making him wish they had all night instead of a snatched hour in an impersonal hotel room.

He would take her…soon. But he would delay his own satisfaction. This particular moment was about establishing control. He stroked her thighs, touched her center still hidden beneath satin and lace. Bryn groaned even at that light caress, her eyes now closed. He rubbed her gently, feeling her heat, the dampness that signaled her readiness for him. He increased the pressure, the tempo. Her hips lifted instinctively.

Slowly, wanting to give her every iota of pleasure, he slipped two fingers beneath the narrow strip of cloth between her legs, and then thrust inside her with a quick motion. Bryn gave a sharp, keening cry and moved against his hand, riding the waves of pleasure that caused her inner muscles to squeeze his fingers.

The eroticism of her release made him sweat. His erection throbbed with a burning ache. But he drew on his iron will and refused to allow himself to be at her mercy. Trent couldn't lie to himself any longer. He was soft when it came to Bryn. And it pissed him off that he didn't really want her to leave. His hunger for her was a weakness. And that vulnerability was trying to persuade him that she was innocent. That she was telling the truth.

Which made him the world's biggest jackass. Powerful men were brought down by scheming women all the time. He hoped like hell she was being honest with him. But if worse came to worst…if she had lied about Jesse…well…Trent's loyalties were clear. Protecting Mac…and protecting Jesse's memory.

But the effort to maintain the upper hand cost him.

He looked down at her broodingly. "You're right. One of us should be at the hospital. And I need to deal with the mess in Denver. I shouldn't have started this right now. I'm sorry."

Her flushed cheeks and tousled hair made her even

more beautiful than usual. He stroked her cheek. "Say something."

Her smile was wry. "What's left to say? I can wait until you trust me...but can *you?*"

Seven

Bryn's heart slugged hard in her chest. She had let herself fall in love with Trent Sinclair.

In the beginning she had fooled herself, thinking that all she wanted was for Trent to forgive her, to believe her and to show her the same gentle camaraderie and friendship they had once shared.

Later, she had told herself it wouldn't be hurting anyone if she dared to enjoy Trent's bed. After all, she'd been living like a nun. She deserved some pleasure.

But now...oh, God...now...

She had done the unforgivable. She had tumbled head over heels, gut-deep in love with a man who was as inaccessible to her as the moon. Trent didn't trust her. Might never trust her. And even if the truth eventually came to light, Bryn had a child. Jesse's son. A boy whose existence might drive a permanent wedge between Bryn and the man she had always loved.

Even if Trent finally accepted her at face value, the situation was hopeless. Even the least intuitive person could see that a happy ending was an oxymoron in this situation.

She turned her head to look at the man who had wreaked such havoc in her life. He was seated on the far side of the opposite bed with his back to her. His voice on the phone was different...sharper, more commanding. She could almost see the employee on the other end of the call scrambling to follow orders.

But Trent was not an ogre. He was disciplined. Fair.

He would hate the description, but he was a beautiful man inside and out. Completely masculine, tough, steady, honorable.

She couldn't fault him, really, for choosing to believe his brother instead of Bryn. Jesse was his flesh and blood. And Trent had spent a lot of years looking after Jesse, making sure he was happy.

Much like Bryn felt about her son. She would do anything for Allen. Including risking Trent's wrath to prove that Allen deserved to be recognized as a Sinclair.

But what she could *not* do was let this thing with Trent go any further. No matter how much she wanted to...no matter how wonderful it was to be in his arms, his life, his bed. Already, her heart was breaking. They had no future...none at all.

She dressed quietly and slipped from the room. Mac

was just rousing as Bryn arrived. "You look good," she said. "Let me help you with that dinner tray."

"Hospital food tastes like crap."

Despite his grumbling about the bland food, Mac polished off a piece of baked fish, green beans and carrots. His protest was halfhearted and she knew the collapse had scared him.

Mac sipped tepid iced tea through a straw. "Where's Trent?"

"He was on the phone when I left. He'll be here soon."

"What's going on between you two?"

She winced inwardly, but managed not to react. "Nothing but the usual. He still isn't sure he can trust me."

"The boy's a fool."

"You were on the same page not so long ago," she reminded him gently. "Until Jesse died and you had to face the truth. Give Trent some slack. He's doing his best. Losing Jesse has shaken him. Especially since it came out of the blue."

Guilt washed over Mac's face. He poked at a carrot with his fork. "I didn't want the three boys to know how bad it was. I thought I could whip Jesse into shape, keep a close eye on him. I'm responsible for his death as much as anyone."

Seeing the proud Mac Sinclair with tears streaking down his leatherlike cheeks was almost more than Bryn could bear. She moved the dinner tray and scooted onto the bed beside him, putting her arm around his shoulder. "Don't be a horse's hiney," she said softly. "You were a wonderful father to all four of your boys…and a dear grandfather to me."

"I sent you away." He rested his head against her chest, his eyes closed.

"You did what you thought was right."

"Can you ever forgive me?"

"Of course," she said simply. "Aunt Beverly was so good to me. And Allen adores her. I'm fine, Mac. No harm, no foul."

They sat there in silence, both of them lost in thought.

Finally, Mac gave a wheezing sigh and moved fretfully in the bed. Bryn stood up and smoothed the covers.

He folded his arms across his chest, wrestling with the IV. "Trent thinks we should get a test…as soon as possible. So there won't be any questions. But I don't want to."

The packet of letters in her room mocked her. Would a paternity test destroy her hope of securing her son's future? "Why not, Mac? We all need to know the truth."

"I trust you, Brynnie, my girl."

At that very moment, Trent walked in. If he had heard the end of their conversation, he gave no sign.

"You're looking better, Dad. Nothing like a visit from a beautiful woman to perk up a man."

Mac chuckled, but the bland glance Trent sent Bryn's way made her knees weak. It was hard enough to deal with a suspicious, angry Trent. How on earth was she supposed to find the strength to resist the charming, seductive version? One glance from those dark eyes and she was ready to drag him into the nearest broom closet.

She cleared her throat, forcing herself to look at Trent. "I'm going to stay with Mac tonight. The nurse said they can bring in a cot for me. Why don't you go back to the ranch to check on things and then come back in the morning to pick us up."

"I thought we were both going to stay at the hotel." A frown creased Trent's forehead.

"It was great to have a place to nap, but I'll be fine here. And Mac says he promised several of the men the weekend off. Isn't that right, Mac?"

"Yep. Brynnie will be here if I need anything, and they're predicting storms tonight. I'd feel better if you were at the ranch. Do you mind, son?"

"Sounds like I've been outvoted." Trent's lips quirked. "But, sure. If that's what you want, Dad."

Bryn and Trent sat with Mac until almost eight o'clock that evening. Trent brought cafeteria food up for Bryn and him to eat. In some ways, it was almost like old times, the teasing, the laughter. They avoided any and all topics that might be upsetting to Mac.

But finally, it was time for Trent to leave. He touched Bryn's shoulder. "Walk me out to the car."

She did so reluctantly, unwilling to be alone with him but unable to think of a good excuse. They stopped off in the gift shop and Bryn bought a toothbrush and toothpaste. She tucked them in her purse with the sales slip and followed Trent outside. "Call my cell," she said, "and I'll let you know when the doctor says he can be dismissed."

Trent leaned a hip against the car. "Okay. I doubt you'll get any sleep tonight. Are you sure you don't want to keep the hotel room and let us take turns?"

She shook her head. "Mac will feel better about the ranch this way." A suddenly gust of wind sent her hair flying. The skies were darkening as storm clouds built. "You should go," she said. "So you won't have to drive in what's coming."

Trent smoothed her hair behind her ears, both of his hands cupping her cheeks. His gaze was troubled. "I want to believe in you," he muttered.

The husky words went straight to her heart. Was she imagining the caring and tenderness in his voice? She stepped away from him, gathering her courage, though all she wanted to do was rest in his arms. "But you can't," she said, the words barely audible.

He thrust his hands in his pockets. "You expect a lot."

She forced herself to say the words. "I can't be intimate with a man who despises me."

For a split second, he stood, poleaxed, before his face closed up and a mask of arrogance cloaked his inner emotions. "I don't despise you, Brynnie. That's the problem."

She shifted from one foot to the other, wincing as thunder rolled in the distance. "Perhaps in light of Mac's most recent incident, we need to concentrate all our focus on him."

Trent's black scowl sent a shiver down her spine.

She held out a hand. "Let's face it. We have nothing in common, Trent. You're leaving very soon…as soon as Gage gets here. Mac might get the wrong idea if he realizes we've been…"

"Screwing?"

His deliberate crudity hurt. "You were always special to me, Trent. And what we did this afternoon was—"

He grabbed her wrist. "If you say *fun,* so help me, God, I'll shake you, Bryn. But don't worry, sweetheart." A sneer curled his perfect lips. "I get the message. You have a short attention span when it comes to men. Maybe Jesse was right about you after all."

He lowered his mouth to hers, giving her no time to protest. But his lips were gentler than his mood, less combative, coaxing rather than demanding her submission. His tongue invaded her mouth, devastating, as he mimicked the sex act. Her knees went weak. She clung to his arms for support. Even now, with intense emotion radiating from his big frame, she felt no fear, no urge to run.

His hips were melded to hers, leaving no doubt about his state of mind. His erection pressed insistently against her lower abdomen. He was giving her what she craved… perhaps for the last time. And all she wanted to do was meet his raging hunger with her own desperate need for him.

It was over too soon. He shoved her away, his chest heaving. "We're not done with this, Bryn. Not by a long shot."

He got in the car, slammed the door and sped away, leaving her on the sidewalk.

* * *

Trent swore violently. How in the hell had she done it to him again?

Was she scared? Or was this part of a Machiavellian plan? Did she think she could turn him into a sex-starved, drooling idiot?

How dare she throw their lovemaking in his face? He'd begun to trust her, to believe in her. And she was deliberately trying to drive him away. He sent the car careening down the road, mile after mile, until reason prevailed and he eased his foot off the accelerator. He'd be no good to anyone dead. Mac was depending on him, and Trent didn't have the luxury of letting his temper reign.

Back at the ranch, he dealt with the various chores on autopilot, his brain racing madly to understand Bryn's behavior. The storm struck with a vengeance, drenching him as he ran from barn to stable to house. When he was finally done for the night, he showered and prowled the halls, wandering from room to room, the electricity in the air keeping him on edge.

He would have bet his entire fortune that Bryn's responses to him had been real...heartfelt. Thinking about last night and this afternoon made him hard as a pike again, and he stood at the large plate-glass window, nude, watching the fury of the storm.

In his memory he saw the smooth perfection of her skin, the way her body responded to his touch. Her warmth. Her scent. His chest hurt, and he rubbed it absently. Jesse stood beside him in the night, a wraith, a painful puzzle.

"Why did you do it, Jesse?" He put his hand on the cold glass. "Why lie about Bryn? Why the stealing? The drugs?"

His only answer was the howl of the wind and the beating of his own heart.

"Hey, boss. Good to have you back."

Trent grinned at the young intern who had the temerity to poke his head into the private office. "Get to work, Chad. Or we'll cut your pay." The cheeky twenty-year-old from the University of Colorado was smart, self-motivated and had fought hard for this unpaid position. He reminded Trent a little of himself at that age.

When the door closed once again, Trent got up from his broad cherry desk and paced the expanse of thick royal-blue carpet. The huge plate-glass window on the opposite wall showcased Denver's downtown skyline, but Trent barely spared it a glance.

After making sure Mac was safely back on his home turf, Trent had come to Denver again to wrap up the business that had been interrupted. He'd half expected the adrenaline of his usual routine to keep his mind off Bryn.

It hadn't worked.

He told himself that he was glad to be back in the office…that the rush of trying to pack two weeks of work into seventy-two hours was exhilarating. And to some extent it was. But for the first time in forever, his personal life took center stage, no matter how hard he tried to pretend otherwise.

His secretary, Carol, was the next to interrupt. "Just wanted to remind you that Mr. Greenfield will be here in twenty minutes. Will you be using the conference room?"

"Yes. And please make sure Ed and Terrence are there."

She nodded and started to leave.

Trent held up a hand to stop her. "Carol...do you think I'm a good judge of character?"

She laughed and then realized he was serious. "I've never seen anyone put anything past you."

"Thanks." He was embarrassed suddenly.

"Is there a problem I can help with?" Her head tilted at a quizzical angle.

"No, not really. Just a situation with a woman."

Her eyebrows went up, and he felt himself go red. "Never mind. Forget I said anything."

The older woman grinned. "One piece of advice, if you don't mind. Don't ever assume you can use business principles in a personal interaction with the female sex. That will blow up every time."

When she closed the door quietly behind her, Trent scrubbed his hands over his face and groaned. He should have a plan before he went home, but he was damned if he could think about anything but getting Bryn in his bed.

He hadn't talked to her once since he left. On purpose. And Mac continued to evade questions about Jesse and the past. Trent felt like everyone was keeping secrets from him, but that was going to end. It was time for a showdown.

* * *

When business was tied up and Trent felt comfortable that his staff could handle things for another couple of weeks, he flew home.

It was late when he arrived at the ranch. He'd used a car service from the airport. His first stop was his father's bedroom. Mac was sleeping peacefully.

When Trent stopped at Bryn's door, he called himself all kinds of a fool. Before his knuckles could make contact with the wood, he jerked his hand back. He turned on his heel and headed for the barn, his forehead covered in a cold sweat. If something didn't break soon, he was going to go mad. He saddled one of the powerful stallions and led him outside. Only then did he see the silent figure perched on the corral railing. Had she been there all along?

He led the horse to where she sat. Before he could say anything, she beat him to the punch. Her features were shrouded in shadow. "It's dangerous to ride at night." Her voice was low, musical. He felt it caress him like a physical stroke down his spine.

He shrugged, putting one foot into the stirrup and sliding easily into the saddle. It creaked beneath his weight. "I *feel* dangerous," he said bluntly. "So you'd be smart to stay out of my way."

With him on horseback, they sat eye to eye. Heat shimmered in the air between them, despite the chilly Wyoming night. The emotions that had consumed him… anger…disbelief…disillusionment…all receded, leaving in their wake a sexual hunger so intense he had to grip the reins and clench his teeth to keep from letting her see.

Bryn held out her hand. "Take me with you."

Bryn was done with denying the inevitable. She wanted Trent. She *needed* him. She'd deal with the fallout later. His big body vibrated with something… anger…desire. He had every right to be furious with her. She'd run hot and cold like the worst kind of tease.

Was he still angry? Did she care? She ached with missing him.

For long, quivering seconds, he didn't move. Then with a noise that was part exasperation, part muffled laugh, he edged the animal closer to the rail and extended his arm. "Why not," he muttered, helping her sling a leg across the horse's back and settle between his arms.

She felt the warmth of his body against her back and was excruciatingly aware that his big, hard thighs bracketed hers. Her bottom pressed intimately to the area where he was most male. She tried to scoot forward a few inches, but he dragged her back, letting her feel the imprint of his erection.

Her breath seemed caught in her chest, her lungs starved for air. All around them, mysterious night sounds broke the silence, but Bryn could hear little over the pounding of her own heart in her ears.

Trent held the reins easily, his body one with the horse. Bryn had ridden since she was four, but she had no illusions about her horsemanship. Without Trent, she would never dare attempt a night ride.

They started out slowly, picking their way out of the

yard toward the road. It would be the only safe place for what Trent had in mind.

He bent his head. She felt his breath, warm and intimate, against her ear. "Forget about everything," he murmured. "Forget Jesse, my dad, your son. Let's outrun our demons while we can."

She nodded slowly. He was right. They both needed this. In the house, they were always tiptoeing, literally and metaphorically, Mac's welfare foremost in their minds.

Tonight, in the scented darkness, nothing existed but the two of them.

Trent urged the horse to a trot and then a gallop. The powerful animal complied eagerly, his hooves pounding the hard-packed earth, kicking up tiny clouds of dust. The speed should have frightened Bryn, but with Trent's arms around her, she felt invincible.

The horse ran for miles. The air grew colder as the night waned. Bryn's nose and fingers were chilled, but everywhere else she was toasty warm. Her head lolled against Trent's shoulder. She could swear she felt his lips on the side of her neck from time to time.

Finally, the horse tired. They were miles from home when Trent reined the stallion in and lifted Bryn to set her on the ground. Moments later, he joined her.

For a few seconds, she was confused, but then her eyes cut through the darkness. They had stumbled across a cabin far out on the property. The ranch hands used it mostly in the summers, either for work or when they wanted to cut loose and have some fun.

Had this been Trent's destination all along? Or had he come here subconsciously?

She swallowed hard. Trent was right. Danger cloaked them, locked them in a vacuum that allowed nothing in, nothing out. Her heart beat in her throat like a frightened bird's. She wanted him. Even if it led to heartbreak later. Tonight was all that mattered.

A narrow stream, much of the year nonexistent, flowed beside the cabin. Trent tied the animal with access to grass and water, and then turned to face Bryn. He was little more than a phantom in the dark night. Only his white shirt glowed. When he held out his hand, she stepped forward to take it. Their fingers linked… comfortably, naturally.

Once inside, Bryn waited impatiently as Trent lit a kerosene lantern and began building a fire. He squatted in front of the fireplace, his broad shoulders stretching the seams of his starched cotton button-down. His jeans were ancient, but the shirt was one of a dozen just like it. The Trent uniform, as she liked to think of it.

The combination of ragged jeans and pristine dress shirt summed up the mystery that was Trent Sinclair. He could go from polished businessman to rugged rancher in the blink of an eye. And both personas exuded confidence and sexuality.

Bryn felt the first ribbons of warmth from the fire. The room was small. Trent had created a roaring blaze that soon knocked the chill off the unadorned space. Other than the wooden chair where Bryn perched, the only furnishings were the straw tick mattress and the iron bedstead.

Trent opened a metal chest—thankfully mouseproof—and extracted a couple of old quilts, clean but worn. Bryn's pulse jerked. Trent spread one over the mattress and dropped the second one at the end of the bed.

He stared at her. "You can take off that jacket, Bryn. It's plenty warm in here."

Was there a dare in his voice? She removed the garment slowly, aware that Trent's narrow gaze tracked every movement.

She wore jeans like he did, though hers were newer, and a simple, long-sleeved tee. Because of the jacket, she'd decided to forgo a bra. Trent's hungry expression signaled his approval. Her nipples hardened. He made no pretense of looking away.

He stalked her then, and she hated herself for backing up against the door. She wasn't afraid of Trent Sinclair. But tell that to her ragged breath and trembling limbs.

When they stood toe-to-toe, Trent lifted a hand and touched her chin, just her chin. "Is this want you want? Sex with me?"

A brutally honest question. No euphemisms about *making love*. She inhaled sharply. "Do you believe me about Jesse?"

He stepped back, enough that she could breathe again. "I don't know. Not yet. It's too soon to tell."

Her head dropped. "I see."

He touched the soft fall of her hair. "I'm not sure that you do. He was my brother, Bryn. And I loved him. He died in suspicious circumstances, and I can't wrap my head around that."

"So what are you saying?"

He shrugged. "I don't know what the future will bring. I'm not convinced of your motives or your reasons for being here. But I can put that aside for the moment if you can."

"To have sex."

"Yes. We ache for each other. Don't pretend you don't know it. We've been waiting six years for this. That's a long time to want something. I need you."

I need you. The stark statement was a gift in its own way. The unflappable Trent Sinclair had allowed her a glimpse of his vulnerability. She could throw it in his face…try to hurt him. But any pain she inflicted would ricochet and shred her heart in the process.

She shoved her hands in her pockets, feeling as if she might fly apart. "And afterward?"

A flush of color marked his cheekbones, and his dark eyes glittered with desire. "I don't think once will be enough. I want to take you over and over and over until we're both too weak to stand."

She gasped and covered the sound with a cough. The image painted by his stark words made her tremble with yearning. He wanted her. He needed her. Could she bear it if he turned on her when the deed was done?

"I'm scared."

His wicked grin was a slash of white teeth. "You should be, Bryn. You definitely should be."

Eight

A violent crack of thunder made them both jump. Bryn's shaky laugh held nerves. "At least you're honest."

He sighed raggedly, wanting to make her happy, wanting to reassure her. "Nothing on earth could stop me from taking you in the next five minutes, Bryn," he said. "Unless you change your mind."

His outward calm was hard-won. He wanted to ravage her, rip the clothes from her body, and plunge inside her until the torment in his gut subsided.

"I won't." Her gaze was steady.

Suddenly he was consumed by a wave of tenderness. "Come here," he said, the simple words guttural and low.

She hesitated long enough to terrify him, and then she closed the small gap between them. She lifted her hands to his face, cupping his cheeks, staring into his eyes as if she could delve the secrets of his heart. "I'm here," she whispered. "I'm here."

He lifted her in his arms and carried her to their makeshift bed. He had imagined having sex with Bryn a million times over the years, but in his fantasies, there was always a luxurious bed, scented sheets, quiet music. Reality was a stark contrast, but he couldn't have stopped if he wanted to. His only regret was that Bryn might be disappointed.

He laid her down carefully and stood over her. "If you want to say no, now is the time." If she did, it would cripple him. But he was damned if he'd let her accuse him of forcing her.

She curled on her side, one hand tucked beneath her cheek. "I won't say no. But I'm not sure this is wise."

He groaned, ripping off his clothes and tossing them aside. "It isn't wise. It's insane, Bryn. But to hell with everything else. Surely we deserve this one night."

The bed creaked as he knelt and made short work of undressing her. Her skin was smooth, pure cream. Naked, she looked infinitely smaller and more fragile. Innocent. But she had the curves of a woman, and his hands shook as he touched her reverently.

Her breasts were sensitive, and he spent what seemed like hours kissing them, weighing their plump firmness in his palms, teasing the pert, dark pink nipples with his tongue and teeth. Each gasp and moan fed his hunger.

When he saw her bite her lip, he put the back of his hand to her hot cheek. "Don't be embarrassed. I love watching you respond to my touch. You're beautiful. Even more now than when you were eighteen."

"I have stretch marks." Her eyes shadowed with insecurities.

He stilled, not wanting the intrusion of the past to ruin the present. An unseen little boy came between them for a moment, and Trent's brain shied away from acknowledging the conflict that lingered just offstage.

With a shaky hand, he swallowed hard, forcing himself to trace one faint silvery line at her hip. "No mother should ever apologize for that. You are young and lovely and sexy as hell."

He wasn't sure if what he saw in her eyes was gratitude or doubt. "No regrets," he said huskily. "Tonight's all about pleasure."

The pupils in her eyes were dilated, her breathing rapid. "Then I want to touch you," she said. She pushed at his shoulders. "Lie on your back."

Bryn hadn't seen a naked man in six years...and in truth, Jesse had been more a boy than a man. So, the reality of Trent's tough, toned body was enough to make a woman swoon. His skin was a light golden-tan all over except for a paler strip at his hips.

She paused a moment to wonder jealously if he vacationed in the tropics at some wildly expensive private island with a string of girlfriends, but she doggedly pushed the thought away. He was here with *her* now.

He tucked his hands behind his head, leaving her free to explore at will. His chest was firm and lightly sculpted with muscle. A smattering of silky, dark hair emphasized his upper chest, slid between his rib cage, and arrowed all the way down to his… She gulped, feeling gauche and in way over her head. Trent was an experienced man with sophisticated tastes.

What did she know about pleasing him?

Hesitantly, she placed her hands on his shoulders. His skin was hot and smooth. His chest rose and fell once…sharply. He closed his eyes. She leaned over him awkwardly, kissing his eyelids, his nose, his full, sensual lips. She didn't linger at his mouth. Too much danger of him taking over and derailing her mission.

Even his ears fascinated her. She traced them with a fingertip and repeated the motion with her tongue. She was shocked when her simple caress made him groan and shake.

His sharp jawline bore the evidence of late-day stubble. She liked the rough texture, because it made him seem more human, less polished. With his eyes closed, he appeared docile, but she was not stupid. Trent Sinclair was powerful in every way. For him to allow her such intimate access was a concession that was only temporary.

She moved her splayed fingers lightly down his chest, pausing to rub her thumbs over his small, brown nipples. He flinched, but didn't open his eyes. His jaw could have been chiseled stone.

Her palms burned from the heat he radiated. She reached his hip bones and lost her courage.

Trent moaned and, still with his eyes closed, took one hand from behind his head and grasped her wrist. Gently, but inexorably, he placed her fingers on his erection. He was long and thick and fully aroused. She gripped his hard flesh and felt a rush of excitement fill the pit of her stomach.

Carefully, she stroked him. His flesh tightened and flexed in her grasp. He was hot as fire, hard as velvet-covered steel, and so amazingly alive. Without weighing the consequences, she bent her head and tasted him. His hips came off the bed, and he gasped.

His eyelids flew open. He looked at her with an expression that sent heat pulsating wildly between her thighs. He managed a tight smile. "That feels good, Bryn. So damned good."

The guttural words bolstered her confidence. She had no experience to guide her, but she wanted to know everything about Trent Sinclair. What made him smile, what made him shiver, what made him shudder in passion.

She loved the intimacy of the act, the feeling of power, the exultation of being able to please him despite her naïveté. But he stopped her too soon, his expression rueful. "Not all the way. Not this time. I want to be inside you when I come."

Her face went scarlet. She could feel it. And for a moment, she panicked. Trent was a male in his prime, a dominant animal, a man set on a course with only one possible outcome. What was she doing? What was she thinking? Could she seriously spend one night in Trent Sinclair's arms and not pay the consequences?

His smile was more a grimace as he lifted her on top of him. "My turn. And this way I can see all of you."

The position made her feel horribly vulnerable. He

had not joined their bodies. His erection brushed the folds of her damp sex and made her quiver helplessly.

He studied her body intently, his gaze drifting from her face to her breasts to the place where their bodies were so close to consummation. His hands gripped her hips. "You're beautiful, Bryn. But back then you were so young...."

His voice trailed off, his expression troubled.

She was the one to take *his* hand this time. She placed it on her breast. "Nothing matters outside this room, remember? We're taking this night for us. Don't think about the past or the future. Touch me. I've never wanted anything more."

Her impassioned speech broke the spell that held him still. He toyed with her breasts, plucked at her taut nipples, tugged them until she cried out. His eyes flashed, and he came to life suddenly, dragging her down to crush her breasts against his chest as he kissed her wildly.

He thrust his tongue between her teeth, taking what he wanted. She tasted the wine he had drunk earlier in the evening, felt the urgency of his hunger as he explored the recesses of her mouth.

Her head swam dizzily. The acrid smoke from the lantern and from the fire mingled with the scent of aroused male. She smelled his familiar aftershave and the tang of his soap.

For a split second, as he put her beneath him, fear pierced her muddled senses. She should tell him...

"I want you, Bryn." His voice cracked as he nibbled her earlobe. "I can't wait." He reached blindly for his pants on the floor, found his wallet, and extracted three condom packets, still linked.

Her stomach clenched. "Are you always so prepared?" she asked petulantly.

"No. Actually, I'm not." His eyes locked on hers with determination. "But I've been carrying these around since the first day you arrived...for insurance. I knew how I felt about you. I've always known. And I wasn't going to let bad planning on my part put you at risk. Do you believe me?"

His eyes were warm. She saw the essence of the man he was in their depths. "Yes," she whispered. "I believe you."

She flinched involuntarily as he parted her thighs and she felt the tip of his erection enter her.

"Relax, sweetheart. I won't hurt you," he said gruffly. He stilled and kissed her eyelids.

But he did. It was inevitable. When he pushed forward, filling her steadily, he met resistance, tightness.

A half-dozen years of celibacy made her body unused to penetration. She gasped once, and then clenched her teeth. It was getting better already. The painful fullness was morphing into a stinging sensation that might be pleasure.

He reared back in shock, but didn't disengage their bodies. "Brynnie?" His incredulous gaze bore a hint of panic.

She squeezed her eyes shut, wanting to concentrate on the incredible sensation of having him fill her completely. "It's okay," she panted. "Really. I can handle it."

But something changed. He continued to take her in deep, long thrusts, but he was so gentle, so protective, that her eyes stung with tears. He wouldn't say the words anytime soon, perhaps never, but his body was making love to hers.

His hips pressed her to the mattress, but he kept his considerable weight on his arms, looming over her in the flickering light. Sweat sheened his chest. He was breathing like a marathon runner, his eyes glazed with hunger. She whimpered as he ground his pelvis into hers, putting maximum pressure on the tiny bundle of nerves that controlled her release.

She wrapped her legs around his waist, needing to be closer still. This was what she wanted, what she had dreamed of for years. And the reality far surpassed her limited imagination. She hovered on the edge of climax.

She wouldn't have objected if he had maintained the incredible sequence of penetration and release all night. It was that good. But his body got the best of him. She felt his sudden tension, heard his muffled shout, and then groaned with him as he took his release in a rapid-fire series of thrusts that toppled her over the edge, as well, into a starburst of sensation that seemed to last forever. Trent Sinclair was well worth the wait.

Trent felt remarkably similar to the time he'd been half trampled by one of his father's prize bulls. He could barely catch his breath and his heartbeat wouldn't slow down, no matter how much he tried to relax.

In contrast, Bryn slept in his arms like a limp, weary,

dark-haired temptress. He brushed a strand of hair from her cheek and sighed. He was in big trouble, because now that he'd had her, there was no way in hell he'd be able to let her walk away. She was his. That much he knew with a visceral, inescapable certainty.

He looked down at their bodies. The way she clung to him was natural. Right. His arm tightened around her waist, and he wondered how long a gentleman would let her sleep before instigating round two.

He wasn't a completely terrible son. His cell phone was in his jeans pocket, so if Mac woke and needed anything, Trent was accessible. But the truth was, Trent and Bryn had the whole night to themselves, and some invisible, pivotal moment had occurred…though he wasn't quite sure what it all meant.

Bryn was almost a virgin…if there was such a thing. Her body hadn't accepted his willingly. She'd been fully aroused, no doubt about that. But he'd had a difficult time penetrating her incredibly tight passage.

Which must mean she had gone without sex for a very long time. And that picture sure as hell didn't jive with Jesse's description of Bryn as a seducer and a promiscuous teen.

He tucked the quilt around her bare shoulder, lingering to smooth the faded fabric against her warm body. He was in deep now. He'd made such a big deal of trusting his brother because of blood ties, but more and more it was becoming apparent that Jesse was not what he seemed.

Jesse had stolen from the ranch, from Mac. And the money had been used to buy drugs…at least once.

Though Trent fought the sickening knowledge with everything in his heart, it only made sense to admit that Jesse had funded a secret addiction via his access to the ranch accounts.

Jesse had described Bryn as a manipulative, sexually active girl. But the woman to whom Trent had just made love was innocent and inexperienced, her body barely able to accept his at first. So in all likelihood, Jesse had lied about that, as well.

For the first time, Trent allowed himself to think about Bryn's little boy. Somewhere in Minnesota there was a kid who might be a Sinclair. If Bryn was telling the truth, then Mac and Trent had treated Bryn abysmally. But what motive would Jesse have had for lying about his relationship with Bryn? Surely Jesse knew that Mac would have welcomed Bryn as a permanent member of the family.

Perhaps for Jesse the answer was painfully simple. Perhaps Jesse hadn't wanted the responsibility of a wife and child. Trent would never know for sure.

Too many questions. Too few answers.

He eased carefully from the bed and stoked the fire. It was 3:00 a.m. Soon he and Bryn would have to go back to the house. And then what would happen? Nothing was resolved. Was Trent going to confront his sick father with the evidence of Jesse's perfidy? Or should he clean up the mess and say nothing?

The trouble was, the Sinclairs had too many secrets already. Secrets that had caused pain and heartache. And Trent was no closer than ever to knowing how to sort it all out.

He slid back into bed, chilled, and groaned his appreciation when Bryn's soft, warm body pressed up against his. Unfortunately for her, his cold skin wasn't nearly as welcoming.

She stirred and sat up. "Trent?"

His heart stopped. The firelight danced across her face, her shoulders, her full breasts…painting an impossibly lovely Madonna. Her dark hair fell in soft waves, framing her face. She was like a vision, a fantasy…

But when he touched her, his heart beat again. She was real. She was here. And he would take what he could, give what he could…as long as the night survived.

He was on his back looking up at her. All it took was a smile to make him hard. Her eyes were shadowed with exhaustion, her tousled hair a testament to their earlier lovemaking.

"I'm glad you came with me tonight." He couldn't resist stroking her leg.

"Me, too. I missed you while you were gone." She pulled her knees to her chest and laid her head on them, regarding him sleepily.

Despite the awkwardness of the question, he took a deep breath and made himself ask it anyway. "Why was it so difficult for you to…"

"Have sex with you?"

He grimaced. "Yeah."

"Why do you think?"

She was asking for something from him. But he felt as if he was traversing a minefield. "I don't think you've been with a man in a very long time. Is that right?"

Her lashes fell, and he could no longer judge her expression.

"I've had sex in my life a total of five times...all with Jesse. I had already decided to break it off when I found out I was pregnant." She sighed. "Since then... well, *you* try being an unwed mother, a full-time student and a grateful niece. Boyfriends were way down on my radar."

A sharp pain in his chest made it hard to breathe. She had been through a hell of a lot, and the responsibility for all of it lay firmly at his family's door. They had all let her down. Mac. Jesse. Trent.

He couldn't bear to think of it anymore. Not right now. Not with the epitome of every one of his fantasies just a hand's width away.

"Come here, Bryn. It will be better this time, I swear."

A smile flitted across her expressive face, but she allowed him to pull her beneath the covers. "It wasn't all that bad before," she teased gently.

She insisted on being the one to put on the condom. Her clumsiness was both amusing and arousing. He moved half on top of her, shuddering at the sense of homecoming. "I can do better."

He put his hand on her thigh, between her legs. She was wet already and warm, so warm. Being with Bryn was like basking in front of a fire on a rainy winter's night. She chased away the cold. And she filled him up in places he never knew were empty. Why was he so afraid to take her at face value? What more proof did he need?

She wasn't content to be passive. As he caressed her, she set about to drive him over the edge. She was a fast learner, and she was uncannily attuned to his body's responses. Her small, soft hands touched him everywhere. He burned. He ached. He struggled to breathe.

He heard her laugh once, and a shiver snaked its way down his spine. It was the sound of a woman discovering her power. And his weakness.

In the distance, the sound of rain drummed steadily on the tin roof. The seclusion lent a surreal note to the night's events. A wild, windswept ride, a deserted, ramshackle cabin. A man and a woman discovering each other's intimate secrets.

If he hadn't known better, he might have thought it was all a dream. He leaned on his elbow, winnowing his fingers through her hair. His body insisted he seal the deal, but he was desperate to make the night stretch beyond its limits. He brushed a thumb across each of her eyelids, replacing urgency with tenderness. Passion slowed to a quiet burn.

"I wish we could go back and change the past," he muttered.

Her expression, even in the firelight, was bleak. "I have a child, Trent. I wouldn't change that if I could. Whether or not you can come to terms with Allen's existence will decide how all of this plays out. I won't hide my son and I won't apologize for him."

He was struck by her quiet confidence. She might be a novice in bed, but she was a mature woman with undeniable strength…an appealing mixture of vulnerability and determination.

Already her taste was like a drug he couldn't resist. He slid an arm beneath her neck, pulled her to him and kissed her. He shoved aside all the questions, the problems, the uncertainties. One thing he knew for sure. Bryn Matthews was his. He'd worry later about the details.

Tonight was not the time.

Their tongues mated lazily. He was on his side with Bryn tucked to his chest. In this position, he could play with her breasts at will, could caress the inward slope of her waist, the seductive curve of her hip. One of her legs slid between his, and his heart punched in his rib cage.

The hunger blindsided him, not blunted at all by earlier release. "Bryn," he said hoarsely, "let me take you."

She spread her legs immediately. A rush of primordial exultation burned in his chest. He lost the ability to speak. Softer emotions were incinerated by his drive to find oblivion in her embrace.

He tried to remember her lack of experience, wanted to be careful with her, but his control had reached the breaking point. He thrust hard and deep, drawing groaning gasps from both of them. Her tight passage accepted him more easily this time, but still he saw her wince.

"I'm sorry." His voice was raw, his arms quivering as he tried to still the unstoppable pendulum.

She lifted her hips, driving him a half inch deeper.

"Don't stop." She whispered it, pleading, demanding. "I want it all."

He snapped then, driving into her again and again, feeling the squeeze of her inner muscles as she climaxed, and still he couldn't stop. Over and over, blind, lost to reason or will.

The end, when it came, was terrifying in its power. He'd built a life on control…on dominance. But in those last cataclysmic seconds, his body shuddered and quaked in a release that was like razor blades of sensation flooding his body as he emptied himself into hers. It went on forever. He lost who he was. He forgot where he was.

All he could see through a haze of exhaustion was Bryn.

Bryn was everything.

Nine

They made it back to the ranch before daybreak, but only barely. The storm had passed on, leaving only faint flashes of light in the distance. Bryn was boneless with exhaustion. Were it not for Trent's strong arms surrounding her, she might have fallen from the horse.

The return was no mad gallop. The horse was tired, as well, and they made the trip at a slow amble. Bryn wanted to cry with the knowledge that their stolen moment in time was over. Tomorrow, in the harsh light of day, all the problems would still exist. Mac's illness. Jesse's tragedy. Allen's paternity. The letters.

Just before they reached the barn, Bryn turned and buried her lips at Trent's throat. She felt his heart beating in time with hers. Awkwardly, she curled one arm around his waist, wanting to hold on, craving one last moment of believing that he cared about her.

Perhaps some of his hostility had been erased for good. But she was under no illusions. Trent hadn't said he believed her. Not yet.

He helped her down from the horse and held her close for several seconds before he bent his head and kissed her.

His voice was hoarse with fatigue. "Go get some sleep. I'll see you later this morning."

She knew he had to tend to the animal, but she felt rebuffed even so. Was that how it was going to be? Trent being his usual aloof, self-contained self, Bryn desperate for any scrap of affection he might offer. The picture that painted made her wince. She'd spent six years proving to herself that she was a strong woman who could put her life back in order. She couldn't let her feelings for Trent make her lose sight of the fact that she was first and foremost Allen's mother.

She had come here to secure her son's future. And to care for Mac. What happened tonight changed nothing.

Trent recognized the watershed moment in his life. As much as it hurt, he had to admit that Jesse was not what he seemed. Trent's baby brother had lied to, stolen from and hurt the one woman who had always been dear to the Sinclair family. The woman who above all deserved their support and protection. But Jesse wasn't the only villain. By their cruel actions, Trent and Mac were partly to blame.

Mac had begun the process of reconciliation. It was up to Trent to carry it through.

He decided on the front porch as neutral ground. When Mac headed off for his usual post-lunch nap, Trent lingered for a heart-to-heart with Bryn. She seemed oblivious to the gravity of the moment, and followed him outside without question.

Trent took her wrist. "Sit down for a minute. I want to talk to you."

She sank into a chair, her expression cautious.

"I realize that you were telling the truth all along about Jesse. Your son is Jesse's boy."

Her smile was watery. "Yes. Thank you for believing me."

He shrugged. "I still think we need to do some testing. For legal reasons. But Mac seems reluctant. Do you have any idea why?"

She shook her head. "I really don't know. He's admitted that he believes me, too. But I get the feeling there's something he's not telling me."

Trent took a deep breath. "Is there anything *you're* not telling me?"

Her unmistakable hesitation sent an arrow of astonishment to his gut followed by a painful shaft of disappointment. He knew her well enough to see the little flash of guilt…the way her gaze shifted from his. *Well, hell.*

The sense of betrayal he felt was crushing. He could persuade himself to believe her response was nothing important, but even his increasing desire for her couldn't make him ignore her telling reaction.

He clenched his jaw. "Bryn?"

She was pale, and her eyes implored him to understand. "There *is* something we need to talk about… but not in Mac's hearing."

"Well, that's convenient. When were you going to tell me this big secret?" Acid churned in his stomach.

She bit her lip. "It's not that simple. People can be hurt."

"People?"

"You. Mac. Your brothers."

His blood pressure spiked. His hands fisted. "Tell me. Now."

She held her ground, though she was trembling all over. "I will. I swear. But now is not the time."

"Dammit, Bryn." He slammed a fist on the unforgiving wood of the railing.

"Your family destroyed my world," she cried. "And I've managed to forgive you all. But I won't let you boss me around. Your money has spoiled you, Trent Sinclair. It's turned you into an arrogant jerk. You think you can make everything and everyone dance to your tune. But you can't. Not me, anyway."

When she stood up, he took her arm, halting her progress. "Tell me."

She nodded slowly. "I will. Soon."

They maintained an unspoken truce throughout the afternoon and during the evening meal. Trent's frequent absences from the house made things a lot easier, though he did show up at the dinner table on time and carried his end of the conversation.

Bryn avoided looking at him, her attention fixed on Mac. But she was hyperaware of Trent sitting only a few feet away. He was rumpled and weary, his jeans stained, his white dress shirt no longer crisp. But in a room of tuxedo-clad men, he would still command attention.

He was an alpha male, and he had the confidence of twenty men. She wondered bleakly what it must be like to always be so self-assured. She'd second-guessed herself a hundred times as a new mom, and even now, she often worried at night, when sleep came slowly, if she could give Allen everything he needed.

Not so much *things*. Between her and Aunt Beverly, they had a nice life of modest means. But sooner or later, Allen would need a father figure to guide him. Someone to toss a football with, to go on Scout outings, to learn what it meant to be a real man.

Mac might fill that role in part, if he were willing. But he was getting older, and his heart attack pointed out the reality that he would not always be around. Bryn couldn't bear to think of the Crooked S without him.

It was a relief when the two men left her to her own devices and headed off to the study. Bryn decided to make her evening phone call a little earlier than usual. She missed Allen fiercely, and she wanted to listen to his high-pitched voice telling her all the silly inconsequential things that made his day special.

In her bedroom, she shut the door, not wanting to be overheard. Her throat was tight, and if she got emotional talking to her son, she didn't need any witnesses.

Before she could dial the number, her phone rang,

and the caller ID was Beverly's. Bryn smiled to herself. *Great minds think alike....*

"Hey, there," she said, her heart lifting. "What's up?"

Beverly's voice was solemn. "Don't freak out, my love. Little Allen is in the hospital."

Bryn's legs collapsed beneath her. She sat down hard on the bed. "What happened?"

"He's going to be okay. It was a severe asthma attack. I had to call an ambulance. He's stabilized, but he's crying for you."

Bryn had never felt so helpless. She swallowed hard. "Can you put him on the phone?"

"Of course."

There was a small silence, and then her son's weak, pitiful voice said, "Hi, Mommy."

"Hello, my sweet boy. I'm so sorry you're sick. Is the hospital taking good care of you?"

"I got ice cream for supper."

She closed her eyes. "That's nice."

"I miss you, Mommy."

The knife in her heart twisted. It was hard to speak. "I'm going to get on a plane, and I'll try to be there when you wake up. I promise."

"Okay." He sounded drowsy now.

Beverly came back on the line. "Don't panic, Bryn. He's perfectly fine. They'll probably release him in the morning. But I do think he needs you."

"I'll be there as soon as humanly possible."

Trent seated his father in the leather desk chair and pulled up a stool beside him. He put a hand on Mac's, feeling the slight tremor of his dad's fingers. Trent had gone back and forth about what to do, but the doctor had reassured him this morning that Mac was more than strong enough to face the truth about Jesse.

Trent pulled up the file he had saved on the computer and sighed deeply. "Dad, I don't know how to tell you this without just blurting it out. I've been working on the books every day during the last two weeks. I've combed through the accounts repeatedly. And I keep coming up with the same answer. Jesse was stealing from the ranch. From you."

Mac's expression didn't change. He turned his palm upward and squeezed Trent's hand. "I know, son. I know."

Trent gaped. "You knew?"

Mac took his hand away and leaned back in the chair, his gaze pensive. "I wanted him here so I could keep an eye on him. Offering him the so-called job of keeping the books straight was supposed to give him direction. But I track every column of those ledgers. I saw the first instance where he shifted funds—I knew what was happening from the beginning."

"And you couldn't confront him?"

"I was scared. He'd developed a terrible temper, exacerbated by the drugs, I'm sure. He was trapped in a downward spiral, but I couldn't seem to find a way to stop it. I was a helpless old fool."

"Why didn't you ask Gage and Sloan and me for help?"

Mac rubbed his eyes. "I didn't want you to think badly of him. You were his big brothers. He idolized all three of you. And I knew how much you loved him in return. If he had managed to get clean, he would have been so embarrassed that you knew, so I kept his secret."

"But Bryn knew."

Mac winced. "Apparently so. I didn't know it at the time, but Jesse often called her when he went on one of his binges."

"She told me. And I called her a liar."

"Aw, hell, son. We didn't deserve that little girl. She hit the first crisis of her adult life, and we kicked her out."

Trent didn't protest being included in the *we*. He could have stood up for Bryn six years ago, but he hadn't. His jealousy and pride had blinded him to the truth of Jesse's poisonous lies.

"We really need to get a test done right away." Trent stood at the window staring into the dark night. "I think we both know that Bryn was telling the truth all along, but I want everything to be on the up-and-up."

"We'll tell her we believe her…that we're sorry we ever fell for Jesse's innocent act. And we'll redo my will to include the boy. But I think doing a test would be insulting to Bryn."

"She will probably welcome the idea."

Mac shrugged. "We'll see…"

"You'll want the boy to spend some time here."

"Of course. Maybe Bryn can stay over while Gage is here, bring the kid out, and she and Gage and I can show him the ropes."

A sour feeling settled in Trent's stomach. He didn't

want his brother bonding with Bryn's little boy...or worse yet, Bryn.

Suddenly, the door to the hall flew open, and Bryn stood framed in the archway. Her dark eyes burned in a face that was ghostly pale. "I have to go." Her chest rose and fell with her rapid breathing. In one hand were the keys to her rental car, in the other, her purse.

Trent was at her side in one stride, gripping her shoulders. "What is it? Are you hurt?" He ran his hands down her arms, searching for clues to her near hysteria.

She put her head on his shoulder, her voice a pained whisper. "Allen's in the hospital. He's had a terrible asthma attack. He's asking for me. And I'm not there."

It was a mother's worst fear. Trent felt her anguish as if it were his own. His eyes met Mac's over Bryn's bent head, both men thinking the same thing. How many nights had they kept vigils at a young Jesse's bedside when he had struggled so pitifully to breathe?

Trent held her close, stroking her hair. "Don't panic. I'll take you. We'll use the next thirty minutes to pack and check plane schedules, and we'll be out of here."

Mac held up his hand. "Wait a minute. Let me order the jet, Bryn. You call the doctor and see if the boy's stable enough to fly. We'll bring Allen and your aunt out here and I'll hire the best private nurse money can buy to accompany them. It will give the kid something to be excited about and you'll enjoy showing him the ranch."

"I can't ask you to do that. It's too expensive." Bryn's face was tear-stained.

"I'm an old coot." He lumbered to his feet and laid a hand on her shoulder. "What am I going to do with all that money, anyway? Let me do this, Bryn. It won't make up for the past, but it would make me feel better. It's late now…they probably have him sleeping. In the morning your aunt can tell him he's going on an exciting journey."

"Would he be comfortable on the plane?" Bryn looked at Trent, her expression troubled, vulnerable.

"It's damned luxurious." Trent chuckled. "He can play video games if he feels like it. There's a bed where he can lie down. He'll be pampered, I promise."

She nodded slowly. "I'll have to call the doctor right away."

"Use my BlackBerry. You don't mind us listening in, do you?"

She frowned. "Of course not."

Trent carried on a conversation with Mac while Bryn was on the phone. "We can give the aunt and the nurse and the boy the suite of rooms at the end of the hall. They'll be close to Bryn, and she can keep an eye on her little one."

Mac gave him a narrow-eyed, knowing gaze. "Staking out your territory, are you?"

Trent didn't rise to the bait. "It's healthy for children to have their own rooms. Even I know that."

"Well, I'll tell you this, boy. If you have designs on Bryn, you'll have to move fast." Mac snorted. "She won't be here much longer."

Bryn finished her call. The doctor had given the go-ahead, so Mac got on the phone in turn and started barking orders. Trent did his part, as well, and soon all the pieces were in place. By 8:00 a.m. the plane would be staffed with a nurse and every medical convenience necessary to make sure Bryn's young son would receive top-notch care.

Trent went in search of Bryn. He found her huddled in a quilt on the front porch swing. The night air was crisp and the stars numbered in the millions. He sat down beside her and pulled her against his chest. "He'll be okay, Bryn. Try not to worry."

She shrugged. "It's what mothers do."

"Did you ever think about getting an abortion?"

She didn't answer for a long time, and he wondered if he had offended her. "I'm sorry. That was very personal."

She tucked the quilt more tightly around her neck. "No, it's okay. Honestly, I don't remember ever thinking of that as an option. I'd wanted for so long to be a real Sinclair. You five were the only family I knew. I had a hazy memory of meeting Aunt Beverly, but the ranch and you and Mac and your brothers were my real family, at least in my heart. So when I realized I was pregnant, my first emotion was joy."

"But that didn't last long, thanks to us."

"I knew Jesse and I were young, but we were in a better position than most kids our age. Finances wouldn't be an issue, and we had all of you to support us."

"So you intended to keep the baby all along."

"Yes. I assumed Jesse would be happy. But that was naive. He wanted to be with me because he thought *you* wanted me. A baby made everything too real. So he lied."

"And we believed him."

"Yes."

"What did your aunt do?"

"She was wonderful from the beginning. No questions, only her unconditional love and support. Which was amazing, because I was almost a stranger to her. She did want to sue Jesse for child support, but I convinced her not to."

"Was she financially comfortable?"

She put her head on his shoulder, her body limp. "No, not really. But I held out this faint hope that one day I'd be able to reconcile with all of you, and I was afraid if we sued for child support, you'd hate me."

"Ah, Bryn." He held her close, feeling sick to his stomach as he realized anew how badly the Sinclair clan had played their part in this scenario. She had believed herself to be one of them, and they had tossed her out on the proverbial street.

Bryn yawned hugely as he stroked her hair. He nuzzled her cheek. "You need some rest, Bryn. It's been a tumultuous forty-eight hours."

She yawned again. "I know."

The memory of all that had transpired between them hovered in the sudden awkward silence.

Bryn stumbled to her feet, nearly tripping on the quilt. He scooped her up in his arms, bedding and all.

"Trent…" she protested halfheartedly.

"Let me pamper you," he muttered, holding her close. "Relax. I've got you."

He carried her all the way to her bedroom and laid her gently on the bed. She was already in her nightgown, and her hair was clean and damp from her shower.

He smoothed her cheek with the back of his hand. "I want to stay with you tonight."

The only light in the room was a dim lamp on the bedside table. But he could see her expression clearly. "Trent, I don't think I can—"

He bent to kiss her. "I'm not talking about sex. Give me some credit. I only want to hold you, I swear."

She nodded. For a moment, shy pleasure replaced the worry in her eyes. She scooted over on the mattress, making room for him. He shed everything but his knit boxers and climbed in beside her. It would be hell not to make love to her, but she needed him tonight, and he was going to be here for her. He had a lot to atone for, and maybe this would be a start.

She nestled in his arms as if they had been lovers for years. The pain in his chest returned, and he rested his chin on her head, inhaling her scent and keenly aware of her soft body and silky skin. He cared for her. Bone deep. It had begun as an invisible tie between them as she grew up. And when she reached womanhood, he'd known deep in his psyche that he wanted her.

But he hadn't been smart enough to understand that some opportunities weren't always available. His ambition and drive to succeed had taken precedence. As an arrogant young buck out to conquer the world, frequent sex had been available and plentiful. Perhaps in the back of his mind he'd assumed Bryn would always be waiting.

It would never have occurred to him to try and win her from Jesse. He loved his little brother too much. But he'd been well acquainted with Jesse's attention span, and he knew, even then, that one day in the near future Bryn would be free. Jesse didn't have it in him to settle down with one girl.

But nothing had turned out like it should.

Bryn cared for him now, he knew that. Otherwise she never would have let him make love to her. But a mother's love and loyalty were fierce commodities, and she would stand by her son first and foremost.

Whether Trent had a shot at convincing her he would welcome Jesse's son was by no means a sure thing. And honestly, he had qualms about being a dad. His own father had lived by the "make 'em tough" model, but Trent doubted that was what Bryn wanted for her son.

And what if Trent had children of his own? Would he be able to love Jesse's son in the same way? He and his family had hurt Bryn in the past. It would be inexcusable to compound that mistake.

Bryn moved restlessly, turning in his arms to find his lips. She moved her mouth over his drowsily, murmuring her approval when he slid his tongue between her lips and deepened the kiss.

His shaft hardened, but the lust he felt was overlaid with a patina of contentment, seemingly an odd match-up, but true nevertheless.

He wanted her, but the need to protect her was stronger.

As she lay on her side, her breast nestled in his palm. He felt its weight and ached to undress her and caress her everywhere. She had become as necessary to him as breathing, and for once in his life, he didn't have a course mapped out. He didn't know if determination was going to be enough. No business model existed to tell him what a woman was thinking. No amount of money could buy her trust.

And there was still a secret between them…something she was hiding.

She fell asleep, her breathing slowing to a gentle rhythm. He reached for the lamp and plunged the room into darkness.

It was hours before he slept.

Ten

Bryn woke with a dull headache and a sensation that something was wrong. Then it all came flooding back. Her aunt's phone call. Her son's illness.

She scrambled out of bed and dressed haphazardly, pulling her hair into a messy knot on top of her head. It was almost nine. For God's sake, why had Trent let her sleep so long?

She made her way to the kitchen, dialing her cell phone as she walked. Mac was there, drinking coffee, looking old and tired. Corralling Jesse would have been his main focus for many years, a drain on his time and energy. With Jesse gone, and once the grief dulled, surely Mac would regain his customary vigor.

She clicked her phone shut and paced. "Beverly's

not answering her phone. What if something has happened?"

Mac reached for her hand as she passed his chair for the third time. "Relax, Brynnie. The plane is in the air. They'll be landing in a little under two hours. And all reports are good."

Bryn couldn't sit still. She went to the sink and stared blindly out the window. Allen was on the way...and Beverly. Now if only Gage and Sloan were here, she would have everyone she loved under one roof.

When she had herself under control, she sat at the table. The cook set a scrambled egg and some toast in front of her. Bryn was too excited to eat, but she forced herself to get it down. Mac passed her a section of the morning paper. One of the ranch hands' jobs was to make a run into town early every weekday to pick up the three papers Mac devoured without fail. It was an expensive habit given the gas consumption, but Mac refused to read newspapers online, though he was fairly computer savvy.

Bryn was too jittery to concentrate on the printed words for long. "When should we leave?"

Mac grinned. "Trent's going to bring the car around in thirty minutes or so. Think you can be ready?"

She punched him on the arm. "Very funny."

The trip to the airport lasted forever. Trent drove, of course, and he and Mac sat in the front seat talking ranch business. Trent had kissed her briefly when he appeared, but there hadn't been time for anything more personal or intimate. Bryn sat in the rear, her legs tucked beneath her, and leaned her head against the window, watching the world go by.

She loved Wyoming. And as much as she missed her son and her aunt, she wouldn't have traded this time for anything. Being home—and it *was* home—had healed the dark places inside her. She didn't know what the future would bring, especially because of the unrevealed letters, but it was enough to be here for the moment and to know that Mac and Trent no longer mistrusted her.

There had been no overt apologies, no verbal acknowledgment that Jesse had lied repeatedly, but she sensed in Trent and Mac a softening, a willingness to listen.

Soon, maybe tonight or tomorrow, she would pull Trent aside and show him the letters, even if it meant finding out that Allen wasn't a Sinclair. Trent, as Mac's eldest son, would have to make the decision about whether or not to let Mac see what his ex-wife had written to Jesse. And after that, who knew what would happen.

They pulled in to the parking lot of the small Jackson Hole airport and parked. Mac stayed in the car, but Trent and Bryn got out and leaned on the hood, hands over their eyes as they watched for landing aircraft. Prop planes were common. Occasionally a larger, commercial airliner.

But it was the sleek, small jet with the blue-and-green stripe and the Sinclair logo that caught Trent's attention. "That's it," he said. He tapped on the window. "C'mon, Dad."

Bryn walked on shaky legs, Trent and Mac at her side.

This was more than just a normal visit. A new Sinclair was about to step foot onto the land of his heritage. And if he wasn't a Sinclair by blood, he was still Jesse's son.

She waited impatiently in the small concourse. Another jet had landed moment's before, and Bryn had to clench her fists and bide her time as the stream of tourists meandered inside from the tarmac.

At last Bryn saw the familiar outline of Aunt Beverly's gray head, with its short, tight curls. Her heart leaped in her chest. An unfamiliar woman in a white uniform walked at Beverly's side, but it was the third member of the entourage who spotted Bryn first and shouted at the top of his lungs.

Allen broke free of Beverly's hold and, despite her admonitions to go slowly, raced forward. "Mommy, Mommy!" His face was aglow.

She ran to meet him, scooping him up in a tight hug as she went to her knees. "Hello, my little sweetheart. I've missed you so much." He smelled of sweat and peanut butter and little boy.

He suffered through a moment of Bryn scattering kisses on his freckled cheeks, but then pulled away impatiently, already asserting his manly independence even in the middle of a reunion. His skin was pale. Dark smudges beneath his eyes emphasized his pallor, but he had certainly recovered his high spirits.

"Who are they, Mommy?" He tugged her to her feet and looked past her with curiosity.

Tears clogged her throat and she had to try twice to speak. "That's Trent and his father, Mr. Sinclair." She lowered her voice to a whisper. "Remember how I taught you to shake hands."

Allen grinned at the two strange males, his head cocked slightly to one side as he held out his tiny palm. "Very nice to meetcha."

Trent stood silent, unmoving, his features carved in stone.

Mac rubbed a hand across his face. "Oh, my God." He took Allen's outstretched hand and pumped it. "Welcome to Wyoming, son."

Eleven

After that, chaos reigned. They all made their way outside. Aunt Beverly and Allen were installed in the backseat with Bryn. Trent hadn't missed a trick. The booster seat he had purchased for Allen was exactly the correct size and model.

The nurse rode behind in a rental car with a hired driver. All the bags went with her, as well.

By the time the caravan got back to the ranch, Bryn was frazzled. Allen was hyperexcited, Aunt Beverly was exhausted and Trent had yet to say more than a couple of terse words to anybody.

Mac was the one to show the new arrivals to their quarters and to help Bryn get everyone settled in. She was pleased that Allen's room was so close to hers. Even with two other caregivers watching out for him—one highly trained—she liked knowing that her son was where she could check on him during the night.

Lunch was quick and simple, sandwiches and fruit. Allen begged to explore the ranch, but the three women who controlled his fate insisted on a nap.

Mac took pity on the boy. He smiled down at him, his eyes misty. "How about I tell you a couple of stories about your—." He stopped short, sending Bryn a visual SOS. His face creased in distress.

She ruffled her son's blond hair, automatically trying to smooth the eternal cowlick. "Mac raised four sons on this ranch, Allen. Trent was one of them. I'll bet Mac can tell you lots of great stories about the trouble they got into."

That seemed to convince Allen, and the old man and the young boy wandered down the hall to Allen's new bedroom.

Which left Bryn and Aunt Beverly alone in the kitchen. Trent had disappeared, and the nurse was taking a much-deserved hour for herself.

Beverly hugged Bryn for the dozenth time. "I missed you, honey. The house was empty without you."

"I missed you, too. Did Allen really do okay...until he got sick?"

"He was a sweetheart." Beverly eased into a chair at the table. "I'm stiff from the plane ride, even if it was the equivalent of being treated like a queen. Good grief, Bryn. These folks have some serious money. They should have been helping you all these years."

Bryn bent her head. "It was complicated." Aunt Beverly knew most of the story, though she had no clue that Bryn had harbored a crush on Trent. She sat down beside her aunt. "Mac hasn't said so, but I can tell from his face that he thinks Allen is Jesse's son. He practically melted, just like a doting granddad should."

Beverly extended her feet, clad in sensible walking shoes, and stretched. "How long will we be staying?"

Panic welled in Bryn's chest. Mac was back in fighting form. Once Allen had a chance to immerse himself in ranch life and the nurse declared him fully recovered, there would no longer be any reason for Bryn and her son to stay.

Which meant Bryn had to confront Trent with the letters. Soon.

And that was problematic, because Trent had reverted to the coolly reserved, impossible-to-read man she had first encountered in Mac's sickroom when she arrived. She no longer detected hostility from him, but his utter lack of emotion was even worse.

He either refused to believe the evidence of his own eyes, or he had no interest in getting to know his nephew.

When Allen woke from a long nap, he was grumpy, but a juice box and a cookie soothed him. The nurse checked him over, and soon, Mac and Bryn were on horseback, with Allen—wearing a mask as a precaution—riding in front of his grandfather. They covered a lot of ground, and Mac's transformation was miraculous. No longer an invalid, he was suddenly hale and hearty again, his skin a healthy color and his eyes sparkling with enthusiasm.

At one point when Allen was occupied playing with

puppies on the front porch, Mac took Bryn's arm. "We need to talk this evening."

Bryn nodded solemnly, a lump in her throat. "Okay. After I get Allen settled for the night, I'll come find you."

"Trent will need to be there, also."

She nodded again, but couldn't think of a thing to say. Trent's feelings on the subject of Jesse's son were an unknown quantity.

Allen tired quickly. They whisked him back to the house and Beverly occupied him with a simple board game while Bryn talked to the nurse. The prognosis was promising. They would have to be vigilant about inhalers and the like, but there was a very good chance Allen would outgrow the worst of his asthma.

After dinner Allen was allowed to watch one of his favorite Disney DVDs, and then it was bedtime.

When Bryn entered Mac's office a short while later, he was already there. And so was Trent. Mac greeted her with a smile. Trent barely noticed that she'd entered the room. He sat in front of the computer, his forehead creased in concentration as he studied the screen.

For a moment she flashed back to that dreadful day six years ago. But she was not here to plead her own case on this occasion. She was an advocate for her son. Bryn wanted nothing for herself from the Sinclairs unless it was freely given. Not money, not love, not anything.

Mac motioned for her to sit in the big, comfy armchair. It was a man's chair, and it dwarfed her, but she complied. Still, Trent remained apart from the conversation. Mac reached in a drawer and pulled out a five-by-seven silver frame.

He handed it to Bryn. She stared at it, but it took a few moments for understanding to click. The birthday cake in the picture was decorated with five candles. And the gap-toothed birthday boy with the wide grin and the cowlick was Jesse.

He could have been Allen's twin. Her throat tightened. "I don't know what to say."

Mac's eyes glazed with wetness, but he coughed and tried to cover his emotion. "I think you know how sorry we are for what happened six years ago, but Trent and I want to make a formal apology and ask you to forgive us. Isn't that right, Trent?"

Finally, Trent revolved and faced her, his expression unreadable. "Yes, of course."

Bryn squirmed in the chair, bringing her knees up beside her in an effort to get comfortable. For years she had thought an apology was what she wanted, but now that the time had arrived, she realized that it changed nothing. "I appreciate the thought," she said slowly. "But I understand why you did what you did, especially Trent. Jesse was the light of this family…the heart and soul. You all poured your love into him, and it would never have occurred to you that he was capable of such barefaced lies."

Mac scowled. "Trent can be absolved on that account, but even back then I realized that Jesse's sweetness and compliance was an act. I was trying to protect him and you, too, Bryn. But I handled it badly. If I had encouraged you to stay and had challenged Jesse to own up to the truth, I'm convinced that things would have gotten very ugly, very fast."

"So you sent me to Beverly."

"Your mother spoke highly of her older sister, and after you ran out of the study that day, I contacted Beverly to explain the situation. We both agreed that you needed to be with a woman during your pregnancy." He came over to the chair and laid a hand on her shoulder. "But it wasn't that I didn't love you, darlin'. I never stopped loving you."

Bryn reached up to stroke his hand. "Thank you, Mac. And I'm sorry I was such a brat and sent all your presents back."

He grinned. "They're in a closet in my bedroom. You're welcome to them."

Her eyebrows went up. "Ooh…an early Christmas. I might have to take you up on that."

Mac sobered. "Allen is your son, and any decisions about his future are up to you. But I want you to know that I already have my lawyers preparing the paperwork to make him a legitimate heir to my estate."

Bryn looked at Trent, begging him without words to say something, anything.

He was stoic, watchful.

Her stomach churned with tension. What did Trent's silence mean? Was he angry? Would he challenge the will?"

She straightened. "I assume you'll want to do DNA testing to establish the relationship between Jesse and Allen."

Mac snorted. "Allen's a mirror image of Jesse at that age. Any fool can see it. I don't think we need a test."

At long last, Trent spoke up. "It might be important to the boy one day to have the proof positive. So no one can ever doubt him."

Bryn's heart sank. Trent still wasn't sure she was telling the truth. "Does this mean you don't believe me, Trent?" She had to know.

Impatience darkened his features. "Of course I believe you, Bryn. Even before I saw the boy I believed you. But I deal in legalities, and it never hurts to dot the *i's* and cross the *t's.*"

She nibbled her lower lip, not at all certain what was going on inside his head. It seemed as though he couldn't even bring himself to say Allen's name. Was he angry that Bryn had borne Jesse's child?

Mac raked a hand through his thick silver hair. "Today was a big day, and I'm almost as wiped out as the kid. I'll say good night. See you both in the morning."

His departure left an awkward silence in the room. Bryn had hoped to approach Trent in a better mood when she revealed the letters, but the time had run out. No wills could be notarized, nor big declarations made, until the truth about the letters from Etta came to light.

She took a deep breath. "Trent, there's something I need to show you. Something important."

He lifted an eyebrow. "What is it?"

"It will be easier if I show you. It will only take me a minute. Please wait here."

His gaze followed her out of the room, and she went rapidly to extract the shoe box from its hiding place.

When she returned, Trent hadn't moved. His eyes narrowed suspiciously. "What is that?"

She held the box to her chest. "Not long after I arrived—the day you took your dad to the doctor and I was here alone—I realized that Jesse's room had not been cleaned since his death. I did some laundry... straightened up the mess. And in the process, I found a box of letters written to him by Etta. As far as I can tell, they started arriving about the time he turned sixteen."

Trent's eyes blazed with emotion, and he took the box from her hands with a jerk. "Let me see that."

She hated showing them to him, knowing it would cause him pain. "They're bad, Trent...wicked in cases... and cruel. Perhaps Jesse's self-destructive behavior was being fueled by something none of us knew anything about."

Trent reclaimed his original seat at the desk and opened the box. He riffled through the contents for maybe ten seconds before selecting an envelope and extracting the enclosed piece of notepaper. As he read it, his scowl blackened.

She could only imagine what he was thinking. She, herself, had been shocked and dismayed the first time she had read the letters. How much worse would it be for Trent, knowing that his own mother had been so intentionally mean-spirited?

No, it was actually worse than that. A child was supposed to be able to know that his parents loved him unconditionally. Jesse would have been better off thinking that his mother had left for parts unknown and was never coming back. Desertion was a terrible blow to a vulnerable boy. But in writing the series of notes designed to manipulate Jesse's fragile emotions, Etta had moved from abandonment to deliberate harm.

Trent read every word of every letter. Bryn sat in silence as the clock ticked away the minutes. The house was quiet. Everyone else had gone to bed. Trent's face was terrible to see. His shoulders slumped, his skin grayed, his lips tightened.

When he finished the last one and turned to face her, his eyes were damp. She had expected him to be angry... and perhaps that would come...later. But at this precise moment, he was in so much pain, he was unable to hide it, even from her.

He swallowed hard. "Why? Why would she do such a thing?"

Bryn clasped her hands in her lap, searching in vain for the right words to ease the torment etched on his face. "I don't know, Trent. Maybe she thought that if she could worm her way back into Jesse's life, Mac would let her come home."

He dropped his head in his hands, elbows on his thighs. "Jesse must have been so confused, so torn. He adored Dad, but she insinuated—"

Trent had seen it, too. Bryn squeezed the arms of the chair. "Etta made it sound as if Mac wasn't Jesse's father." The words scraped her throat raw. "And if that is true, then Allen is not a Sinclair. Not at all."

Trent was so still, he worried her. She went to him

and put her arms around his neck from behind. "I'm so sorry," she whispered, putting her cheek to his. "She was your mother. I know this hurts."

He shrugged out of her embrace and got up to pace, his hands shoved in his pockets. She took the seat he had vacated and wrapped her arms around her waist, trying not to let him see how upset she was. Trent had enough to deal with at the moment without comforting her.

Intense emotion blasted the air in unseen waves. He ranged around the small space like an animal trapped in a cage. He paused finally and leaned against the wall, fatigue in every line of his posture. "Why didn't you show them to me when you first found them?" he asked dully.

"I was afraid. Afraid of hurting Mac…hurting you."

"Afraid of losing your quarter of the Sinclair fortune?"

Her actions hadn't been blameless. She shouldn't have been surprised by the question. But Trent's question sliced through her composure and left her bleeding.

"Fair enough. I understand why it might look that way. But I was always going to show you these eventually. I had to. You deserved that from me. Because sometimes the only way to help with grief is to find answers."

"Did you think about destroying the letters?"

"No," she said bluntly. "I would have had to live with guilt for the rest of my life. I *want* Allen to be a Sinclair, but only if it's true. If Jesse was not Mac's son, we'll deal with it somehow."

"You didn't show these to Mac." It was a statement, not a question.

"No. He's been so frail. I did wonder if maybe he knew about them already. They weren't exactly hidden. The box fell off the top shelf in the closet when I was putting things away."

"But Mac wouldn't have snooped in Jesse's room."

"No, I guess not."

They both fell silent.

When Trent didn't say anything more, apparently lost in thought, she pressed him. "Do you think we should show them to him now? He's like a new man since Allen came."

Trent frowned. "True. But if he *didn't* know about them, then the contents might give him another heart attack. And I don't know if I can risk that."

"We can't let him change the will if he's not Allen's grandfather. It would be wrong…unethical…"

"But if bringing Allen into the family makes Mac happy, who are we to stand in the way?"

It was her turn to frown, her stomach knotted. "You made it clear six years ago that being a Sinclair is a bond all of you shared, and I didn't. My growing up here meant nothing. So what would make you soften that stance now?"

Trent's expression was inscrutable, his mouth a grim line. "Six years ago I hadn't lost my baby brother to a drug addiction. Six years ago I hadn't watched my father nearly die of a heart attack. Six years ago, I was a self-centered jackass."

His unaccustomed humility made her uneasy. She

counted on Trent to be a rock. She didn't need his self-abnegation. Not now. Not with so much riding on the outcome of the next several days.

She glanced at her watch. The hours had flown. It was midnight—the witching hour. That dark moment when everything bad in life was magnified into a crushing burden. No longer able to sit still, she stood up and went to the window, her back to Trent.

Her breath fogged up the chilled glass. "So what do we do?" She wanted him to come to her, take her in his arms and tell her everything would be all right.

But as always, Trent was not a man to be easily understood or bent to a woman's will. She sensed him watching her, but he remained where he was. "I have to think," he said gruffly. "Too much is at stake to make any snap decisions. Will the boy take a nap tomorrow?"

The boy. Trent still couldn't say her son's name. "Yes." She drew a heart in the condensation on the windowpane.

"Then let's you and I take a ride in the afternoon. We'll go to the far side of the meadow…where the creek cuts through the aspen. No one will interrupt us. We'll talk and decide what to do."

Trent was speaking matter-of-factly. Nothing in his tone or demeanor suggested a hint of passion. But unbidden, her mind jumped to memories of the night they'd shared in the cabin, and she felt her face heat. It might as well have been happening again at this very instant, so vivid was the recollection of each perfect minute.

Her moans and cries. His hoarse shouts. The rustle of the straw beneath the quilt. The snap and pop of the fire. The comforting drone of rain on the metal roof.

His touch lingered on her skin. She breathed in his crisp masculine scent. His hard body moved over her and in her. Soft sighs, ragged murmurs...pleasure so deep and swift-running she drowned in it.

She was glad they weren't facing each other. Her face would have given her away. She stiffened her spine, drawing on every ounce of self-possession she could muster. She turned to look at him and almost flinched at the intensity of his gaze.

For one blazing instant she saw raw, naked hunger beyond comprehension in his narrow gaze. A predatory declaration of intent. But he blinked, and it was gone.

Had she imagined it? Did he still desire her, or had her actions in concealing the letters destroyed the fragile bond between them?

She bit her lower lip, unsure how to proceed.

Trent's posture had relaxed somewhat. He leaned against the wall, looking tired and discouraged. Seeing him so vulnerable hurt her somewhere deep in her chest. He had taken on so much responsibility in the last few weeks. And her revelation about the letters, necessary though it was, had only added to the load he carried.

She toyed with the cord that controlled the wide-slatted wooden blinds, unable suddenly to meet his gaze. "I'll be glad to go with you tomorrow," she said quietly. "To talk things through. But in the end, it has to be your decision, Trent. Mac is your father. You know what's best for him and your family. I think he could help us get to the bottom of Etta's correspondence and what it means. But if you think he can't handle it, we'll destroy them and no one will be the wiser."

He ran a hand through his rumpled hair. "This is a hell of a mess. I need to call Gage and Sloan."

"Can they come back so soon?"

"Gage is due here in a week anyway, because we all agreed to give the old man a month of our time to help get things at the ranch back up and running. And Sloan, well, I'm pretty sure he'd come back under the circumstances. They deserve to know the truth about Jesse's problems, but I don't know if we can wait to talk to Dad about the letters."

It hit her suddenly that Trent was planning to leave… and soon. His month was up. He'd be going back to Denver. Without her. She'd known it was going to happen…eventually. But she had deliberately closed her mind to the thought of it. It hurt too much.

She went to him and laid her head on his chest, circling her arms around his waist. "I'm so sorry, Trent."

His hand came up to stroke her hair. Beneath her cheek she felt his heart thundering like a freight train. "Go to bed," he said softly. "Get some rest. I'll see you in the morning."

Twelve

Trent saddled his horse and headed out, following the route he and Bryn had taken to the cabin. But tonight Trent pushed his mount, skirting the edge of recklessness, trying to outrun the barrage of thoughts whirling in his brain. Every word of the damn letters was emblazoned in his memory. And it hurt. After all these years, his mother's betrayal hurt.

And then there was Bryn. What was he going to do about Bryn? From the moment he'd set eyes on Allen, he'd been consumed by guilt. The kid was Jesse's son, no question. Yet, six years ago they had thrown Bryn out in the street. Like she was some sort of sinner. And all along, Jesse had stood by and let it happen.

Dammit. What an unholy mess.

Trent couldn't lie to himself any longer. He was head

over heels in love with Bryn. And it wasn't something that was going to magically go away. Hell, he'd been half in love with her for years. She was his heart, the very essence of who he was. And whatever it took, he couldn't lose her.

He'd been an ass about Allen. He didn't know much about children, and the fact that the boy was Jesse's son hit Trent hard. He was only the uncle, but the bare truth was, he wanted to be the boy's father. And if Jesse wasn't Mac's son… Good God.

And still he rode on, paying penance, seeking answers, looking for absolution.

Bryn barely slept. Every time she rolled over to look at the illuminated dial of the clock, only an hour had passed…sometimes less. Her whole life hung in the balance. For years she had assumed that her son would one day take his place as a Sinclair. And she had believed that such a moment would cement the fact, once and for all, that the ranch would always be her home, no matter where she actually chose to live.

Deep in her soul she recognized a connection to the land here. Perhaps it was unwarranted. Her parents had been no more than hired help on the Sinclair ranch. But that reality couldn't change the way she felt.

And Trent…dear, complicated Trent. She loved him beyond reason. Loved him enough to know that no other man would ever measure up. She didn't want to spend her life alone, but it would take a long, long time to forget the imprint Trent had made on her soul.

Jesse might have been the one who took her

virginity, but Trent had showed her what it meant to be a woman.

An early morning walk calmed some of her agitation and made it possible for Bryn to greet her son and aunt across the breakfast table with some degree of equanimity. Beverly and the nurse carried on a lively conversation. Mac's mood was jovial, and no one remarked on Trent's absence. An empty cereal bowl and coffee cup were evidence that he'd been up early.

Allen finished off his pancakes and turned, bright-eyed, toward his mom. "What are we going to do today?"

Bryn had thought about letting him explore the attic—she'd loved doing that as a child—but she worried that the dust might aggravate his asthma. He wasn't going to be content with puzzles and board games now that he was feeling better. Inspiration hit her. "Come with me," she said. "I have a surprise for you."

With Allen bouncing along beside her, she went to the large family room and opened the cabinet that stored all the leather-bound picture albums. Gage, Mac's second son, had developed a passion for photography early in life, and Mac had indulged him with fancy and expensive cameras, lenses and developing equipment. Mac could never have imagined in those early days how Gage's love of photography, combined with a strong wanderlust, would take him to far-flung places across the globe.

Bryn opened one of the early albums and spread it in Allen's lap. Her throat tightened as she recognized a long-forgotten photo. It was one of the rare instances where Gage was actually "in" the picture, and Mac had been the photographer. Five children, four boys and a girl, sat on the top corral rail, their legs dangling. The three older brothers bore a striking resemblance, though Trent, probably twelve or thirteen, stood out as the eldest.

Bryn and Jesse sat side by side with the bigger kids, their arms around each other's shoulders. Bryn's hair was in pigtails…Jesse's blond head gleamed in the morning sun. All five children looked healthy, happy and carefree.

When Allen wasn't looking, Bryn took the photo and slipped it in her pocket. Soon, very soon, she'd tell him about his father. And she wouldn't lie, if possible. There were plenty of good memories to share.

She flipped the pages…showing Allen a montage of county rodeos, family Christmases, impromptu picnics on the ranch…all chaperoned by a much younger Mac. Allen drank it all in with avid interest.

The final album was smaller than the rest. Inside the front cover was a faded Post-it note in Mac's handwriting that read *For Bryn*. Every photo inside was of her parents, sometimes together, sometimes smiling alone for the camera, many times holding their little girl.

She touched one picture she barely remembered. "That's my mom and dad," she said softly. "I wish you could have known them. But they died a long time before you were born."

A frown creased Allen's small forehead. "Did my daddy die, too? Is that why he doesn't live with us?"

The question came out of the blue and took her breath

away. Allen had never once asked about his father. Bryn had been prepared for some time now to launch into an explanation when Allen seemed old enough to understand, but until today, he'd never questioned their nontraditional family.

She had lain many nights, sleepless, wondering how to explain to a small child that his father didn't want him. Now she didn't have to.

She swallowed the lump in her throat, desperately wanting to point to a photo of Jesse and say, "That was your dad." But she couldn't. Not yet. Not until things were settled.

"Yes," she said simply. "Your father died. But he loved you very much." Perhaps God would forgive her for the lie. A son needed to know that his father thought the world of him. Even if it wasn't true.

In the way of five-year-olds, Allen suddenly lost interest in the past. "Can we go see the puppies now?" he asked, wheedling in every syllable of his childish plea.

"You bet." She laughed. "I'll get Julio to bring them up from the barn."

Lunch was a scattered affair. Bryn and Allen took sandwiches out into the sunshine to eat, spreading a quilt on the ground and enjoying their alfresco meal. It had been a long, hard winter in Minnesota, and the spring warmth was too appealing to resist. But by one o'clock, Allen was flagging. Bryn turned him over to Beverly and the nurse.

When she left her son's bedroom, Trent appeared

suddenly in the hallway, his expression somber. "Are you ready?"

She nodded, her stomach flip-flopping with nerves. "Yes."

One of the ranch hands insisted on helping Bryn saddle her horse, though she could have done it on her own. Trent mounted a beautiful stallion and waited for her to put a foot in the stirrup and leap astride the gentle mare assigned to her. She was self-conscious about Trent watching her, but she managed not to embarrass herself.

They rode side by side in silence, crossing a meadow bursting with flowers and sporting new green in every shade. Trent had rolled up Bryn and Allen's luncheon quilt and tied it to the back of his saddle. He'd also brought along a couple of canteens of fresh water.

When they reached the creek, Trent helped her dismount and tied both animals to trees so the horses could eat and drink as needed. He spread the faded blanket and dropped the canteens to anchor the fabric against the capricious breeze.

Nearby, the crystal-clear, frigid water burbled gently over smooth stones that were as old as the mountains themselves. Trent faced her, his expression unreadable.

The breeze tossed her hair in her face. She took a rubber band from her pocket and bound the flyaway mess at the base of her neck. "Where do we start?" she asked. The calm in her voice was a complete fabrication. Her knees were the consistency of jelly, and her heart fluttered in her chest.

Trent took one step in her direction. "With this," he said gruffly. He took her in his arms, and instantly her fear and anxiety melted away to be replaced by heat and certainty. It was a homecoming, a benediction, a warm, wicked claiming.

Did he know? Did he have any idea that she was his in every way that mattered? She met the urgency of his kiss eagerly. The hunger that consumed both will and reason no longer frightened her.

She would have followed him into hell for the chance to have him again, to know the searing touch of his hands on her damp flesh.

He was inside her jeans, his big hands cupping her bottom, drawing her tight against the hard, pulsing ridge of his erection.

"Trent. Oh, Trent." She wanted to say more, needed to say more. But it was all she could do to remain standing.

They ripped at clothing, hers and his, unashamed to be naked beneath the gentle afternoon sun. Bits of shade dappled their bare skin.

She barely noticed when he drew her to the soft caress of the quilt. He went down on his back, taking any discomfort from the rocky ground and making it his, while she sat cradled astride his hard thighs.

His thick, eager erection was impossible to miss. It lifted boldly between them, filled with life and purpose.

The gleam in his eyes made her blush. "Stop that," she hissed, unable to hold his gaze. She looked around, knowing they were alone, but feeling bashful nevertheless.

He gently traced the curve of one breast, lingering to coax the nipple to hardness. "Stop what?"

The innocence in his question might have been more convincing if he hadn't simultaneously brushed his finger in the wetness between her legs. Where his touch trespassed, her body went lax and soft, ready to take him. Eager for more.

She cleared her throat. "I thought we were going to talk," she said. It seemed as though one of them should make an effort to be sensible, but it was difficult for a woman to be taken seriously when she was sprawled in erotic abandon beneath a cloudless sky.

A shadow darkened his face for scant seconds, but he shook it off, his hands clenching her hips hard enough to bruise.

"Later," he groaned, rolling on a condom and lifting her to align their bodies. "Watch us," he muttered. "Don't close your eyes."

He entered her inch by inch, and though she squirmed and shivered, her gaze never wavered from the spot where his hard flesh penetrated her. The act was as elemental as the cry of the hawk overhead, as life-affirming as the advent of new life in the wild.

He filled her completely, his mighty arms straining as he lifted her repeatedly. Her knees burned, her thighs ached. The intentionally lazy tempo drove her mad with longing. She bore down on him, squeezing, pressing his shaft so he would go faster.

But Trent Sinclair had an iron will, and his control

was frustrating for a woman whose patience unraveled with every upward thrust of his hips. She was so close to the moment of release, she held her breath.

Acting on instinct, she lightly touched his copper-colored nipples, circling them and making Trent flinch and groan hoarsely. Within her, he grew. Harder. Longer. More insistent.

She was stretched. Impaled. Held captive to the madness that drove them both to the brink of insanity. And it *was* insane. There was no future for them. No hope for a positive conclusion.

All they had was the present.

She put her hands on his shoulders. He reached behind her, and with a brutal twist of his fingers, snapped the band that held her ponytail. The long silky strands tumbled over her breasts and onto his chest. He stroked her hair with wonder and reverence in his gaze.

Then his hands fisted in the silken fall and he dragged her down so his mouth could ravage hers. Teeth and tongues and clashing breath. His sweat-slicked chest heaved, her thigh muscles quivered. He tortured them both, making them wait, drawing out the anticipation of the end until she wanted to scream at him and scratch his bronzed muscles with her fingernails, anything to hasten the promised pleasure that shimmered just out of reach.

He seized her face in his hands, his fingers sliding into the damp hair at her nape. His rapier gaze locked on hers. "You should have been mine, Bryn. He didn't deserve you. You should have been mine." Something in the rough, aching words made her heart hurt. But then he kissed her again, and the joy returned.

They were helpless, lost in the windswept eroticism of the moment. He laughed at her, laughed at them both. Nothing could have torn them apart. She lay on his chest, exhausted. The new angle sent tingling sensations from her core throughout her body.

His strength and stamina amazed her. He grunted and thrust more wildly. She was limp in his embrace, desperately aroused, but unable to summon the energy to sit up again.

"Tell me you want me, Bryn. I need to hear you say it." He rolled them suddenly, coming on top of her, but bearing most of his weight on his forearms.

She licked her lips, her throat parched. "I want you."

"Tell me you need me."

"I need you."

"I wish I had been your first."

Her slight hesitation sent lightning flashing in his dark gaze, dangerous, potent.

"I was immature," she said softly. "I think I used him to make you jealous. And I am so sorry for that. But I was never *in love* with Jesse."

She waited for him to say he loved her. Prayed with incoherent desperation that he would say the words that would change her life forever. The simple phrase that would make all her dreams come true.

But no such words were forthcoming.

Trent's face was unreadable. He was a man in the throes of passion…nothing in his features to express anything other than a dominant drive toward completion.

And finally, when she was boneless in his embrace, he rode her hard and took his own release with a ragged shout that echoed across the plain.

Trent pulled the edge of the quilt around the sleeping woman in his arms and checked his watch. The minutes ran away from him like rivulets of water on a rain-soaked windowpane. He wanted to preserve this slice of time, keep it pristine in his memory. But the moment of reckoning was fast approaching and it might be very ugly indeed. No matter how much he wanted to protect Bryn and her son from pain, his efforts might be futile.

He closed his eyes, feeling the sun burn into the skin of his eyelids and face.

He stroked her hair, abashed to realize that he was no longer jealous of his dead brother. Jesse had held Bryn like this…had made love to her. The knowledge was painful. But he loved his brother. Would always love him. And Jesse's premature death was a tragedy that would forever mark their family.

He was hard again. It seemed to be a perpetual, inescapable condition in her presence. He shifted her gently onto her side so they were face-to-face. Carefully, he lifted her leg across his hip. Breathing hard, he probed gently at her swollen entrance.

Bryn murmured, and the ghost of a smile teased her lips as her eyelids fluttered and opened. He pushed until he was seated fully in her still-slick passage. He moved slowly, savoring the way her body grasped his shaft. She felt small and fragile in his embrace, but she was strong in ways he could never match. She'd made a home for her son as a single mother.

Beverly had been a source of strength…true. But Bryn was a good mother, a woman of backbone and grit, much like the pioneer females who helped settle the wild and dangerous West.

She kissed him and murmured soft words of pleasure. He gritted his teeth as his climax bore down on him. He'd taken her like a crazy man less than a half hour before, and already he was at the edge again.

He slowed his strokes, relishing the position that enabled him to kiss her as he moved in and out with deliberate thrusts. Dark smudges beneath her eyes tugged at his heartstrings. Sleepless nights. Endless worry. But her smile was pure sunshine.

When he thought of the way he and Mac had thrown her out six years ago—a naive, pregnant eighteen-year-old—he was sickened. He'd never be able to make that up to her, but God knows, he could try.

He shuddered as his brain ceded control to his baser instincts. Tremors shook him. The base of his spine tightened.

"Bryn…" He spoke her name urgently, needing to see her forgiveness, wanting absolution.

She caught her breath. "Trent…ohh…"

Their position was intimate, sensual. He put his hand on the soft curve of her bottom and pulled her in to his downstroke. Her back arched. Her eyes closed. She was so beautiful, he was blinded. He told himself it was the sun.

But it was her. It was Bryn. Until she came back to the ranch, he'd had no clue his life was an empty shell. But she had shown him the truth. And all she'd had to do was be herself…pure, generous, charming.

He'd been lost from the first moment, though he'd fought hard to believe she was a liar and a cheat. It was much easier that way.

He brushed a kiss across each of her cheeks, her nose, her eyelids. The urgent need for climax had retreated to a muted simmer. His primary emotion at the moment was quiet contentment. And for a man unused to examining something as hazy and insubstantial as feelings, it was a significant shock to realize that the woman in his arms was as necessary to him as breathing.

The knowledge was exhilarating and scary as hell.

He pushed her over onto her back and urged her legs around his waist. Her skin was soft and luminous in the unforgiving light of day. What would it have been like to be her pioneer husband, bound inside a tiny log cabin for weeks at a time as blizzards howled?

Isolation. Nothing to diffuse the interaction between male and female. Nothing to run interference when one of them was in a bad mood. Nowhere to escape when tempers flared.

He'd have taken her night after night, wrapped in a world of only two. And it would have been as close to heaven as a man like him was liable to get. He'd said Jesse didn't deserve her, but the truth was, neither did he.

She smiled at him, a secretive curve of soft pink lips that made him shake. Her gaze was slumberous.

The look of a woman who had been well loved. Any man in his right mind would move heaven and earth to make her his. He'd grown up believing that everyone and everything had a price. But not Bryn. She had never asked for a single thing.

And he wanted to give her the world.

He moved in her, wanting to imprint his touch on her heart so that she could never forget him.

She dug her heels into his lower back. "Whatever happens, Trent, I'll always remember this." Her gaze was solemn, melancholy.

He nuzzled her neck. "I'll work it out. Trust me."

A slight frown appeared between her perfectly arched brows. "Work what out?"

He withdrew almost completely and chuckled when she said an unladylike word. He dropped his head forward, resting his brow against hers. "Mac. Jesse. Allen. The letters. You'll see."

She tightened her legs around his waist with surprising strength. "Less talk. More action."

He tried to laugh, but it came out as a groan. He let it snap…the cord he'd bound so tightly around his need, his control. Again and again, he entered her, holding back until he heard her sharp cry and felt her body spasm around his rigid flesh. And then he buried his face in her neck and leaped into the unknown, feeling only the soft pillow of her breasts and knowing that there was nowhere else he wanted to be.

Sweat dried on their skin. The sun moved lower, brushing the mountains with gold and lavender.

He came so close to blurting out his love for her. But

the habits of a lifetime were deeply ingrained. Never operate from a position of weakness. Make a plan. He'd get everything worked out in his head, and then he'd tell her. When the time was right.

Bryn was so silent and still beneath him, he felt panic tighten his throat.

He sat up and gathered her in his arms, warming her skin with his hands. The words rushed from his mouth, shocking the hell out of him. "Marry me, Bryn. Make Allen my son."

Thirteen

Over the years Bryn had entertained dozens of fantasies in which Trent declared his everlasting love for her, went down on one knee to offer her a ridiculously extravagant ring and begged her to marry him. None of those scripts bore any resemblance to what had just happened.

She stood up awkwardly, painfully aware of her nudity, and scrambled to pick up her clothes and put them on. In one quick glance she saw that Trent was frowning. No less magnificent and commanding in the buff than he was fully clothed, he stood with his hands on his hips.

When she was ready, she folded her arms across her waist and made herself look at him. She managed to swallow against a tight throat. "Thank you for asking," she said quietly, "but, no." He hadn't technically asked her at all. It had been more autocratic than that. An order. The mighty Trent Sinclair telling a minion what to do.

She hated that she was suspicious of his motives, but her instinct for self-preservation had kicked into high gear. She couldn't be one of his *acquisitions*. Her heart couldn't bear it.

Trent's scowl was black enough to make a grown man cower, but Bryn held her ground. His jaw was clenched so hard, the words bit out in sharp staccatos. "Why the hell not?"

The naive Bryn grieved for the ashes of fairy-tale romance. But practical Bryn had more to consider than hurt feelings. "If Allen is a Sinclair, then of course I want him to get to know his grandfather and you and Gage and Sloan and the ranch. But if it turns out that he's *not,* I'll take him back to Minnesota with me and we'll make a good life there with Beverly."

His eyes narrowed. "You said that whether or not to show Mac the letters was my decision. I say we destroy the damn things and move on…as a family."

The temptation to give in was overwhelming. She would be Trent's wife. Allen would be his son. There might be other children.

She bit her lip and shook her head. "I was wrong. I've had all night to think about it. Secrets are never the best course of action. Mac needs to know the truth. And afterward…"

He shoved his legs in his pants and buttoned his shirt. "And afterward, your son will either be very rich, or just another illegitimate kid being raised by a single parent."

She flinched. His deliberate cruelty shocked her. Was this his response to not getting his own way? "It's about more than the money," she whispered, her throat raw from the effort not to cry. "You know that."

He faced her, barefooted. Most people would appear vulnerable in that condition. Not Trent. "The world revolves around money, Bryn. And if you don't realize that, you're more of an innocent than I thought."

She was chilled to the bone though the day was warm. "Why are you being so hateful?" What had happened to tender, caring Trent? Had the gentler, kinder man been no more than a ruse to get her into bed?

He shrugged, the smile on his face mocking. "If I'm not in the best of moods, Brynnie, you'll have to take the blame for that. It's not every day I get a marriage proposal tossed back in my face. Forgive me if I'm not so cavalier about it as to go on with life as normal."

For the briefest flash of a second, she thought she saw hurt flicker in his cold gaze, but then it was gone. She couldn't hurt Trent. He was impervious, thick-skinned. That was the only way to make it to the top.

She bit her lip. "Why did you ask me to marry you?"

He propped his foot on a stone and bent to put on the left boot, then the right.… Was he hiding his expression deliberately? His voice was muffled. "We owe you. Maybe not Gage and Sloan, but certainly Jesse and Mac and I. You suffered at our hands, and that can't be erased. Sinclairs always repay their debts."

Disappointment and grief tangled in her stomach, destroying any last hope that Trent felt something for her beyond simple lust. "I absolve you," she said dully. "There's plenty of blame to go around. I kept Allen away from you all for five years. So let's call it even."

She picked up the quilt and rolled it with jerky motions. "I need to get back to the house."

The hours until Bryn and Trent could meet with Mac in private passed like molasses on a cold day. Allen's high spirits frayed Bryn's nerves, yet finally, by nine o'clock, Allen was sound asleep. Bryn didn't waste any time. She retrieved the box of letters and made her way to Mac's study.

The two men were already there.

Her heart thumping, she entered hesitantly, searching out Trent with her gaze to see if his face gave any indication of what was to come. What had he said to Mac? Anything? She sat down and waited.

Trent ran a hand over the back of his neck, looking uncustomarily frazzled. "How are you feeling, Dad?"

Mac frowned. "I'm great. What's all this about?"

At Trent's almost imperceptible nod, Bryn smiled wanly. "We have some things to tell you, but we don't want you to get upset."

Mac snorted and rolled his eyes. "I may have a contrary ticker, but I'm not some damned pansy who's going to wilt over a little bad news. For God's sake, spit it out. You're making me nervous. You and Trent look like you've swallowed bad fish. Tell me what it is. Now."

Bryn gripped the box in her lap. When she looked at Trent, he was no help at all. He simply shrugged.

She stood up and moved to where Mac sat in the leather chair that was his version of a throne. "I found these," she said. "When I was cleaning Jesse's room. They're letters. From Etta. Did you know Jesse's mother had been writing to him?"

"God, no." Mac paled.

Bryn winced. "I was afraid of that. They're bad, Mac. She tried to poison his mind. And her deliberate mischief-making may have contributed to the drugs. Jesse would have been confused. And hurt."

"Let me see." He tried to take the box, but she held on to it for a moment more.

"That's not all." She was surprised she was able to speak. Her throat spasmed painfully. "Jesse may not be your son."

Mac's big hands trembled. He jerked the box away from her. "Damn it, girl, quit coddling me."

The room was silent when Mac tossed the last letter in the box and replaced the lid. He set the innocent-looking cardboard container on the desk and laid his head against the back of his chair. His eyes were closed. Bryn was not in the mood to indulge him.

She got to her feet and paced. "Talk to us, Mac. Please."

He scrubbed his hands over his face and turned his head in her direction. His entire body had deflated. He looked like an old man.

Trent exhaled an audible breath. "Dad. Come clean with us. What's going on?"

Mac sighed. "I didn't know about the letters, but I've known where Etta was every day since she left."

Trent looked thunderstruck.

Bryn managed to speak. "I don't understand. I thought she ran away. Left her kids. Left you."

Mac nodded. "She did that for sure. And I checked her into a mental facility, because she had a complete, devastating breakdown. She split with reality. Etta has been a patient at the Raven's Rest Inpatient Facility in Cheyenne for almost two decades."

Trent gaped. "For God's sake, Dad. Why did you never tell us? Why did you let us think she ran away?"

"She did run away. At first. But when I found her, she was cowering in a bus station like a wounded wild animal." Mac's voice broke, and Bryn saw that even after all the years that had passed, he still loved her.

He continued, his voice thick. "I took her to the hospital. And she was never able to come back home. She was a danger to herself and others. There were a few good days here and there, but for the most part, she lives in an alternate world. I'm honestly shocked that she was able to remember Jesse well enough to be able to write to him."

"You think Jesse inherited some of her mental instability, don't you?" Trent's face had paled, as well.

Mac nodded slowly. "I wanted him to see someone… to get help…medication. Anything that he needed. But he never gave me an inch. Denial was his friend."

Bryn leaned forward. "So the other men she talks about in the letters? Did they exist?"

Mac's silence dragged on for tense moments. He was

suddenly the epitome of an elderly man. "Yes." His tone was flat. "She never leaves the facility now. But before… when she was still living on the ranch…there were a couple of episodes. Jesse is probably not my biological son. I'd been gone for a few weeks to a cattle show. The timing…well…let's just say the odds are against it. But it doesn't matter anymore. Jesse is dead."

He got to his feet, almost stumbling, and leaned a hand on the back of the chair. "You were right to show me the letters. I'm sorry I didn't tell you the truth about your mother, Trent. But when you were all boys, I didn't want you to know. And by the time you were old enough to understand, I'd kept the secret so long, I couldn't bring myself to expose the truth."

He hugged his son, and Bryn was relieved to see that Trent gave as good as he got. She had feared he'd be furious. But whatever his emotions, he kept them in check for now.

Mac hugged Bryn, as well. "I love you, Brynnie, my girl. And you've always been family to me, with or without Jesse."

She kissed his cheek. "Sleep well, Mac. I'll check on you before I go to bed."

When it was just the two of them, Bryn studied Trent's face. He wasn't doing well. She could see it in his eyes, though he stood as proud as ever, his spine straight and his broad shoulders squared off against the world. She took his hand. "Come to the kitchen with me. I'll fix you something to drink. And I'll bet Beverly tucked away some of those sugar cookies."

He cocked his head, pulling his hand out of her grasp and stepping backward behind an invisible fence. "You don't have to pamper me. I'm not dying. But I guess you were smart to say no to my proposal. Who knows what crazy genes are rattling around inside me? I don't know which is worse—a mother who will abandon her children on a whim, or a raving maniac."

His sarcasm made her flinch. "Don't do that, Trent," she said urgently. "Give yourself time to process this. You've had a shock." She turned to Mac's desk. He'd been known to keep a flask for emergencies. "I'll pour you some whiskey. You deserve it after the day you've had."

Trent's laugh held little amusement as he took the tiny shot and tossed it back. He wiped his mouth with the back of his hand, his eyes bleak. "There's not enough whiskey in the world to fix this."

"It will be okay," she said, trying to believe it.

It was as if he never heard her. "I'm going to have to be the one to call Gage and Sloan. I can't make Mac do it. He could barely tell me. Damn it to hell." Trent hurled the small glass against the wall and smiled with grim satisfaction when it shattered into a dozen pieces.

"You don't have to do anything tonight," she insisted. "It can wait until morning. When you've calmed down."

"I'm perfectly calm," he said, his tone blistering. "Go to bed, Bryn. This doesn't concern you."

"*You* concern me," she said. He was trying to hurt her…and he succeeded. But her own concerns had to be pushed aside temporarily for his sake. He needed to let go, let the anguish out, and hang on to someone else for a few minutes. But such perceived weakness wasn't in his repertoire. He was a Sinclair male. That particular animal was trained not to show weakness. Not to anyone.

She knelt to clean up the mess, and Trent barked at her.

"I said…go to bed." His eyes blazed in a white face.

She finished her task and dropped the pieces into the trash can. "I don't want to leave you right now. You need me."

He went still, and in that split second, she knew she had made a mistake. His lip curled. Any tenderness she'd ever imagined in his steely gaze had been obliterated by fury and suffering that was painful to witness.

"I don't *need* anyone, Brynnie. So leave me the hell alone."

Bryn gave herself and her son one last, precious twenty-four-hour period to enjoy the ranch. Their return flights, along with Beverly's and the nurse's, were booked for the following day.

She did her best to make her mind a blank. All that mattered now was ensuring that Allen and Mac spent time together and that Allen had one last opportunity to explore the ranch. She was the one making a decision to leave this time, but the end result was the same. She had to say goodbye to the two men she loved. And to the home where she had grown up with so many happy memories.

Allen ran circles around her when she lagged behind on their walk. Her sleepless night was catching up with her. She held up a hand. "Mommy needs to rest a minute." They were climbing a slight rise, and the two or three hours of sleep she'd had during the long, bleak night weren't enough to give her any energy at all.

She spied a boulder up ahead near the trail, one of many left behind when the glaciers retreated, and made a beeline for it. They were in sight of the house. Their trek had taken them in a big circle.

They sat down and Allen put his head in her lap, a move that said louder than words that he wasn't entirely back to normal. She stroked his hair. "I have something to tell you, sweetheart."

He yawned and swiped at his nose with a dirty hand. "Okay."

She hadn't expected it to be quite so hard. "You know how I told you I lived here when I was growing up?"

He nodded.

"Well, Mac had a son, Jesse, who was my age. I fell in love with him and that's how you were born."

"But my daddy died."

"Yes."

"Why didn't we live with him?"

This was the tricky part. Allen sat up and looked at her with big curious eyes. She bit her lip. "Ah, well… your dad was very sick and he couldn't help take care of a little boy."

Allen cocked his head. "Like strep throat?"

"No. Something that never got better. But you

were very lucky because you had me and your aunt Beverly."

"Why didn't my dad ever invite me to come here?" Allen was sharp.

"He didn't want you to see him feeling bad. And he didn't tell Mac and Trent that you were his little boy. But now that they know, Mac wants you to visit as often as we can."

"Can we live here?"

Bryn groaned inwardly. "We already have a place to live…you know? And Aunt Beverly would miss us if we were gone."

Allen grinned. "Yeah. I guess." Then as usual, his focus shifted. "Can we go back to the house now? I'm hungry."

She ruffled his hair. "You're always hungry."

They took off at a trot, and Allen pretended to race her, giggling when she panted and bent to put her hands on her knees. She took a deep breath and made one last sprint.

Two steps later, she cried out in shock when she stepped in a hole and her body kept going. There was a sickening crack, dreadful pain shot up her leg and she catapulted forward to meet the ground with a thud.

The first thing she remembered was her son's little hand patting her cheek. When she opened her eyes, she realized he was crying. "I'm okay," she said automatically.

He wasn't stupid. Fear painted his face. "Mommy, your phone's not in your pocket."

Oh, God. "I left it at the house." Throbbing pain made it difficult to enunciate.

"I'll go get help," he said, looking sober and not at all childlike.

"No. You'll get lost." She blurted it out, terrified at the possibility of letting her baby boy wander alone.

Allen took her face between his hands, his expression earnest. "Mommy, I can see the house. It's over there."

He was right. The roof was visible through the trees. Her brain spun. What choice did she have? If she passed out—and it was a good possibility given the way she felt—she'd be leaving Allen unattended anyway. Was there any difference in the two scenarios? The pain made nausea rise in her throat as sweat beaded her forehead.

Desperately, she gazed at her small, brave son. "You must stay on the trail. And if you get confused, stop and come back. Be careful. Promise me."

He stood up. "I'll bring Trent, Mommy. He'll know what to do."

Trent was in the corral, examining the left rear shoe on his stallion, when a small figure out of the corner of his eye caught his attention. It was little Allen. Alone. Trent ran to meet him, his heart in his throat. "What happened? Where's your mother?" He dropped down on his knees, so the two of them were at eye level. Allen was wheezing a little bit, but his color was good. He was scared and trying hard not to show it.

He laid his head on Trent's shoulder in an innocent

gesture of trust. "She stepped in a hole. Her ankle might be broken. I can show you where she is. It's not far."

Trent's brain buzzed. He scooped the little boy into his arms and tucked him up on the horse. "Hold on to the saddle horn. We're going to ride fast." Allen's eyes were huge, but he nodded. Trent put a foot in the stirrup and vaulted up behind him. "Let's go. I'm counting on you to show me the way...."

One arm wrapped around Allen's waist, Trent rode hell for leather. Thinking about Bryn, hurt and alone, made him crazy, so he did his best to concentrate on getting to her as quickly as he could.

Thankfully, the kid was right. It was less than a quarter of a mile. But when they reached Bryn, she was unconscious. Trent felt his world wobble and blur. She had to be okay. She had to be okay. She had to.

He jumped down and set the boy on his feet. While Allen hovered anxiously, Trent took a handkerchief from his pocket and wet it with water from the canteen on the ground beside Bryn. He wiped her face gently. "Wake up, Bryn. I'm here. Wake up, sweetheart."

It was a full minute before Bryn responded. She was ghostly white, and her lips were pale. "You came."

The words were so low he had to bend his head to hear them. He reached out his hand for Allen, pulling him close. "Your son is a hero," he said softly. "I'd never have known where you were without him."

She tried to wet her lips. "I've hardly seen you speak to him. I thought you were angry because he was Jesse's son," she whispered, her voice almost inaudible.

He lifted the canteen to her lips and made her drink.

"Angry?" Had she hit her head after all? She wasn't making sense.

"Because he's not yours and mine."

It was his turn to frown. "Don't be ridiculous. I love Allen. He's my flesh and blood. I'll always love him."

It was a nightmare ride that took far longer than it should. The sun dropped lower in the sky as they made their halting way back toward the house.

When they finally reached the edge of the corral, Trent barked out orders, and ranch hands came running. Beverly took charge of Allen, and the nurse was at Trent's side as he carried Bryn into the house. He put her in his bedroom. It was larger and more comfortable than hers, with a massive king-size bed. Bryn moaned as he laid her carefully on the embroidered, navy silk duvet.

There was really no choice what to do. The ankle was clearly broken. The nurse confirmed Trent's amateur diagnosis. Mac summoned a helicopter and Trent and the nurse boarded with Bryn for the brief trip to Jackson Hole.

Fourteen

"How is she, son?" Mac, Beverly and Allen had lingered at the ranch for a couple of hours, not wanting Allen to get restless at the hospital during what could be a lengthy surgery.

"She should be coming out of recovery any minute now." Trent was hollow inside, feeling the aftermath of adrenaline. The sterile waiting room had been a cage he'd prowled for several hours. "Why don't you go on in so she can see Allen first thing. It's room 317. I'm going to grab some coffee and a sandwich."

He didn't linger at the snack machine. It was almost nine and he knew Mac and Beverly wouldn't want to keep Allen out too late.

When he approached the room a quarter hour later, he could hear Allen's excited chatter and Bryn's softer voice. He drew in a sharp breath, swamped with a wave of relief to hear concrete proof that she was okay.

He hovered in the hall, wanting to give the others plenty of time to reassure themselves that Bryn had come through the surgery with no ill effects. Finally, the door opened, and Bryn's visitors exited. The nurse would ride back to the ranch with them.

Mac squeezed his shoulder. "Take care of our girl."

Now Bryn was alone. Trent took a deep breath, knocked briefly on the partially open door and stepped into the room.

Bryn shifted in the bed and winced. Even with really wonderful drugs, her ankle throbbed mercilessly.

When Trent appeared in the doorway, her heart jumped. She hoped he couldn't tell on the monitor. She was in pain. It had been a terrible, stressful day. And she felt in no condition to hold her own with him.

He looked like hell. "You should have gone home with the others," she said quietly. "You're exhausted."

He pulled up a chair beside her bed. "I'm not leaving you." His angular face was creased with fatigue, his eyes shadowed. She wanted to smooth a hand over his hair, but she felt the invisible wall between them.

"There's no need for you to stay. I'm fine...really." She touched the neck of her hospital gown and sighed inwardly. Her hair was a mess. She would kill for a shower. And Trent had to see her like this. It wasn't fair. She always seemed to be at a disadvantage when it came to their interactions.

He took her hand in his, examining the shallow cuts and scrapes that covered the palm. She had tried to catch herself when she fell. It was a wonder she hadn't broken an arm. He ran his thumb gently over the worst of the wounds. "I lost ten years off my life today."

He looked at her, for once his dark gaze completely unguarded, and her breath caught in her chest. Was she imagining the agonized concern she saw there?

She curled her fingers around his palm. "I'm so sorry. I should have had my phone with me."

He shrugged. "Reception is sometimes spotty once you get away from the house. It might not have been any help. Your son, on the other hand, is one hell of a smart kid."

She might have taken offense at the "your son" reference, if not for the fact that Trent's face beamed with pride.

No mother could resist praise for her offspring. "He *is* pretty amazing," she said smugly. The she sobered. "I was terrified to let him go off on his own, but what choice did we have?"

"He took me right to you. He was a trooper."

The room fell silent. She was tremblingly aware of the fact that Trent stroked the back of her hand, almost absentmindedly.

He stood and reached forward to tuck a strand of hair behind her ear…then kissed her cheek. "Why did you turn down my marriage proposal, Bryn?" He propped one arm on the bed rail and stared at her intently.

She plucked at her IV nervously, unable to meet his eyes. "I'm able to provide for my son."

"That's not what I asked."

She slanted him a sideways gaze. "I didn't want to be an obligation to you...a wrong you have to right."

He frowned. "That doesn't even make sense. I offered to make you my wife."

"Like a business merger." She heard the petulance in her own voice and winced inwardly.

A smile began to draw up the corners of Trent's sensual mouth. "I may be good at a lot of things," he muttered, "but that was my first proposal. It possibly lacked finesse."

She pouted. "It lacked *something*."

He grinned fully now, picking up her hand and kissing each scrape. "Would it have helped if I told you I adore you...that I've loved you since you were a little girl in ragged shorts and scabbed-up knees. That what I felt for you changed over the years into something far deeper. But that I was too much of a self-centered, ego-driven jerk to recognize what I had before I lost it. That I need you so much it hurts, and I didn't even know there was anything missing in my life until you showed up in Wyoming."

Bryn lay, openmouthed, and thought her heart might break. For Trent, the self-contained, tightly controlled man that he was, to humble himself in such a way was a gift she had never expected. She was speechless.

His smile was wry. "Is that a second *no?*"

She gulped. "No. I mean yes. Oh, Trent, I don't know what to say." She sniffed, blinking rapidly.

He shook his head and wiped her cheeks tenderly with the edge of the sheet. "You're killing me, little one. Any kind of answer would be appreciated. A man can only stand so much suspense."

She grabbed his hand in hers and squeezed. "Are you sure?" She couldn't bear it if he was confusing affection with love.

He kissed her again. Harder this time. With echoes of the passion they had shared. "Do I strike you as indecisive, Brynnie? *Yes*—I love you. And I promise you I'm not going to change my mind in five minutes or fifty years. So you might as well get used to it."

She tugged him closer. "Sit on the bed."

He lowered the bed rail and complied, but he pretended to look toward the hall with apprehension. "I'm scared of that nurse. Please don't get me in trouble."

She wanted to laugh, but her chest was a huge bubble of happiness that made it hard to breathe.

He put an arm around her shoulders and settled her against his chest, her cheek over his beating heart. She decided there and then that a broken ankle was a small price to pay.

"Yes," she said with a soft sigh.

He kissed her temple. "Yes to what?"

"To everything. To laughter. To forever. I love you, Trent."

He stretched his long legs out on the mattress, one ankle propped over the other. "Are you sure?"

He was mocking her, but she was too happy to care. "I'm sure," she said, grinning uncontrollably. "So kiss your calm, ordered life goodbye."

He nuzzled the top of her head and sighed from deep in his chest. "I can't wait, Brynnie. I can't wait."

* * * * *

Desire™

HONOUR-BOUND GROOM by Yvonne Lindsay

Alexander Del Castillo was betrothed from childhood. So the CEO doesn't expect his beautiful bride to get under his skin...

CINDERELLA & THE CEO by Maureen Child

Tanner found himself saddled with a gorgeous housekeeper he couldn't keep his mind—or hands—off, who also turned out to be his annoying neighbour!

BARGAINING FOR BABY by Robyn Grady

Queensland sheep-station owner Jack Prescott was all bad boy sex appeal, but he'd inherited his baby nephew and feisty Maddy!

THE BILLIONAIRE'S BABY ARRANGEMENT by Charlene Sands

Suddenly Nick Carlino was face-to-face with a woman from his past...and her five-month-old baby.

EXPECTANT PRINCESS, UNEXPECTED AFFAIR
by Michelle Celmer

Samuel Baldwin had seduced Princess Anne to quench his own desire. Chipping away at Anne's icy façade had been pure pleasure...

FROM BOARDROOM TO WEDDING BED? by Jules Bennett

He'd been faced with the toughest decision of his life—a future full of wealth and power, or the love of Tamera Stevens. What would it be, love or money?

On sale from 15th July 2011
Don't miss out!

Available at WHSmith, Tesco, ASDA, Eason
and all good bookshops
www.millsandboon.co.uk

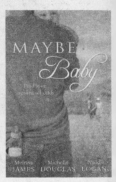

New Voices is back!

New Voices
returns on
13th September 2011!

For sneak previews and exclusives:

 Like us on facebook.com/romancehq

 Follow us on twitter.com/MillsandBoonUK

Last year your votes helped Leah Ashton win
New Voices 2010 with her fabulous story
Secrets & Speed Dating!

Who will you be voting for this year?

Visit us Online   Find out more at
www.romanceisnotdead.com

Discover Pure Reading Pleasure with

Visit the Mills & Boon website for all the latest in romance

 Buy all the latest releases, backlist and eBooks

Find out more about our authors and their books

 Join our community and chat to authors and other readers

Free online reads from your favourite authors

 Win with our fantastic online competitions

Sign up for our free monthly eNewsletter

 Tell us what you think by signing up to our reader panel

Rate and review books with our star system

www.millsandboon.co.uk

 Follow us at twitter.com/millsandboonuk

Become a fan at facebook.com/romancehq

FREE BOOK
AND A SURPRISE GIFT

We would like to take this opportunity to thank you for reading this Mills & Boon® book by offering you the chance to take a specially selected book from the Desire™ 2-in-1 series absolutely FREE! We're also making this offer to introduce you to the benefits of the Mills & Boon® Book Club™—

- **FREE home delivery**
- **FREE gifts and competitions**
- **FREE monthly Newsletter**
- **Exclusive Mills & Boon Book Club offers**
- **Books available before they're in the shops**

Accepting this FREE book and gift places you under no obligation to buy, you may cancel at any time, even after receiving your free book. Simply complete your details below and return the entire page to the address below. You don't even need a stamp!

YES Please send me a free Desire 2-in-1 book and a surprise gift. I understand that unless you hear from me, I will receive 2 superb new 2-in-1 books every month for just £5.30 each, postage and packing free. I am under no obligation to purchase any books and may cancel my subscription at any time. The free book and gift will be mine to keep in any case.

Ms/Mrs/Miss/Mr _____ Initials _____

Surname _____

Address _____

_____

_____ Postcode _____

E-mail _____

Send this whole page to: Mills & Boon Book Club, Free Book Offer, FREEPOST NAT 10298, Richmond, TW9 1BR